DRIFT

DRIFT

James Hanley

LONDON:
NICHOLSON & WATSON

BOOK
PRODUCTION
WAR ECONOMY
STANDARD

PRINTED BY LOVE & MALCOMSON, LTD.
LONDON and REDHILL

DRIFT

CHAPTER I

THE wind was coming down the road. It was a fine strong wind, salt-laden, and it was sweeping in over the river. And now, as it was coming down the road, it sang and shouted for joy. There was an old man standing in the gutter and he was singing a little song ; and it was a nice little song. It was about a cat and a fiddle. And the wind was coming down the road, and the old man was singing this song when the wind caught him flat-handed, upon the mouth, and he gasped for breath—" O Jesus ! O Jesus ! " he said, and ran after his cap which had blown into the gutter. He picked it up and came back to where he had been before, and then he started to sing his little song again : that nice little song about a cat and a fiddle.

Then the wind that was coming down the road struck the house with the queer smell. It was a strange little house. And then the rain fell and it tapped-tapped upon the window-pane. And there was a little old man in the kitchen. He was sitting by the fire, sucking his thumb. He had a bald head, a beak like a bird, and a mouth like a knife-slit in a rotten pumpkin. He was a funny little man. When he pulled his thumb out of his mouth he spat in the grate. He turned round to look at the clock upon the dresser and then you saw he had a fine head. And you said to yourself—

" That's a fine head."

A man came in through the back-kitchen door. He was John Magee.

John Magee was fifty-five, and he used to run messages for the midwife in Twist Street. He had dull roving eyes.

The man who sucked his thumb had a nice name. His

name was Anthony. His mother gave it to him. He got up from his chair, and gave Magee a dig in the ribs.

"Just in time, Martha's just cooked a lovely pig's cheek," he said ; adding, " an' how's the widow ? "

Magee went as white as a corpse's shroud and said—

"What's the matter with ye now ? "

"You're an excitable man," remarked Anthony and sat down.

Martha Rourke came in then. She was a nice large fat woman. She was Anthony's daughter. Her husband was named Michael, and he killed bulls and things at the abattoir.

"Just in time to feed your face, John," said Martha.

"I like a drink of tea about seven," replied Magee. "How's the boyo ? "

"He's lovely. Surely now, Mr. Magee, won't you sit in to the fire ? "

Martha commenced to lay the table. The bread smelt sweet. Martha baked her own bread. She used to make the sign of the cross over the dough. St. Anthony helped to make the loaves bigger when you did that. And the rain kept singing its song on the window-pane, and the wind blew over the chimney-top.

They all sat in to table.

"You've a great belly for pig's cheek," said Martha, cutting a big slice.

Magee winked, and went on lapping up the cabbage like a dog lapping up water from a brook.

Anthony had no teeth. With one of her feet Martha kept time to the rise and fall of his jaw.

"Have another slice of the ambassador's face," invited Martha.

"I think I will," said Anthony, and helped himself.

"That's a great tale I hear about spit-Dick," said Anthony. There was silence. Neither Martha nor Magee took any notice of him. Anthony went on lapping up his cabbage.

"I'll have another slice of the beauty," said Magee, drumming on the table with his fork.

" It's a great tale," burst in Anthony, his mouth half full of cabbage.

" There you are, John," said Martha, and passed him a slice of the pig.

" Yes, a great tale," went on Anthony.

" Keep it to yourself then," said Martha quite smart and pucking her brows.

" Yes, keep it to yourself," said Magee, " nobody wants to hear it."

" Well, Theresa Corby's in the family way, so there," blurted Anthony.

He smacked his lips, and thought to himself—

" H'm—got them guessing now."

Martha and Magee laughed. Anthony suddenly said "Ah !" It sounded like an angel playing an arpeggio upon a harp.

Then they all laughed together. The house with the queer smell fairly rocked with the laughter. And the rain kept tapping on the window-pane. Night fell smoky-scarved, and plunged the street in darkness. Martha got up to light the gas. Martha had a broad back like a fisherman's.

She drew down the blind, and turning said to Anthony:

" Poke up the fire ; Mick will be here soon, you know."

Anthony poked up the fire and whistled a few bars of " Wrap the green flag round me." Then he fell to sucking his thumb again. Magee rose and said he must be going.

Anthony said he was sorry and Martha said he would get drenched going out in that pouring rain. Magee laughed. He said it didn't matter. He had a good wife at home. She would dry his clothes for him.

" I've been sitting on your hat, John," said Martha, and handed it to him.

" You're a proper suck, d'you know that, Mrs. ? " said Magee, and banged the door after him. Martha thought he said sulk and asked Anthony if he had ever seen her sulk to be treated that way.

"Well now, I never did ; although," said he, "you sulked somewhat when Father Harry dropped Joe at the Christening."

"But," said Martha, "that was entirely his fault, not mine."

"Ah, well ! let bygones be bygones ; I think I'll have a walk before I go to bed."

He got up and put on his coat and went out. Martha poked up the fire again. There was a knock at the door and she thought it was Mick, but it was only little Annie Rooney calling to say that her dad had sent her to inform them that Mick would be working late and would be home about nine o'clock.

Martha said "Come in," and the girl came in and sat down by the big woman in the house with the queer smell. She was a nice little girl—she was thin but she had fine eyes as clear as the waters of the river, and hair like ripe corn, and her skin was like dead ivory flushing into life. She snuffed and that made a funny noise.

"Why don't you blow your nose," said Martha, "haven't you a hanky ? Here ! " She gave a corner of her apron to the child. The child blew hard. She thought it was the most awful apron she had ever felt in her life.

"It smells like the devil," she said to Martha.

Martha laughed and said the apron was hard and smelt bad because she had been cleaning fish for Mick's tea, adding—"but it wouldn't do you any harm, me chucks."

She gave little Annie a kiss and a penny, and said she had better go home.

"Is Joe in ? " asked Annie.

"He's gone to confession," says Martha,. and busied herself with trying to stir some life into the now fast-dying fire in the grate.

It was a nice little room. There was a large holy picture of the Sacred Heart right over the door, and a little shelf in front of it. On the little shelf a candle burned. The table was laid for Mick's tea, and the fire was soon blazing ; in the back kitchen the little boiler-fire was blazing too, for Martha had such a big wash to do. It was a bad day too for the clothes, for you couldn't do anything, with it raining cats and dogs. She had such a big wash ! All the clothes from number eighteen were there too. She would never have consented to wash such a pile, only that the poor woman in number eighteen had just had a child. Last Sunday Father Harry had preached a powerful sermon about helping those who trespass against us, and Martha remembered how the poor woman had trespassed against her son, because he called the poor woman's husband a " dirty big tub of guts." Joe was twenty, and worked at the docks when he could ; but more often he sat in the library reading the best he could find in modern poetry. He had a little book at home and there were forty poems in it, about love and the stars, and devils and angels and things like that. And the man in the library used to say to him—" Well, Joe, what d'you want now, eh ? "

That man had a face like an owl. It was a very hairy face. One morning at communion he had dropped the Host out of his mouth just as the priest was saying, "*dominus vobiscum.*" There was a terrible to-do about it. He had to scrub white the spot where the Host fell. He scrubbed for an hour. The priest said that if he didn't visit the pubs so often he would not be so shaky of a morning. The poor chap had never done right from that day. One day he gave Joe the wrong book and Joe, little knowing, left it lying on the table in his room. Martha burnt the book ; it was such a bad book and the man was bad, but the Pope was a good man. She had to pay five shillings and sixpence to the library committee for destroying the book.

Joe had a rough time. He used to clear out on Sundays after Mass and take his book with him. The fresh air was so fine. After the holy smell, so warm, so clinging, so clammy and sickly.

He had a scab on his right knee, which made it painful for him to kneel. Once he fell asleep during benediction. That was when the bishop, wearing his big hat, came to confirm a lot of boys and girls. It was a funny hat. The bishop was a long thin man who had a face like a wolf, and when he laughed he looked like a dog with his two rows of bright little teeth shining. But Joe had seen him laugh only once, and that was when a little girl gave him a little purse with money in it for the bishop's funds. He patted the little girl on the head and made the sign of the cross over her and she smiled. Then her mother took her home and kissed her and was proud of her little daughter because she had kissed the bishop's gold ring. Then the bishop drove away in his carriage. As he passed the church door one of the wheels of his carriage went over the toes of a little boy named Simon Dart. The little lad had squealed like a stuck pig, but his mother had gathered him to her tremendous breast and said—

"Why duckins, it was only the bishop's carriage."

The dream of Joe's early life had been to kiss the bishop's hand, but he never brought enough money for the waifs and strays. He once asked his mother if he could be a bishop. That was just after little Annie Rooney had walked into his mother's kitchen and whispered into Martha's ear that she would like to be a midwife when she grew up. Martha laughed and told her that her hands were too clumsy for anything. Then Annie cried her eyes out, and Mrs. Rooney, who was passing at the time, stopped when she heard her daughter crying so bitterly. And she accused Martha of hitting her. Martha said she had told her she would never make a midwife, and Mrs. Rooney with fine scorn said—

"I'm surprised, fancy you teaching a child that—for shame!" She took Annie home. Annie got no tea but when her father came in, Mrs. Rooney told him about finding her daughter crying in Martha's house.

"Give her her tea, after she has made a good act of contrition," said Mr. Rooney, who was a medium-sized man, soft cheeked, and his hair cut like a monk's. He was a very nice man. He had a scar over his right eye. It was an ugly scar. He got it carrying the banner in the summer procession. There had been a dirty row; the banner pole had been knocked out of his hand by a gang of Billies and someone had hit him over the eye with a bottle. He was a proud man that day. He had been carrying the banner of St. Brigid. It was a hot day. And the sun was like a huge ball of fire hanging up there in the sky. Mr. Rooney was a fine singer. He sang in the choir. He always led off the singing in his big bass voice. Everybody loved him because he sang so well. He worked in the abattoir with Martha's Mick. Mick was an outsider. But his child was the apple of his eye, and of his mother too. That was Joe, and Joe was a good boy. Father Harry used to have him help serve Mass. He once asked Joe if he would like to be a priest. Joe said he would rather be a bishop. The priest laughed. He said one had to be very clever to become a bishop. Joe said he was clever, as clever as Paddy Dolan, who worked in Donovan's. He had won a scholarship But Joe hadn't, although he was a good boy.

"But you have to be very clever indeed," said Father Harry; "oh, very clever."

Joe gave it up as useless. He told his mother he wanted to be a bishop. Martha said it would cost a lot of money. Joe said that didn't matter. The parish would help to pay for him. They were all good people.

"But there's nothing but debt for every parish in the land, my child."

Martha had said—"Why, there's the roof has to be paid for, and the high altar is going to cost about five thousand pounds, and then Father Harry wants a new room for the two priests and himself. How could the parish help you, my child?"

Joe had wept—then he had got suddenly angry and said he would be nothing. Martha burst into tears, and said that if he wished she would get him away as a foreign missionary. Father Harry would certainly help in that. But Joe stuck by his guns and said it was to be a bishop or nothing.

Then his mother shut up. Mick heard all about it and said to Martha—

"What you say and what I say is two different things

—you say he'll be this and I say he'll be that—but what does he say himself?" Mick had asked.

Joe up and said he didn't want to be anything if he couldn't be a bishop. Mick laughed and said, getting Joe by the neck—

"You'll be what your father says, remember that—not what your mother says."

But Martha never asked Joe to choose what he really wished to be, following his refusal to become a foreign missionary. And Martha's Mick never asked either. Joe went to work at the docks. Then he forgot all about the bishops and their big hats and the foreign missionaries. Martha cursed the day that saw her husband send Joe down to the docks to work.

"My son's intelligent," she said, "why couldn't you have got him a job in an office? Somewhere where he'll wear a collar, and not be mixing up with the gang of dirty bitches that hang around the dock road." Mick up and shook himself and roared like a bull giving full vent to its rage on the pampas.

"He'll stay where he is; his job is to get out and work, same as his father did, see; what next? and the likes of us always seven days off the workhouse."

Martha said nothing. But a great pain seated itself underneath her heart. For she loved her son; she was a woman and a mother, and a woman, where her child is concerned, is as ready to give her blood as she is to give her milk. Mick stormed and raged for a week. He got drunk on top of it, and smashed up a table which Martha's grandmother had left her in a will. Martha bore the pain bravely, as bravely as she was bearing her seventh, which was pleased to turn over from one side to the other, making her feel sick. So Joe went each morning to the docks, and when there was no work, he came home again, and sat down to read his poetry. But Martha stormed and raged with him because she had seen in the book a poem by a man named Shelley, and he was a bad man. She brought him down a book of the life of St. Francis de Sales. Joe said that it was too dry, that he wanted something lively . . .

" Mick's late indeed," murmured Martha to herself.
She poked the fire once more. When a heavy boot was
heard kicking against the door she knew it was Mick. He
came in with a hang-dog expression and his boots squelch-
ing with blood. He yawned and sat down.

" Killed a bull to-day and saved me soul and me
bacon at the same time," exclaimed Mick.

Martha placed a steaming jug of tea on the table, saying as she poured out a cup for her husband, who was
already helping himself to herrings and bread—

" Indeed ! That was fine."

Mick yawned again. Martha asked him if he was
tired. The bed was made.

" Put the food in the oven ; I'm going out for a drink."
He went out the back way. Then Joe arrived. He had
a latch-key and he came in by the front door.

" Any tea ? " he asked, looking curiously at his mother.

" Maybe there is and maybe there isn't, but just let
me tell you this, mister : you've got to cut your Miss Jane
out of your mind. If your father gets to know of it, he'll
break you up. The idea ! A dirty bitch like that who
would think nothing of spitting on your beautiful religion.
Wait till I see her, the dirty low-lived creature. And you
just been to confession. Did you tell the priest that ? "

" What, mother ? "

" Why about your going about with this Protestant
young woman."

" No ! I didn't like to, mother."

" Very well then ; in the morning I'll see Father
Harry myself."

" Can I have my tea then ? " asked Joe trembling.

" No, you can't have your tea ; I might tell your
father yet, believe me ; your doings are disgracing me.
Get to bed out of my sight."

Joe went to bed. For a half hour he lay there, a swift
train of thoughts passing through his mind, the while his
eyes stared vacantly at the ceiling above him.

A voice at the bottom of the stairs—

" Have you said your prayers ? "

" Yes—will you give me some supper ? "

" No, I won't."

The door banged. Martha went to the window and, drawing up the blind, looked out. All was dark and silent, save for the gentle patter of the rain and the low murmuring of the river. Just then the great bell of St. Nicholas rang out the hour of ten. Its dull heavy tones came through the night air like the sound of muffled drum-beats. And always ascending towards the heavens the clouds of smoke and grease and steam. The city was heaving up its guts. There it lay like some huge beast. Martha stirred. She thought she had heard a footstep in the street. But her ears had deceived her. Her nose was pressed flat against the window-pane. She was thinking. She crossed from the window and at the bottom of the stairs shouted up to Joe that he could come down for his supper. Then she went back to the window and peered into the void. And if one had seen her face one would have noticed that it had become deathly pale, that her lips had drawn themselves apart, that there was a vacant look in her large blue eyes. She was unconscious of the fact that her son had come down was and even busy clearing away what was on the plate on the table. He did not know that he was eating the supper prepared for his father. He heaved a sigh of relief and went upstairs to bed again. Martha remained with her nose pressed flat, never moving. Night deepened. The black, mysterious night that seems to calm and soothe the heat and fever of Life. To the woman standing there it seemed deluged by phantom-like movements. It weighed heavily upon her heart. Martha stood stock still. Then she heard a voice and she knew her husband was returning. She heard him singing and knew that he was drunk. She went to the door, opened it, and looked out. She could see nothing, though the voice was now more distinct. She went into the house. She put on her shawl and went out into the street again. She looked about her, wondering. From which end of the street had the voice come. She stopped to listen. Ah ! She ran up to the top of the street. Her

Mick was in the middle of the road and he was kneeling down there in all the rain and slime. And he was repeatedly crossing himself and saying—

"Crucify me! crucify me!" There was a little crowd gathered round him. They were laughing at the strange sight. The rain had ceased, but the cruel wind of the morning had risen again. Martha broke through the crowd. She dragged her husband to his feet. He was covered with slime. The saliva trickled down his shirt front. The crowd laughed again. Martha, strong as a lion, dragged Mick through the crowd. At last she got him into the house. Now he lay on the couch by the fire, dead drunk. He looked at her and commenced muttering to himself.

Martha ran upstairs. Joe was lying awake. He had not slept. For long he had been tortured by strange thoughts. He had been on the brink of an abyss. He had feared to look down. A gust of wind had come upon him and he had all but fallen into the depths. Strange thoughts had poured across the surface of his mind. In a flash he had been drawn down into the gulf of desire. It whirled him down into the abyss. He could not free himself from it. Its tentacles had fastened upon him like a vice, swathing his heart with a gentle mist which stirred his blood. Alone he had lain thus, feverish, haunted by all the demons of the nether world. He had twisted and turned in his bed. He had buried his face in the pillow, seeking vainly to crush out the thoughts sweeping and surging against the floodgates of his soul. It had lain there so long, that desire for being, that desire for creating a something within himself. Like a pin-head of fire it had lurked upon the bosom of his soul, slowly yet surely flushing into life. And now he was in the grip of the beast. He could not stall it off.

"Jesus! Jesus!" he cried.

Martha heard his cry. Frightened, she rushed to her son and placed her arms around him.

"My son! my boy—what is it, are you ill?"

He did not answer. Below there was a sudden shout,

followed by a crash. Joe sat up. He looked at his mother. Then he said slowly—

"Again."

"Yes, again," replied his mother.

They held each other, finding a consolation in that ; they could have remained thus through an eternity of time. Joe kissed his mother.

Again that voice calling to her from below.

She hugged her son the tighter against her breast.

"I am afraid, my son," she said to him.

"There, there," he said, "I am still here with you—I will go down with you."

Stealthily Joe left the room and descended the stairs. His father was lying upon the floor. He had dragged down the table with him when he fell.

His eyes were wide open, staring up at the ceiling. And in those eyes Joe saw the hunger of the animal. He ran up the stairs.

"It is all right, mother," he said in a reassuring tone ; "you can come down, for he will fall asleep soon, and he can do no harm at present, he is helpless."

Together they raised him and got him upstairs into his room.

Then they left the room tiptoeing lest they should wake him. But he was fast asleep. So the remainder of the night was passed in silence. Joe slept on the couch and Martha slept in her son's room.

Dawn came, bleak and grey. Joe heard the hooters. It was seven o'clock.

He ran upstairs and called his father. But his father had already risen and gone out. Joe woke his mother.

Over the breakfast his mother said—

"Joe, I hope you are not going to continue going out with that Protestant girl."

He did not answer. She saw him bite his lip. She was afraid for him, because she was a good mother.

"All right, I will not bother with her," replied Joe and helped himself to a second cup of tea.

But in his heart he knew he had lied. He could not

speak the truth. He dare not, because, because——. No, it was impossible. He could not give her up. He would not give her up. He must continue to lie and bespatter his character, for her sake, and for his own.

"Your father," his mother was saying, "would cut her throat, son, as soon as look at her if he knew about it."

He made no answer. Instead he left the table and went outside to wash himself. He was going down to the docks, he told his mother. There was a big ship expected this morning; there was bound to be work by her. He was going to be first on the stand. Even now there would be many men on their way down, because men fought like wolves with claws and teeth and blood for a day's pay.

Martha began to clear the table. Joe said—"Good morning," and was off.

"My son, my son," exclaimed Martha, "and have I reared a son for such as she! No! I swear he will not carry on with her. Can I suffer disgrace, in a parish where I have spent all my days?"

Meanwhile Joe was tramping along in the direction of the river. The pavements were aflood with life. And the cold tang of the dawn—one saw it in the pinched blue faces. On they swept. Swarming miraculous life. The human ambulance, a mighty phalanx sweeping down, down, down.

The wind from the river cutting into them, and making them shiver. And the bent heads. Hurrying their various ways, on they swept. The hunters and the hunted.

Joe stopped at the large wooden gate. There were a hundred men beside himself. Young and old, they waited, in the first hours of the grey morning, waiting and watching, for that hand, the hand that would beckon to them. The hand appeared, was raised, a finger pointed at Joe.

Then he disappeared. And now a mighty concourse of sound. It deafened one. Trains, cars, ships, all the maggots of civilisation, steaming and tearing and lurching on their way. Whir! whir! whir!

Joe was down a ship's hatch. He was working like a nigger.

Crack ! A man fell beside him.

His skull was smashed. " Ha ! ha ! " laughed the crane, " come again ! "

* * * * * * *

Holiday of Obligation. Feast of the Holy Souls. The church is crowded. Joe is there with his mother. Mick has been at the first Mass, at five o'clock. The mission starts next week. The famous Brothers of St. Bernard coming for a fortnight. The priest is in the pulpit. He has a cracked voice.

" Ah !—my dear brethren in Christ, we all know that this day is in honour of the holy souls. We must remember, my sisters and brothers in Christ, what this day means to them. They are appealing to us to intercede for them to Our Blessed Lord."

The priest coughed and took up the red book from the pulpit desk.

" Seven o'clock Mass this morning will be for Patrick Tooley—the eight o'clock will be for Henty Ryan, the half-past eight will be for the deceased relatives and friends of the congregation. Ahem !

" Your respected prayers are requested for the following whose anniversaries occur about this time,

> Martha Pierce,
> Thomas Dolan,
> Georgina Flanagan,
> Arthur Benjamin,
> Mary Ann Kelly.

May their souls and the souls of the faithful departed rest in peace."

" Amen."

" The Children of Mary will assemble in the school-room at three o'clock. The members of the Third Order are requested to be in attendance at three o'clock to-morrow, Monday, for their quarterly meeting.

" There will be no Sunday school for the children to-day.

" In his monthly letter to the churches of the diocese, the Bishop calls upon the faithful to show their generosity in the matter of the new church of the Holy Land, which is now being built in a neighbourhood that has long been without a church or indeed a school.

" The brothers of St. Vincent de Paul kindly call your attention to their hand-boxes as you leave the church. Ahem !

" My dear brethren, we all know how the love of God is the one thing by which we receive His divine grace. But I am afraid there are in this congregation some who have not learnt the lesson of the love of our Blessed Lord. The attendance at the confessions has been bad. Last Sunday there were only two hundred and eighty who received the Blessed Sacrament."

The priest returned to the altar.

The elevation bell rang. All bowed their heads.

" *Mea culpa, mea culpa, mea maxima culpa.*"

The last gospel. Then home. The crowds filed out. The two men who were standing at the door with the boxes gave these an occasional shake. A penny dropped in. Another penny. Soon the place was deserted. Joe and his mother continued their way home. Martha had her arm in that of her son. Neither spoke. Both were thinking independently. Martha was thinking of the priest who would be calling to-day. She imagined she could hear the priest again—

" Father Harley will call to Pine Street, and I will call to Hinsley Road and Addio Street."

They reached the house. Martha started to cook the dinner. Joe took his book and was on the point of leaving the house when Martha called him back—

" Where are you going in such a hurry ?—why you are not a minute back from Mass yet—what's the book you have in your pocket ? "

Joe pulled out the book, and handed it shamefacedly to his mother.

" 'The Dream,' by Emile Zola—my God ! Who gave you this book ? "

Joe would not answer. He was angry with himself at not getting away. His mother dragged him by the arm.

"Bad luck is visiting this house, and it is through you, you devil," said his mother; "wait until your father returns."

She sat down. Her face was red with bending over the fire and the gas stove. The beads of sweat were standing out on her forehead.

"My God in heaven!" she exclaimed again "Where did you get this book?" she asked

"Mr. Flint gave it me," replied Joe.

"Well, I'll take it back myself to Mr. Flint, and we will have no more of such books coming into the house to put bad luck on us. The likes of you reading such a book!"

"There is no harm in it," said Joe.

"No harm in it, you flamer," shouted his mother. "Wait till Father Harley comes."

Joe shivered. He was in a fix. He wanted there and then to shout aloud—

"I do not believe—I do not believe."

But he dare not. His father would kill him. Besides it would kill his mother. His whole being trembled with anger. He wished in that terrible moment that the earth would open and swallow him up.

Instinctively he wished to be drawn down again into the abyss. To be sucked under by the spout of desire, ever lurking within his soul. To escape from himself. To be himself for one single moment. He stared at his mother. She glared at him like some frightened animal. The minutes sped by. Martha got up and said she was going to look for his father. Joe got up also. He turned to his mother and said—

"Burn the book then, but I'm going out, you can't prevent me!"

"You're staying here until the priest comes, my fine young man, he'll hear all about you, and your carryings on. Ever since you met that Protestant girl down the road you have been going to hell. After all I have done for you: worn my poor old bones out for you, given you the last of everything I ever had, created something out of nothing many a time, and starved my own belly to do it, and this is how I'm treated."

She burst into tears. Joe stood there, looking down on her.

"But you must listen to reason," he said.

"That's enough! I don't want any of your high knowledge displayed in this house, and you only consecrated to the Sacred Heart a month ago. Oo-hoo."

There was a bang at the door, and Mick came in. He looked at his son, and then across at his wife.

"What's the matter now, another row I suppose?"

"Look at this," exclaimed Martha, flinging the book to her husband.

Mick looked, walked across to the fire, and flung the book into the flames. Then he turned to his son.

"How many times have I told you not to bring those cursed books in here. They're all atheistic, every one of them, and all foreign books at that. I am responsible before God for your soul."

He raised his fist and struck his son a blow across the mouth.

"Get out," he shouted in his son's ear. "Go on, out of my sight, for I'd kill you as soon as look at you, you bloody worm. You're breaking your mother's heart as well as my own."

"Can I not read what I wish?" asked Joe.

He looked straight into his father's eyes. He saw there suddenly magnified the temper and anger of a wild beast.

"There's the priest" said Martha as a knock was heard.

Mick opened the door. There was Father Harley standing outside.

"Good morning, father, come in."

The priest came in. He was a thin, medium-sized man of about forty.

He saw Joe sulking in the corner.

"Hello!" he said, "what's the matter with this young man?"

"Ah," said his mother, "my son is breaking my heart, father; he is indeed."

The priest laughed.

"Well, well," he said, "let us hear all about it Joe."

Joe remained silent.

"Why don't you answer the priest," screamed his father.

But Joe would not speak. He wished that the floor would open and swallow him.

Father Harley went across and put his hand on the boy's shoulder. "Come, my child," he said, "tell me all your trouble."

But still he did not answer.

"He's reading bad books, father; this morning I found a book by Zola, that French writer, under his pillow, and last night he had a most horrible book by a filthy Irishman named Joyce, who please you, still considers himself a true Irishman. H'm. And he's carrying on with a young lady, father, who's a Protestant."

Silence. Joe took out his handkerchief to blow his nose. But he did not carry out that function. He had not the strength to do anything. He sat there silent, staring down at the floor. The priest put his hand under the boy's chin and gently raised his head, until he was looking right into his face. Joe felt the priest's hand caressing his face. It was a nice soft hand. He had never before felt a hand with so velvety a touch.

"You know our holy father the Pope forbids all Catholics to read such books."

"Yes, father," said Joe.

"And, my dear child, such books can do you infinite harm. They can blast your soul into the depths of hell. Woe to him who is damned! They are the weeds that tear up the beautiful flowers of one's soul. You will not read such books again?"

"No, father."

"And surely you will not carry on with a young woman not of the same religion as yourself, you know what our holy father has said of such marriages? Why, you are yet a child. Look after your parents, my son, who brought you into the world through the grace of God; look after them as is your duty to those who have reared you. You will, won't you ? "

" Yes, father."

" And again, my dear child, think of the mission, it is for such as you, you will come, won't you ? "

" Yes, father."

" And you will make a good confession and receive a good holy communion ? "

" Yes, father."

The priest patted him on the head. Joe liked to feel that fine soft hand caressing him. His mother and father looked across at him.

And upon their countenances Joe perceived a something he had not seen there before. To him they seemed infinitely happy. But they did not know that they were attaining that happiness by the travail through which their son was passing.

" Promise now that you will come to benediction to-night, and that from this day you will do your duty to your parents and to our holy mother the Church."

" Yes, father."

" On your honour ? " asked the priest, taking up his hat.

" Yes, father."

" God bless you, my child."

He turned his attention to Martha and her husband.

" He is a good boy ; he will look after you and after his own soul. Joe was always a boy of sound sense ; he has been led away ; but he will repent ; he has promised me that he will."

" I hope so, father," said his mother, looking with her large eyes into those of the priest.

" Yes, I think he will turn out a good lad," said his father, adding, " I must say that I struck him in a temper, father, but I am sorry. Really he has nearly killed his mother, for if he had kept on with such doings she would not have been able to hold up her head, father—and we have been in this parish for thirty-five years, father."

" Ah, well ! " said the priest, " I must be going."

"Yes, father," said Martha, and followed him to the door.

As he was leaving she pressed a shilling into his hand, saying—

"I'm sorry, father, but that is all I can spare this time, my husband hasn't had such good work lately, the works are very slack, you know."

"Yes, yes," said the priest, "I understand."

"And the boy here, he has not had much work lately you know; he gets an odd day here and there at the docks, father, but it was his father who sent him down there. It was not my wish, father. The last place I should think of sending a pure clean Catholic boy."

"Well, well," said Father Harley, "there are worse places than the docks, my dear sister in Christ; one has to have strength, and must be able to prevail against all evil. A good Catholic is no exception even in such a place as that. Well, good-morning"—calling in through the half-open door—"Good-morning, Joe, good-morning, Mr. ——" Then he was gone.

Martha came in and started to get ready the dinner. It had all been delayed both by her terrible son and by the priest's visit. Mick went upstairs, saying he was going to lie down. Joe remained seated in the chair. He would not speak. He would not look into his mother's face. He was sorry in his heart for giving his mother this worry and heartache, but what could he do? He said to himself as he sat there—

"I have lied. In my heart and soul I know I cannot go on with this. I hate it. Curse the day that I was born! Is there no escape?" The blood whirled in his body; it boiled in his heart. He was angry with himself. He had said to the priest "Yes," knowing that he lied. He had said to his suffering mother "Yes," knowing that he lied.

He had bespattered his soul with mud. He was not noble; he was not truthful; he was nothing.

He sat there silent, thoughts running riot in his mind. Could he never be free? Must he remain chained forever to a thing which he despised? Ah! little did they know of the struggles that had been going on in his soul. Little did they know of the desire lurking in his heart. They spoke not. They knew nothing. They would never know. They could not know.

The dinner was ready. Mick came down. They all sat together at the table. Martha was smiling. She said—

"Let us start now, this day, and live good holy lives— say the grace before meals."

The three bowed their heads.

When the grace was over his mother said—

"Eternal rest give unto them, O Lord, and let perpetual light shine upon them, and may they rest in peace."

"Amen," said Mick.

"Amen," said Joe.

They ate in silence. After dinner, Mick said he was going down for a walk to the docks. Martha reminded him that he had promised to attend benediction.

"All right," he said, put on his hat and coat and left the house.

"Now if you like you may go for a walk, because I am going down to attend to the Third Order. Will you go?" asked his mother.

"No," Joe replied, "I much prefer to remain at home."

"Will you come with me down to the schoolroom? You know you ought to join the Young Men's Society, all the young fellows are in it, there's that Tom Scully, he's in this long time."

"He drinks like a fish too," remarked Joe.

"Well I don't know anything about that," said Martha, "but I do know that he is a good living Catholic and that he attends his Easter duties as every good man should do."

"He has a proper boozer's face," went on Joe, "there's quite a clique of them! For all their running to church they can take their pint of ale."

"Well, now, Joe, try not to be so envious of everybody ; they do you no harm."

"It's not that, mother," replied her son, looking up suddenly at her, "but it's the fact that they can go and get drunk every night, and be good Catholics just by belonging to the society, and attending their Easter duties and going to Mass on a Sunday, but because I pick up a book, which has more force, more of the stuff of life in it, than most of the modern novels, you condemn me, and blacken my name everywhere. I know my duties as well as anyone else, although I don't run down to the church at every hand's turn."

"There, my son," said Martha, "you'll make yourself ill. Stay in if you wish—have a little rest, then you'll be able to come with me to-night to benediction."

She went upstairs to get herself ready for the monthly meeting of the third order of St. Francis.

Joe sat in his chair, looking straight before him. He sat thus for fully five minutes, then he rose, crossed to the fireplace, and sat down. Then he went to the foot of the stairs and shouted up to his mother—

"Have you seen the ' Sunday Post,' mother ? "

"I think it's in the cupboard, your father had it last —why he buys such rubbish I don't know. He's nearly as bad as you. The paper's full of nothing but divorces and filth."

Joe slammed the kitchen door. He had heard enough for the day.

Then he searched in the cupboard, and found the Sunday paper. He lit a cigarette, and sat back to read in comfort.

His mother came down, dressed in black. She had worn the clothes ever since little Pat had died, through falling down a large grid in the street. Soon she would have to lie up.

"I'm going now," she said to her son.

"All right," replied Joe, without looking up from his paper. She stood there looking at him, her hand holding the knob of the door. Once she thought of going straight across and tearing the paper out of her son's hands, and pitching it into the fire. But she could not do that now. She turned the knob gently, and slipped out into the street. Joe heard the door close, glanced up from the paper, and knew she had gone.

At last! To be alone! Alone! He flung down the paper. From his pocket he took a book. It was a pamphlet by Paine. He read on, little thinking of the time. Suddenly he put the book in his pocket. Someone was at the back door. His father came in.

"Where's your mother?"

"Gone to the Third Order meeting."

"Did she say what time she would be back?"

"Said she'd be back in time for tea," said Joe, and picked up the "Sunday Post."

"I see the new ship pulled into the river to-day," said his father.

"Yes, I heard it was coming in," said Joe, without looking up from his paper.

There was a key turned in the lock. That was his mother. The house smelt funny on a Sunday. It smelt of roast beef, oranges, stale papers : a musty smell that now seemed too strong for Joe's nostrils. He got up and went out into the back yard.

He heard his mother calling him ten minutes later. He went into the house. The table was laid for tea. He sat down next his father. Mr. Rourke ate in silence. He did not raise his head when Martha said she felt ill and left the table. Mick knew what that meant. He went on with his tea. Joe also ate in silence. He did not look at his father. He did not wish to look at either of them after the affairs of the morning.

The tea over, Mick went upstairs to change into his best clothes. Joe found his mother sitting on a chair by the window in the front sitting-room. He knew she was ill, because her face was pale. He could see that she had been crying. He went over to her, and said—

"Are you ill, mother, perhaps you'd better stay at home to-night, you do not look at all well."

His mother raised her tea-stained face, and said—

" I am going to-night if I have to crawl there, if I die on the doorstep. Joe," she went on, in her low voice, " you promised you would go, and I am going because of you."

" All right," replied Joe. He left the room and went upstairs to his own room to get ready. His father was coming down the stairs. They looked at each other for a moment, and Mick's glance seemed to say—

" I do not trust you, you are lying."

Joe sat down on the bed. He did not know what to do. If he refused to go, there would be a terrible row, and yet he hated all the paraphernalia of church-going. He got up, and put on a clean collar and tie. He heard his father shouting up the stairs to him—

" Are you nearly ready ? "

" Yes," he shouted down.

" Hurry up, it is nearly a quarter-past six."

" All right ! "

Below his mother was up and ready. She had dried her eyes. Joe came down. He was dressed in his blue serge suit and had on a clean white collar. His brown shoes had been polished by his mother.

" I am ready," he said.

" Your father has gone down the yard—he will be here directly."

They both sat down opposite each other, each trying not to look at the other. The awkwardness of the situation was stemmed in time by the return of Mick, who was trying to fix his braces.

" Why don't you buy those braces Andy Flanagan wears, these are no use at all. You never seem to do the right thing, Mick," said Martha.

She went over and fixed the braces which had got all tied up into knots.

" There," she said, " I suppose you are ready now."

" Yes," he replied.

They were just leaving the house when Mick called out to Joe—

" Run and get my pipe, Joe, I left it upstairs."

" You're a terrible man," said Martha, and waited for Joe, fearing he would not carry out his promise to the priest.

Mick walked off up the street. She watched him turn the corner. Just then the bell of the church commenced to ring. Martha looked vexed. She shouted through the door to Joe to hurry up. Joe shouted back that he couldn't find the pipe.

" Never mind the thing, come along, we'll all be late."

Joe came out. Martha shut the door. Then they started after Mick. But when they turned the corner there was no sign of him. He had vanished.

" Your father is probably in church by now," she said to Joe as they hurried down the long road leading to the Church of St. Patrick.

" He always did walk very fast," said Joe.

When they reached the bottom of the road, they found Mick waiting for them outside the pub. Martha went right up to her husband. She could smell his breath. He had hurried to get a drink before the sermon,

CHAPTER II

JANE ASKEW was the bastard daughter of a chemist. She was a tall girl, and had a face as white as marble, and as motionless. She had black eyes, a heavy sensual chin, and hair as black as a raven. Jane was twenty-two and she walked the streets. True she had a kind of protector : an old man of eighty who used to sit on the doorstep all day, looking out of little grey eyes from which tears incessantly flowed. He was a very weak old man ; he had long legs. He used to sit of an evening in his little room reading the Bible.

It was a big house with twenty rooms. A lot of people lived there. (1) Eliza Redmond—prostitute. (2) Tim Larson—a sweep. (3) Mary Ann Sully, widow of whom nothing was known. (4) Johnny Garsides, a rag-picker. They all had children. The house was full of them.

They used to set up a terrible din, whenever any of the people in the house began fighting, and they were always fighting' The prostitute used to fight with the chimney-sweep. The ragman used to belt the heads of the children, whenever they made a noise. There was always a smell of old bones and fish.

" The damned place is always full of someone or others' dung," Tim Larson used to say. He was a funny man. He had only one eye. He drank like a fish, and was a devil for singing. You could hear his cracked voice all over the place. The house was on the river bank. From its windows you could see the broad rolling waters. The wind used to come up of a morning, just when old Tim would be opening his window and starting to clear his throat of accumulations from over night. He was a very hairy man. The children used to shout after him—" Hello there, hairy Larson ! "

He would fly into a rage and catching hold of one of the children between his knees use his belt furiously.

" That and that for you," he would say—" you are only damn nuisances like all children. Your mother should have buried you all in one day. Take that and that."

Jane lived in a room on the top floor. She never spoke to anybody, excepting when she was wearing her little red toque.

" The peacock's there again," Larson would whisper to the sweep.

Then they would laugh and you could hear them all over the house. The old man of eighty reading his Bible, used to raise his head, and cross himself—

" Lord God save us from all evil ! "

One day Tim heard him praying aloud in his room.

He knocked at the door and went in. The old man on his knees against his little wooden bed.

" Say a thimble full for me, old boy," he laughed.

" My son," the old man answered, " revile not the most beautiful religion in the world. God protect us from all evil ! "

" And from short-time Jane, and fresh Eliza Redmond
—ha ! ha ! ha ! "

Then he vanished from the room. The old man went
on with his praying.

Sometimes he used to go up to Jane's room. Once
when he knocked he heard a man's voice say—" Well,
what the devil do you want ? "

That was Joe. For Joe used to sneak up sometimes
after his mother and father had gone to night prayers.
He and Jane were truly in love with each other. Once
Jane asked Joe if he really loved her. He looked at her
for a moment. Then up came the wave of desire—he
stared hard at her, noted her open dress, and swore—

" I would damn myself for you."

She laughed and said, " But you are only a boy yet."

" What matter ? I am as strong as you, and perhaps
more fresh."

Joe wanted her to give up walking the street. But she
would not promise.

" Who will pay my rent—who will buy my clothes—
who will buy me food and light ? "

He remained silent after that—then suddenly he said—

" But I would work for you, Jane. I love you with all
my heart and soul."

" But what would your mother say to that, Joe ? "
she asked him.

" It doesn't matter about her," he replied savagely
—" only you matter."

" Remember you owe them a duty ; they brought
you up—didn't they now ? "

" Yes," said Joe.

" When you start working and make a little money I
will marry you, will that do ? "

Joe hugged her and kissed her mouth, her eyes, her
neck.

He was carried away by it all. The abyss had him
again. Just a little gust of wind, and he was down,
fighting with desire.

He had once asked Jane if she would run away with him. Jane had laughed at him.

"Why, where could we run? the world is a very small place, you know."

But he was determined on something like that. He had said to her—

"Consider what I do for you—I throw up my religion, I disgrace my father and mother at the call of instinct. I break up my home. I abandon myself—for you. Believe that I will work for you. Honest I will."

She laughed again. This taunted him. It was a hot iron burning into his very soul. He looked at her out of his clear eyes.

"Ah well! there will come a time." Then she said good-night. She had a nice little room. It was poorly furnished, but clean. There was a little statue of the Blessed Virgin, standing on a shelf.

That room made her reflect. The little statue was still there for comfort's sake. Sometimes when she was alone, she would reflect upon the ferocity of life, and the badness of men. She had been thrown on the street by an aunt with whom she had lived for ten years, ever since her father had perished in a fire at sea. Her mother went mad with the shock and died in an asylum. And often in the small hours she would sit staring out of the little window, far out over the rolling river, and in imagination she would be carried away down the dark night of the world. She had to work hard for her living, in that she had had to suffer the curses and kisses of men. But then, it was a job like everything else. Otherwise how could she live in the city? How could she live in this place, a dark forest, peopled by human wolves, rushing here and there, spurred on by the energy and ferocity of living? Swarming miraculous life! She saw it in the faces of the men. She saw it in the faces of the women, and of the children. It was there, in their eyes: that hunger, that haunted look. Hither and thither they streamed with their vacant faces, staring down upon the ground, suspicious of every human soul whom

chance threw in their path. And she had to live in this
teeming vortex!

There are moments in our lives that stand out clear
and shining against the sun of the soul, and in those
moments the Being becomes suffused by a radiant light.
This light blots out for a time the dark texture of the
years through which we have passed. The soul becomes
charged with new life ; the heart renewed with hope,
the body with sap, even as the tree, which, though ageing
is pregnant with Beauty. In those moments there seems
to ring in our ears the very music of Being. So intense
is this manifestation of beauty, so strong, that the heart
and soul become trapped in its very trellis-work, blinded
by its light, made feverish by its richness. Those moments
Jane had never known. She had been too early the
victim of that strange, peculiar madness which ever
lurks in cities ; that madness that feeds on life itself.
Jane would turn away from the window with a sigh.

"Ah, dear me ! " she would exclaim.

Her price was everybody's price. That is the art of
living that your price shall suit everybody. That is the
will to live when you shall demand that price. That is
your courage when you will fight for it.

*   *   *   *   *   *   *

In moments of despair, Jane would bow her head and
weep.

And her tears, like those of the old man with his Bible,
would run often and long. As the old man would say—

" I have lived through eighty years and seen through
the book of life, and because I am a gentleman, I do not
close the book forthwith and spit upon it. There is
nothing but evil in our world."

Then he would fall to weeping, even as Jane in her
moments of misery.

Night after night, day in, day out, all through the
years, she would have to say—

" Yes, that will do me ! "

And she would say that because life was hard and she

c

had to live. She would say that—she would utter those
words beneath the dome of heaven because it was better
to say that to the idiots, to the blue-faced apes swinging
on the trees of life between heaven and earth, better to
say that in the sight of the passionless God aloft in the
clouds, his hands upon his emotionless breast. Better,
because one had to live.

And let her not depart from such things ! It was
impossible. One move and would fall into the abyss.
For the abyss was but a stone's throw away. The icy
mist of fear hung perilously over her.

She would light the gas, draw the blinds in the little
room, and turn the statue of the Virgin to the wall.

All is still. All is calm. Peace. No sound. Presently
the wind stirs and traverses the roofs. A child is heard
whining in the night. A voice—

" There, there, my little Christ." All is silent again.

The infant gurgles as one strong little hand clutches
eagerly at the breast. Over all, the low-lying and ominous
clouds. Outside, the low murmuring of the river. Like
the beating of some huge heart. Away beyond the
horizon, the new day, the dawn, holding life within the
lightness of his wings. The sudden scream of a ship's
whistle, outraging the stillness of the night. The moon
milk-white disappearing behind a sheaf of clouds. Black
darkness like a heavy blanket over the city. Outside
Jane's window, ivy upon the wall. It stirs, so gently, the
sound comes to the ears of the pair lying on the bed.
Abyss of dreams and illusions. Nothingness. Nothingness eating out life—life eating out nothingness. Down
the dark night, far away upon ships of fire to the land of
dreams. The wind again stirring the ivy leaves. A cough!
That is the old man. He is very old and very ill. Cough
cough ! cough ! The silence is broken by the hammer-
like coughs penetrating the night air. Then again a
great silence, save for the low moaning of the wind like
great prayers being carried to the clouds. A faint whispering. God ! God ! The night wears on. A voice again—

" This confounded bed is alive with bugs."

" Tell the landlord to-morrow."

" He doesn't give a God-damn."

" Well shut your mouth, and let other people get a bit of sleep."

" Ah Christ ! "

Dawn. The wind has ceased. The sudden barking of a dog in the stillness of the new morn. The pale light filtering through the blinds. A gentle stirring of the bodies in the bed. A sleepy voice speaking in low tones—

" What time is it ? "

" 'Sh——"

A great blowing of a ship's whistle. She is coming down the river. She is hurrying for the tide. A footstep in the street below. Another. And again another. Their feet resound on the setts as they hurry along. All in the same direction. Pilot going to his ship. Tug men going to tow in the ship. Dockers waiting for a day's work. Again the loud blast of the whistle.

" Is it late ? "

" 'Sh—— ; it is only half-past five."

" Jesus, I thought it was nearly eight o'clock."

The great bell of St. Nicholas rings out. The angelus. Life stirs again. The blind is raised in the little room. The man in the bed stirs. Sits up. Buries himself again in the clothes. The pavements are aflood. Tramp, tramp. They hurry down the streets and the roads, turn the corners. The cars commence. From the thousands of chimney-pots rises the first sign of life in the caves of the living. The roar of the first trains thundering on their way, carrying their human loads. Whir ! whir ! Rushing through the tunnel. On, on, never resting, never ceasing. That is the law of life. On, on. There is no turning back. Jane rises from the bed. She washes and dresses and does her hair with the aid of the broken pier-glass standing over the mantelshelf in the little room. The man rises. He looks at her, smiles, as if to say— "I am satisfied." He dresses hurriedly.

A kiss. He is gone. She is alone. She puts two notes

in her little bag. She hurries down the stairs. She puts on the little tin kettle and makes her breakfast. Tim is passing through to the back-yard.

" Good morning, Jane," says he.

" Good morning," she answers, not even looking at him, but intent upon her business of making her breakfast. He laughs. But she does not look up.

" Ha ! ha ! three for the bishop," says he, and marches out into the street.

She goes upstairs with her little kettle and makes some tea in the little enamel teapot. She cuts some bread, takes out some cold meat from the cupboard, makes a sandwich or two, then commences her meal.

Below all is activity. The ragman is busy oiling his handcart. The chimney-sweep is off to his business. The old man is in his room praying. The children are out in the back-yard throwing things at one another. Eliza Redmond is looking out of her window at them. She has a hard cruel face. It is nearly purple in colour, and she has a swollen neck. She stands there for a long time staring at the children. Suddenly there is a wailing sound. One of the children is lying on the ground. There is blood on his face. A voice from the top window—

" Ah, you little bastard, I saw you, wait till I come down."

The boy runs off to his mother. She is lying in her bed. He crawls on to the bed. He wakes up his mother who has been snoring heavily. She yawns.

" Mrs. Redmond called me a little bastard," he bursts into tears.

" What else are you, my little cock, in heaven's name tell me," she says to him.

The old man is coming down the stairs. The wooden stairs creak beneath the weight of his big body. He has a big pop-belly. He is wiping his eyes with a dirty hand-kerchief. Then suddenly he has a fit of coughing. " Oh, dear me ! dear me ! " he wails aloud. He reaches the bottom of the stairs. He stops, looks around him, gazes out into the yard. He sees the little chimney-sweep's son

sitting on the old wooden bench, crying his eyes out
His heart is full of pity, and he makes his way out to him.
He sits down by his side, and strokes the fair curly hair.
The child looks up at him with large innocent eyes.
He smiles at the old man.

"What is the matter, my little man?" asks the old
man.

"Tommy hit me with a piece of iron," replies the
child.

"That is very cruel," says the old man, again stroking
the boy's head. "Never mind," he goes on, "some day
you will grow up to be a man, then you can fight your
way through this cruel world. And remember always
that God is above you, up there in the clouds, that he is
looking down upon you all through the days and years ;
and he is saying to his angel with the great book—
'That is Bobby the chimney-sweep's son. Watch him
because now he is growing up into a man, and will soon
be out in the world of men, working hard like his father.
He is my servant, protect him.' That's what God does,"
said the old man.

The boy loved the old man. He stroked his hairy face
with his little hand. He was his good friend. He would
come to see the old man every morning, and the old
man who was so good to him would tell him wonderful
tales of all the things he had seen in his lifetime. That
was good for the boy, because he had no friend, only a
father. And the old man was so gentle, he spoke so
softly, he had no enemies in the world, save those whose
hearts were filled with evil. So each morning the old
man would look forward to meeting his little friend.
They got to love each other, like two good and faithful
brothers. And the chimney-sweep was happy because
his little son had found a friend in the old man whose
eyes were always running tears, and whose age was
eighty, and who had seen much of life in his wanderings
over half the face of the earth. Soon the sweep would
send his little son to school. But still he would always
have a friend in the old man. For in this sink of iniquity

he was a bright angel. His outlook upon life was so beautiful.

"Build, build," the old man would say, "do not destroy, build a heaven in your hearts, that you will fear no man peering into its innermost depths. Purge your soul of all evil, that it may stand the test of the great winds and storms of life. For if you have God in your heart, you are happy, and this happiness will shine out of you, like the beautiful rainbow, and it will pass on to every living heart. Keep God in you, and all is well."

That was the old man's philosophy of life. Many an evening he would sit on the bench with the sweep, and together they would talk for hours of all the beautiful things on earth. The moon and the sun and the stars.

"The moon is the daughter of the sun, and the stars are her sons," he would say.

"But the evil in men's hearts, Lord on high! it is the cause of all the unhappiness in this world."

And his friend the sweep would look into his poor weak eyes, eyes that were as bright as the sun of truth, and he would hold the old man's hand and say—

"Those are beautiful words you have spoken, father, would that each and every one of us could abide by them."

"Ah!" the old man would reply, "you cannot because you will not open your hearts to each other. How can one live with evil in his heart? His soul is a burden to him, his heart is a millstone round his neck, because of the evil therein."

They would look into each other's eyes, speaking no word, their hearts full of love for each other. And suddenly the little boy would come running into the yard, and he would squeeze himself between his father and the old man, look up into their faces, and say as he stroked the old man's face—

"Ah, granddad, tell me a tale, just like the one you have told daddy."

The old man would take him on his knee. He would smother him with kisses, he would dance him up and down upon his knee.

One evening when he was rather late coming to see
his little friend, the boy's father entered and gave his
son a little brown paper parcel to give to the old man.
And the old man had been delighted and had kissed the
child. He looked at the bright new red handkerchief,
then at the boy, and said—his lips trembling the while—

" My son, God lives in your little heart—I will remember you, for I have lived all my years in sorrow, and
now as I stand with one foot on earth and the other
in the next world, you fill my heart with joy." And he
took the boy in his arms and hugged him to his heart.
And the little sweep was proud of his son, that he had
made such a friend of the old man.

" The old fellow will remember him in his will, he's
plenty of tin, the old miser," said fresh Liza to the sweep
one morning as they passed each other in the hall on
the way to the yard.

" I am not looking for that," he had replied with some
heat. He was angry, because such thoughts had never
entered his mind. And the other children were envious
of the boy. Jane used in the daytime to take the little
fellow for a walk. Once the sweep had told the old man
that he did not like his son going out with the young
woman at all.

" Ah ! " the old man had said, " have pity for her,
it is through the brutality of men that she lives so ; you
know she is the one person in this house whom I love,
although we rarely speak to each other. She is a daughter
to me, because she has no people and no friends save
you and the boy."

The sweep did not answer him for some time, then
he said—

" Well, yes, you are right, father, then I will not mind
her taking out little Bobby for a walk now and again.
Yes, I am sorry for her, I have spoken rashly indeed."

" You have never spoken as rashly to her, as that
rag-picker. He is the devil incarnate. I am sure if she
were alone with him, he would do her some terrible
harm, yes I am sure he would."

The old man fell ill one day. He started to cough terribly. Fresh Redmond, who was having her afternoon nap, woke up when she heard the awful fit of coughing which seized the old man. The boy heard it too and ran upstairs to the old man's room. He found him lying on the bed, his eyes closed, his hands to his throat. Cough! cough! It seemed to shake the very walls of the room. Bobby burst into a fit of weeping and ran out of the room to look for his father. But his father had not yet arrived home from work. He sat down on the bench in the yard, weeping and moaning as if the little heart would break. Upstairs Eliza had heard it too, and was gently cursing the old man for having spoiled her afternoon's rest.

"He coughs in the night, and gives people the shivers, and is not content with that, but he must spoil people's sleep in the daytime."

The boy told his father that his great friend was ill. Without stopping even to take off his clothes the sweep ran upstairs to the room.

The old man was lying very still upon the poor worn bed. He was breathing heavily, and there was a huskiness in his breath. The sweep knelt down by the side of the bed and stretching his hand across stroked the old man's forehead. He was very hot and feverish. He got up and left the room. Below he found his little son sitting on the old wooden bench sobbing.

"Granddad is very ill, run and tell Jane to come to his room. I am going for the doctor."

Jane came into the room. Just then the old man opened his eyes. He looked up at the young woman standing over him, and a faint smile crossed his face. She bent down and took his poor weak hand in her own. Then she knelt down by his side and said—

"Father, father, you must not die, you are the only one I love in this world."

"I will not die yet, my child," he replied, "the good God above knows when His servant is ready; no—I will not die yet, never fear."

The sweep came into the room then. The doctor was with him.

He said in a loud voice, loud enough to waken the dead—

" Open that damn window, and you, what are you doing standing there, get a fire lighted in this room straight away," he added, turning to Jane.

He examined the old man. Then he put on his hat and turning to the sweep he said, this time in a very low voice—

" He will not last the night—his lungs are gone."

The sweep burst into tears. The doctor said something in a low voice to Jane and left the room. The child entered. The old man heard the door close. He raised his great head, ever so slowly, and saw the child. He smiled and said—

" Come here, little one, I want to whisper something in your ear."

The boy climbed upon the bed and leaned over to the old man.

His father turned to Jane, who was busy trying to open the dirty window, and said—

" Let us go outside, he will feel happier alone with the child." They both went down into the yard. And together they sat on the bench, upon which the old man used to sit so often of an evening telling tales to the boy and his father. Neither of them spoke. A voice seemed to have suddenly sprung up between them. They both stared down at the ground. Above in the little room the old man was saying to the little boy—

" My son, remember to love everybody, love everybody—and I have something for you which your father will give you to-morrow."

Then he fell back upon the pillow, yellow with age.

" Granddad," screamed the boy, " wake up ! wake up ! "

Downstairs his father raised his head after staring at the ground for half an hour, and he turned to Jane and said to her in a mere whisper—

"Did you hear what the doctor said, Jane? He said he would not last the night."

They both went upstairs. They found the boy asleep across the body of the old man. His eyes were red with weeping. One of the old man's arms was clutching the boy. The two people knelt down. Their friend was gone. They did not, they could not speak. They could not look each other in the face. Each was concerned with his own sorrow. And that is enough.

CHAPTER III

"Has that lazy devil washed himself yet?"

Mick was shouting down the stairs at the top of his voice. Martha was cleaning her boots. She had one foot up on the old arm-chair, showing off a massive leg encased in a thick black woollen stocking. She was red in the face with the exertion. She shouted into the back kitchen to her son—

"Your father's calling on you, are you deaf?"

"Where's the confounded soap, you can never find a thing in this hole."

"Perhaps it fell down the sink—look for it."

"I can't find the damn stuff."

"Below there!—what's all the row about—I'll screw your neck if you speak like that again to your mother."

Mick came downstairs. He was angry with Joe. He went out into the back kitchen. Joe was swilling himself under the tap.

His father gave him a kick. Joe jumped and turned round.

"What's the matter?" he asked furiously.

"I'll show you what's the matter in a minute, hurry up and get ready to come to the mission, your mother's ready long ago. Come on, shift yourself, or I will, confounded quick."

Joe swore to himself. He felt like rushing at his father

and taking him by the throat ; he felt like pummelling him, and saying as he did so—

" There ! there ! take that ! you've vexed me long enough, take that ! and that ! "

When he dwelt on this aspect of the case, he felt an inward glow of pride. He said to himself as he wiped himself down with the towel—

" Ah ! wait, just wait, my fine beauties, wait till you are old, I'll fix you. Fix you when you have a bent back, and can hardly crawl. You've had the laugh on me long enough. I can't blow my nose in this confounded house. I wouldn't go to this bloody mission, only that it pacifies you. I don't believe a bit of it. Bah ! You wait."

They left the house together. On their way Martha stopped now and again to look at the shops ; Joe hung on silently. His father asked him why didn't he go down to look for a job on the new ship.

He didn't answer. His father was angry with him because of his silence.

So was his mother. She said to him—

" You treat your father like a piece of dirt. You ought to be ashamed of yourself."

" Well, I have my own opinions. I stick by them—he sticks by his—that's good enough for both of us." As they neared the church they saw large crowds of people going in by the iron gate. Martha said to Joe as they were on their way across the road—

" Did you hear that young Samson was ordained yesterday ?—you remember he used to go to school with you."

" I remember him," said Joe. Once again there was a silence. His father was fumbling in his pocket. Martha was fumbling in hers. She had a big one in the side of her skirt. She looked up suddenly at her husband.

" Have you got any coppers on you ? I left my few coppers on the dresser."

" You are always short of something or another," replied her husband. He put his hand in his pocket, and pulling out three pennies gave them to her. Then she turned to her son and said to him as he was entering the porch—

"Here! give that, you—I only pretended to your father, I have my own coppers here."

She thrust the three pennies into his hand. Together they entered the church. A big raw-boned man with a plate took their money. He whispered to them—

"'Ave to go on the high altar, all the seats packed. Yes, up the right aisle."

They went up the right aisle. As they passed the tabernacle they all three genuflected to the Blessed Sacrament. Then they went in through the little gate of the altar rails and up the steps, then turned to the right and took their seats. They could see right down the church from their position.

Martha beamed. She was so proud to see the church packed. She felt an inward flow of pride that she was a Catholic; she hoped that her husband felt the same. She was praying too, that her son would know the same pride. The people were still pouring in. Already they were standing in long lines in the four aisles. Joe sat with head bent, looking down at the rich carpet on the floor, and secretly wishing that he had such a fine carpet in his own room. His mother watched with admiration one of the priests come out of the vestry and look up and down the church. She could read the priest's mind, she knew that he was saying to himself—"Great! that's a parish for you!" Then he went into the vestry again. The big doors at the bottom of the church were left open until it was found that it was impossible to get another single person into the church. They were packed like sardines. And outside there was a crowd also. Some of them were sent up with the choir. They were lucky because there were good seats in the choir. Mick himself was looking steadfastly at the high altar, and admiring the golden tabernacle, the golden candle-sticks, the rich carpets, the beautiful flowers in the big golden vases. He remembered when he was a child, his mother used to help decorate the high altar in the very church in which he was now sitting. He remembered how he had helped to serve Mass. He felt proud of himself in that moment. There was a sudden hush amongst the vast congregation. Everybody sat silent. An altar boy came out and opened the little gate, leading from the altar rails to the pulpit. He was only a little chap about twelve years old. He had a cast in his eye. He stood there, mute, one hand on the altar rail, the other hanging down listlessly by his side, like a Roman sentinel of old. Then a door opened. A long thin man, wearing a brown habit, sandals, and a little round brown cap on his head came out, walked along the foot of the altar, genuflected, then passed on to the pulpit. All the eyes of the congregation were turned up to him, eyes that might well have been those of startled animals, looking up into the face of an executioner. He ascended the six steps to the pulpit, slowly, and stood for a moment scanning the crowd of people. Then he took up a book, looked at it, put it down and said in a loud voice—

" In the name of the Father and of the Son and of the Holy Ghost, amen."

A sudden movement on the part of the congregation. Some coughs. Then silence. The father in his bass voice began the rosary.

" My dear children in Christ," said the missioner in a loud voice as he came to the address, " I am going to speak to-night on the value and importance of the holy Mass."

Up in her seat Martha sat still. Her face was transfigured. She was watching her son, his head hung down, he could not look up. For in his heart he knew he had missed Mass. He was damned then for ever. God might suddenly call on him. He might say to him those terrible words of which the missioner had just reminded them, " Depart ye cursed into everlasting fire."

He was hot. He was wishing it over. He felt tired. The long prayers, during which time he had had to kneel on the floor, had given him a terrible pain in his legs. He wanted to get up and walk out. But he could not do that. He dare not walk out during the sermon, for the people would say he was a blasphemer ; they would stone him ; they would kill his mother with their talk about him. Instinctively his mind turned to Jane, who even now might be sitting alone in her room.

Again the voice of the missioner broke in upon him. He stirred, ever so gently, then fell back again into the torpor of a moment before.

" My dear sisters and brothers in Christ." . . . .

At last, the missioner left the pulpit. He walked slowly up the aisle, across the passage leading to the altar rails, through the little gate, and finally disappeared into the vestry. A sudden coughing on the part of the congregation. The altar boy came out to light the forty candles on the altar. He switched on the electric light, shedding on the whole altar a bright glow, which revealed the magnificence of the scene. The people sat silent. Martha turned to look at her son. He was still sitting in the same position, head bent down, whilst his father was looking with pride in his eyes at the altar boy. It brought back to him memories of his young days. At last. The altar boys came out through the door, six of them, followed by the priest. They ascended the altar steps. The choir started to sing the *O Salutaris*. And the people joined in with the singing. The air was stifling with the smell of the incense which the altar boy was now offering to the Blessed Sacrament exposed upon the altar. The *Tantum Ergo* was sung, and the priest bent low over the altar.

Then he went round and brought down the Blessed Sacrament. The congregation bowed their heads. And the bell rang three times. Then the hymn to the Blessed Sacrament was sung, followed by the priest singing a solo that the choir took up. Then the divine praises.

" Blessed be God."

The organ burst out again. And the people were slowly filing out. Martha was pulling Joe after her. His father had gone by way of the vestry. On his way he saw

Father Dunny. He stopped. An idea suddenly occured to him. He made his way towards the priest.

" Excuse me a minute, father," he said.

" Of course," said the priest, " what is it you want of me, my dear man ? "

" It is about my son, father. I thought you had better know. You know, father, he has the house stocked with these bad French books, father, and the English ones are not much better. I really do not know what to do with him, father, I am afraid he is going fast to hell. He has come to the mission to-night with his mother, but I was watching all through the sermon. I am sure he was not bothering about what the missioner was saying. The other day, father, he brought a book in, lent him by some man, and the book, father, I am sorry to say, is the most blasphemous book I ever saw in my life."

" Did you read it ? " asked the priest, looking him closely in the eye.

" No, father, although I just opened it casually, and saw something on the page about ' les jupes,' concerning the priests of the Society of Jesus, father."

" My dear man, it is useless for you to ask your son not to bring these books in, you must burn them—all of them—do you hear me ? Do you want the curse of God to fall upon your household ? Do you understand me ; you are responsible for the boy's soul, it is you who must do your duty by him, the priests are always willing to help, already I understand Father Harley had a con- versation with you last Sunday, he told me all about it over dinner. You must destroy these books because you are responsible for the boy, as you are his father. I am sorry that such a thing should happen in your house, Michael, because I know how good your wife is. But pray God to guide your son. To-morrow I will say a Mass for him myself, at half-past nine."

Mick looked at the priest. His heart was full of gratitude to him for his kindness. He bowed a little on one knee before the priest, and said—

" Thank you, father, thank you very much—God bless you, father."

Then he left the vestry. Martha and Joe were waiting for him outside. Martha asked him what had been keeping him. He said that he was looking at some of the pamphlets which were on sale in the vestry. He said he had gone out that way especially to look at some new prayer-books, and beads.

" Well, let's get home," said Martha, " I am shivering with the cold and I am sure that fire which I left banked up will have gone out."

They turned away from the church. As they passed one of the little Sisters of the Poor wearing her big white hat and blue dress, Martha stopped, smiled at her, and said—

" Well, well !—how are you, my dear Sister Veronica ?"

The sister smiled and replied, " I am very well indeed, thank you—how did you like the missioner ? "

" Glory be to God and His blessed mother, but he's a fine gentleman, a beautiful man, a lovely man ! Well, there's two pence for your box, it's all I have to spare at the moment, I hope you will call on me some day and bring me a miraculous medal of St. Philomena, because I want one for my son, he is a bit foolish and harum-scarum, sister. Good-night, sister."

Mick and her son had walked on. She started to run. They were just entering their street when she caught sight of them. Instinctively Mick turned round. Something told him that his wife would be on his heels. She had such a habit of standing and talking to everybody she met outside the church door.

Martha came up panting for breath. Mick took her arm and they walked on up the street. Joe had gone ahead to see how the fire was doing and to put on the kettle. When they got in, the fire was burning brightly and the supper things were already on the table. Joe had gone upstairs.

Martha proceeded to cook some fish for the supper. Her husband sat down in his favourite chair and took up a copy of the evening paper. The kettle boiling on the fire then attracted his attention.

"This is boiling, shall I take it off?" he called out to his wife in the back kitchen. She was busy cleaning some herrings on the wash-board.

"Of course take it off, why you'd let it boil over on top of you, you're so interested in your paper," she shouted back at him.

"There you are again," said he, "always looking for a confounded row."

"Me!" she called out, "me looking for a row, indeed it is yourself that makes the rows, you ask shall you take the kettle off, your own common sense should tell you to take it off as soon as it boils."

"All right, have your own damn way," he said and got down to his paper again.

Joe up above was sitting on the edge of his bed. He felt humiliated in that he had had to go down to the very place he loathed. He felt angry with himself. And at that moment he did not know whether he should not do without his supper, just to show some kind of pride or contempt. But there was his father shouting at the top of his voice—

"I say, do you want this supper or not, it'll be cold if you don't hurry up."

He heard the door bang. He asked himself if he should or should not go down. But the belly won, and he tramped down the stairs. When he opened the door his mother and father stared at him. His father was just swallowing a piece of bread. His mother saw that he did not look so very pleased. She said to him—

"What have you been doing up there, surely you are not reading one of those dirty books after what you promised Father Harley last Sunday?"

"I was not reading at all," he said. "I was just think-ing—that's all."

"That's as bad as reading," said his father. "I'd just like to know what lies behind that brain of yours, I would really, so help me God!"

Joe sat down. He would not look at his parents, but took the food which was handed to him. His father went on with his supper unconcernedly. He knew that he would never to get to know what was troubling his son. Martha looked across.

"More tea?" she asked. "There is some more fish outside in the pan."

"Don't want any more," replied Joe, and drank the last drop of tea out of his cup, which had a crack in it, and a painting of the good Queen Victoria on it. Mick got up from the table and went out. When he had gone his mother crossed to her son and putting her arms round his neck, she said—

"My son, tell me, surely you are not reading those books again, tell me the truth. I know something is worrying you, tell me what it is."

"Not that," replied Joe laconically.

"What then?" asked his mother. "Is it that girl? My God! you can't have that girl, Joe, she is a prostitute. Isn't it that, Joe?" He looked up at her as if to say—

"You know well it is."

His father came in, said "Good-night," and went upstairs.

A minute later he shouted down—

"The rain is coming through this roof, you'd better tell the landlord to-morrow, why the wallpaper is hanging down in shreds. It must have been coming in for a long time. Is the slate off the roof?"

Martha went to the foot of the stairs, and shouted up as hard as she could—

"Of course the rain's coming in through the roof, didn't you know that? A fine husband you are!—and the paper's hanging in shreds is it? Dear me! are you just beginning to notice these things?"

"Give me a rest, for the love of Christ. I'm sick of it, I can't open my bloomin' mouth."

"Well, will you tell the landlord to-morrow, and six weeks' rent owing to him and him the very divil if he doesn't get it? Indeed, you won't! but you will roar

and shout like a bull and let the neighbours know everything."

"To hell with the neighbours, give me a rest. I have
to be out in the morning at six o'clock."

"Well, less said the better," Martha shouted back at
him, "only don't be telling me what I have to do and
what I haven't to do. I can look after this place all right
without you. It is the woman who has to do all the dirty
work."

"I'm sick of these bloody rows, day in, day out,"
said Joe rising from the table.

"Indeed," said Martha.

His father had heard him and came rushing down the
stairs.

"What's that," said he, "you are sick of the rows
are you—you b——"

"That's enough," said Joe and made to leave the
kitchen and go to bed. But his father was angry. He
rushed at him and struck him across the face.

Joe stood up, looked at him, and said—

"You are my father—you are sixty years of age ; but
for that, I'd smash you up."

He left the kitchen and went to his room. There he
dropped upon the bed. He was angry with everybody.
He wanted to go away there and then and never return.

CHAPTER IV

For a long time Joe sat on the edge of the bed. He heard
the front and back doors bolted by his mother. He could
look out of his window down into the back yard. The
light from the gas in the kitchen lighted up the wall.
There was no blind drawn. Suddenly the light vanished.
He saw nothing now save the inky blackness of the night.
He heard his mother climbing the stairs. Heard her walk
along the landing, and then close the door of her room.
After a while he heard someone whispering outside his
door. The door had been gently pushed open. He heard
the voice of his father saying in a low voice—

" Good-night, God bless you—I thought you would be
reading one of those books. Have you got a candle,
because there is none in our room ? "

" No," replied Joe.

" Good-night, Joe," said his father.

Joe did not answer him. He heard the door closed
gently. He sat still, not knowing what to do with himself. What use to sleep ? What use to live ? What had he
to live for ? What had he seen around him ? Was this
all that life could offer ? An eternal round of sacrifices
and battling with prejudice and pride and ignorance.
He lay down upon the bed, without troubling to take
off his clothes. His thoughts turned to the young woman.
Ah, if only he were with her alone. He tossed about the
bed, but try as he would he could not sleep. And he
had to be up in the morning as he was going down to
the docks ; there was another big ship coming in. All
was silent now. Of a sudden he rose from the bed, and
feeling his way to the door, slipped out. He crept down
the stairs ; he lighted the gas. He sat by the remnants of
the fire. He was seated thus when the kitchen door
opened. His father was staring at him.

" What's the matter with you—what are you doing
sitting down here at one o'clock in the morning ? "

" Can't sleep ! "

" Can't sleep ; h'm, well you can't sit here with the
gas burning. We have enough to do with our money,
without supplying the gas company with more."

" Well, put it out then," said Joe hastily, " I don't
want it, I only came down here because I couldn't
sleep. I think I'll go out for a bit of a walk."

" You can't go out at this time of the night."

" Why ? "

" Don't answer me, you——"

His father put out the gas and left Joe sitting in the dark.

The door closed. He heard his father climbing the
stairs. He was alone once more. He undid the catch
of the door and slipped out. He closed the door softly
behind him and went off down the street. Where was

he going? To whom was he going? Instinctively his thoughts turned towards his friends—and then to Jane. She would help him—he would return no more. He was sick of it all. He tramped on until he reached the end of the street. Suddenly a form rose up in front of him. Was he dreaming? Was this the young woman he loved, out at this time of the morning? Then he opened his eyes wider, for the form was that of a policeman.

"Out late o' night for a walk, me son," said the officer.

"I have insomnia," said Joe and made to walk off, when the officer caught his arm.

"What do you want?" asked Joe.

"Were you looking for a woman by any chance, because I can get you just the right bit of goods for half a crown."

Joe did not answer, but he felt in his pocket, for he thought that perhaps by a miracle there might be one there. But he had no money.

"No, I have no money," he replied.

"Oh, well, that's no use," said the officer, "but any time you want one just look for me—number 447. I'm on this beat every night for a fortnight. I suppose you haven't a shilling on you by any chance?"

"Not a cent," said Joe—"Good-night."

When the policeman turned round he was gone. He noticed that he had walked down to the edge of the park where the lake was. He climbed the railings and steered about until he found a seat. He sat down. He felt cold. He did not know what to do. How could he find Jane now? It was impossible. There would be a terrible row if he woke up the other people in the household. He remained sitting there for a long time. A slight drizzle came on.

"I'd better get moving," he said, and turned away, and commenced to climb the railings. As he dropped to the ground he beheld a man running down the street at top speed. He was just in time to catch a glimpse of him as he turned the corner. It was his father. He stood for a moment. What was the matter? What could his father want at that time of the night? He asked himself these questions, standing there in the street alone, whilst all the while the rain was drizzling down on him. He started to cross the road. He had better return home. Something serious must be the matter. He started to run. He was muttering incoherently to himself. He passed the same policeman sheltering in the doorway of a large emporium. The officer stared after him.

"That's a queer chap that—wonder what game he's up to," thought the policeman. But Joe had vanished out of sight. He had turned the corner leading into his own street. He ran as fast as he could and coming to the door found it was half open. He crawled in, fearing lest he should wake his mother. But instantly he heard somebody moving up in the room. Then suddenly he heard a moan. Something terrible had happened. Someone was coming down the stairs. His father had left the front door half open and the gas burning full on. A tall woman stood in the kitchen before him. He recognised her immediately. She stared at him, as if he were some being from the nether world.

"Why, where have you been to, Joe, this time of morning," she asked him.

"I went out for a walk," he said, "I couldn't sleep somehow—is anything the matter?"

She saw he was trembling. She put her hand on his shoulder.

"Did you meet your father on the way down—he's gone to bring Mrs. Nolan."

"I saw somebody running hard down the road, as I was coming up," he answered. He knew now. Again came the sound of moaning from up above. He made a move as though to go upstairs. She stopped him and told him to sit down.

"You can't go up now," she said, "your mother's very bad in bed."

He knew what that meant too. He sat down in the corner by the fire, and watched the woman busying herself making some tea, and putting a large pan of boiling water on the gas stove in the back kitchen. That was it, was it? Yes, he thought his mother seemed queer of late. She never told him she was ill. That was like all women : they said nothing, till they were suddenly struck down, then they had everybody's nerves on edge. He sat there crossing and re-crossing his hands. The woman came in bearing a large pan of water. She put this down on the hearth, and said—

" Hadn't you better go to bed, you have to be down at the docks early, so your father tells me. Though you cannot very well go upstairs now, I'll make a bed for you on the couch. There is some tea outside which I have just made. Would you like a cup ? "

He got up to go and help himself to something, when she stopped him again, saying as she did so—

" All right, I'll get it, do you want anything to eat ? "

" No thanks," he replied, " just a cup of tea."

She brought it in. He sat down to the table. Then he noticed there was a draught coming in from some part of the house. He got up to close the door, saying—

" I'm going mad, I'm sure ; there am I looking for a draught ! and the confounded door wide to the wall— as if there were not enough people to know our business. The confounded thing is never closed."

" Jesus, Mary and Joseph ! "

Joe jumped to his feet. The awful moan rang in his ears.

" It's all right," said the woman. " I'll attend to that, you get your tea and lie down."

But he sat there listening to the woman ascending the stairs. He could not stay there idly listening to such moans, knowing it was his mother. He left his tea and went upstairs, and the woman met him as he was making his way into his mother's room.

" You can't go in—you know right well that you can't."

She almost pushed him to the head of the stairs. Then there was a knocking at the door. Joe ran down and admitted his father. He had never seen him looking so ill before.

" Oh ! " he gasped, " I'm nearly dead with running—
I was ten minutes knocking that woman up, and she
cursing and swearing because she had been knocked up
at that hour. That's the way when you are poor, you
have to take all kinds of insults. She would not have
done that to anyone else. But she knows that your mother
owed her some money from the time that John was
born—Lord rest his soul in heaven !—as if those are our
faults. Oh, well she's coming, although you can't blame
these people. She was coughing enough to spit her heart
out. I was sorry for her, I was indeed."

He sat down to recover his breath. The tall woman
from the next house came down into the kitchen then.

" Oh, you're back," she said.

" How is she now ? " he asked.

His face was white, and his mouth was drawn in at
the corners. Joe felt infinitely sorry for him in that
moment, but then he thought of his own sufferings, and
was himself again. Yet he remained anxious for his
father.

" Were you out ? " asked his father.

" Me out ! " said Joe, " no, I never left the house. I
have only just come down."

His father looked hard at him. Joe thought he was
caught. But his father asked no more questions. He lay
down on the couch and covered himself with the blanket.
But try as he would he could not sleep. His mind was
befogged. He had been thinking of so many things
within the last few hours. His mind was turning instinctively to Jane. At that hour Jane would be sleeping. He
had been struggling against a thing he did not believe
in. He had been wounding his mother's heart. He had
been rowing with his father continually since the mission
had started. He had been enmeshed in a network of
passion for weeks and could find no escape from it. He
could not sleep ; he ate little ; was morose ; would
speak to nobody. At times he thought of ending his life,
but the thought of the young woman who was willing to
change her life for him had prevented that. All these

thoughts ran riot in his mind as he lay there. When
again he heard the sounds of moaning he covered his
head. He wanted to shut out the anguish. He could not
stand it. Somebody was hammering at the door. He
heard his father open the door, and a woman's voice
say—

" Is this thirty-two ? "

" Yes, that's right ; she is upstairs in the middle
room," he heard his father say. He heard the woman
climbing the stairs. Heard the room door closed. Then
he fell asleep. When he woke he found his father had
gone out to work. He jumped off the couch, ran into the
back kitchen and hurriedly washed himeslf. The woman
from next door was telling him that there was tea in the
pot which she had just made for his father—adding—
" There is no sugar."

He gulped a cup of tea down and went out. It was
fully half-a-mile to the docks. He hurried along, wishing
that he had had a penny for tram-fare. Suddenly he
turned back.

" To hell with it ! I won't go—I'm really ill myself,"
he said.

When he got back he asked the woman to tell his
mother he had a bad headache and had had to return.
Then he lay down upon the couch.

Upstairs he heard voices. Then he heard moans.

" Jesus ! Jesus ! deliver ! deliver !—come forth for
the love of God ! "

He shut his ears to that.

A stream of people were continually passing the
window. They were going down to the docks as he
should have been going—but how could he go with his head
throbbing like the devil ? He thought he would go and
see Jane. He brushed his clothes, and putting on his
cap went to the bottom of the stairs and called up to the
woman.

" Do you want any messages, because I am going out
for a bit of a walk myself."

" Well, yes," she said, " you might bring in some

sugar and butter, and I don't think there is any bread—
wait, I'll look."

She came back and told him to bring butter and sugar.
She pushed some money into his hand, and disappeared
upstairs again. Joe went off. At the house where Jane
lived all was quiet. Nobody had risen save Larson and
the cobbler. When he knocked at the door, he was
confronted by the ragman standing in his shirt.

" What you want at this time of the morning ? "

" Is Miss Askew in ? "

The man stared hard at him.

" Why ? " he asked.

" I want to see her, that's all," said Joe.

" Wait then, I'll see if she's up."

He went upstairs and came down a moment or two later.

" She's not up yet," he said.

" Damn ! " exclaimed Joe.

" Will you knock and tell her Joe wants to see her
right away? It's important."

The man looked at him stupefied.

" What d' you think I am ? " he shouted, and slammed
the door in his face. Joe felt like smashing in the door
with his fist, but suddenly to his surprise it was opened
again and this time it was the chimney-sweep.

" Do you want to see Jane particularly ? " he asked.

" Yes," said Joe.

" Come in," said the sweep.

He led Joe upstairs and left him outside of her door.

" Knock there," he said.

Joe waited till he had descended the stairs.

Then he knocked gently upon the door.

" Who is it ? "

He recognised her voice immediately, and a smile
appeared across his haggard face.

" It is me," was all he said in reply.

He heard a gasp of astonishment.

" Come in ! "

When he entered the room, he found she was already
up, half dressed, sitting on the chair by the window.

"What's the matter with you—have you lost your head, coming to see me at this time of the morning?"

"I had to come," he said. "I want to talk with you. Oh, I have such a lot to say."

She crossed over to him, put her hands on his shoulders, and led him to the bed. They sat down together. He could feel the beating of her heart. He trembled. He steadied himself—he did not want to fall now—he must guard himself. He felt her hands caressing him. He wanted to tell her so much and in the end when she asked him to tell all he merely said in a choking voice—

"I am sad."

She put her arms round him and kissed him.

"Why are you sad?" she asked, still holding him in her arms.

He poured forth all that had lain in his mind. His heart was open. Like a flood there came gushing forth all the repessed desires of weeks.

She looked into his eyes. He put his arms on her shoulders.

"Help me! help me!—I do not know what to do."

And all the while he was hoping, hoping against hope that she would say—

"Yes, I know what it is, well there you are." But she did not speak. Instead she got up and finished dressing herself. He stood watching her. He was in a fever. What if she should suddenly divine his intentions. What if she should suddenly say to him—

"Leave me, I do not want you to come here any more."

He would be lost. He would have no place to turn. His heart sank at the thought. She turned and asked him if he had had his breakfast.

"No," he answered.

He lied. But then any excuse to remain with her. He was leaning on her with all the weight of his hungry body and soul. He must not fall. He must save himself from that. She went below and after being away about ten minutes returned with a tray containing breakfast.

" Come, have this breakfast with me, and don't be sad any more."

His lips were quivering. He wanted to burst into tears. His eyes were already glistening.

They ate and talked, and Joe told her that his mother was having another child.

She smiled and went on stirring her cup of tea until he reminded her that she was spilling it over the cloth. She sat up suddenly, laughed, and kissed him.

" Why do you live in a place like this, Jane ? " he said. " Couldn't you get another place more respectable ?—when I start working next week at the same place as my father, I am going to save up so that we can go and live together in a quieter place just outside on the borders of the city."

" That will be fine," she replied, " but what will your people say when you leave them to come and live with me ? "

" It doesn't matter about them—let them look after their own business. They have lived their day. I have to start living mine."

" You are thoroughly selfish," she said.

He thought for a moment. What can she mean ? I am selfish. How and why is that ? I am only looking after myself. It is no crime to study oneself. If one does not do that, nobody else will.

" Jane, I am not selfish ; I am the same as anybody else, that's all."

" But you owe a duty to your parents for all that."

" Well, if I send them some money from time to time that is all that I can do. There is nothing else, is there ? They have no jurisdiction over what I shall and shall not do."

" Do you think I want an army of priests descending on me and cursing me to all eternity ? I want to live in peace. You know that your people will certainly follow you everywhere, because your father and mother believe that they are responsible for you."

" But you know I do not love them," he exclaimed passionately.

" You do not love your mother and father ? "

" No !—I hate them—I will love them as people, as individuals, but as parents, never "

She stared at him in amazement.

"What do you mean ? " she asked.

" What I said," he replied. " Most people assume that children are the property of their fathers and mothers, which is a silly idea for anyone to treasure—they think that children must slave their young lives away to keep their parents. I am not responsible for my existence. The onus is on them. Why do they bring us in the world if they will not allow us freedom ? Some day we will settle with them, that's all."

" How did your mother get to know you were in love with me ? " she asked.

" She opened that letter you sent to me the other day."

" Oh, so they opened the letter, did they ?—h'm—well, they won't get another letter to open so quickly. But the blame for that is mine. I should have been more cautious. Did she show you the letter ? "

" No, she burnt it—said it was a disgrace to any Catholic young man to have a prostitute running after him. I said I didn't care. She went down then and told the priest what I said. The priest said I would land in hell one of these fine days—my mother was crying all that day. I was angry too—I smashed down the little altar she had in her room. There was a terrible row. When my father came home we went at it hammer and tongs. He said—' You may think you are clever ; you can go where you like with this woman, but I'll follow you to the ends of the earth, and if ever I set eyes on her, I'll take her life.' That's what he said."

She listened attentively.

" And what did you say to that ? "

" I said I didn't care what he did, but he had no authority over you—you were your own boss. If he started taking liberties like that he would find himself in the law's hands. Anyhow he talked for a long ti

I was sick of listening. When I told him that I had ideas of my own, he said I had no right to have ideas contrary to what were right according to the Church ; and when he asked me last night if I had been reading one of those bad books censored by the Pope, I said, ' No—that I had just been thinking ! ' He said to me, ' Well, that's as bad as reading—I'd like to know what lies behind that brain of yours.' I shut my mouth then and cleared off to bed."

She caressed him, and a semblance of a smile crossed his features.

" Well, don't be sad any more will you ? " she said to him, as she got up from the bed.

He promised that he would try to be happy ; he said that he would always be happy with her—it was only thoughts of her that kept him from destroying himself.

" You must never do that," she entreated, looking up into his eyes. " Never."

He did not answer, but nodded, and got up to go. She pulled his arm as he was crossing the room.

" Good-bye, you will see me again, won't you ? "

" Yes, yes," he said, " of course—won't you come down to the beach some night ? "

" Yes, all right," she said, and half pushed him towards the door, adding—" Here is my old landlord coming up for his rent. Now isn't it a good job that I am able to pay my rent ? "

" Yes," he said, " my mother owes six weeks' rent, and the landlord is a holy terror, the roof's leaking, and the paper hanging off the walls, but we can't do anything until we pay off the arrears. The woman who came up to our house last night, said she had never been in such a cold and draughty house in her life. ' I have a bad cold,' she said, ' and I have to turn out of my bed at one o'clock in the morning, and here I am in a place not fit for a bitch to have pups in.' She was awfully wild—she said something about my mother owing her some money from the last confinement."

She kissed him and watched his figure retreating down

the stairs. Outside the ragman was laughing as if his sides would burst. He looked at Jane.

" That's a fine strong-looking chap you've had there half the morning."

" My second cousin," she replied, and went off down the stairs to pay the landlord, who was sure to be waiting for his money. She found him at the bottom of the stairs talking to the sweep. They were having a hot argument.

" Well, if your place is alive with bugs, that's not my fault, you know, Mr.—er—er—all I have to do is to collect the rent and go about my business."

" Get a box of powder," said the slatternly looking widow who was standing at her door listening to the argument.

The landlord got his rent and cleared off. When he had gone the sweep turned round to the widow of doubtful origin and said—

" Mind your own business next time—I was talking strictly private with the collector—it is his business to see that his tenants enjoy good health and that the houses are fit for human beings to live in that's all— why, my arm's thick with bug bites—just look."

He pulled his shirt sleeve up to the elbow and revealed a hairy arm studded with red pimples.

The woman laughed at him.

" It's nothing to laugh at," he said.

* * * * * * *

" Ha ! ha !—but that's a great little man up above," said Magee.

" A great little man indeed, bedad," said Mick. " I'm proud, I tell you."

" Of course you are," said Magee, rolling his eyes—" of course you are—will you pass me the salt ? "

" Have a bit of corned meat," said the woman from next door.

" Have you seen Donovan lately ? " asked Mick.

" The old ——," said Magee.

" 'Sh—the boy," said Mr. Casey, who was fishing with his fork for a bit of pickle.

" Of course, of course," said Magee—" I apologise, gentlemen, I really do indeed for not being a bit more particular like—what you going to call him ? "

" Same as meself, what you think," said Mick, " although," says he, " the missus wants me to call him Anthony after his grandfather."

Anthony looked up from his chair in the corner. He was not in the spree at the table.

" Divil a bit I care what you call him," said Anthony.

" Not so hasty, man, not so hasty now," said Magee. " Won't you sit in an' have a bite just to show as how we're friends like ? "

" Not now, not now," replied he, " I'm just interested in this book. God ! it's a great tale."

" Indeed," said Magee, helping himself to a slice of ham—" an' what's it about ? "

" Ha ! ha ! you'd like to be knowing how and why and all the rest of it—well now there's a nice little widow in it," said he.

" God bless her," said Magee. " I thought you were a better man than that anyhow."

" Why what's the matter with me, d'you think?" said Anthony.

" Why a man of your years reading such a tale—is it one of those Frenchies, by the way ? "

" You're a funny man," said Anthony, and lapsed into silence.

After the meal Mick and Magee drew in their chairs to the fire.

Joe was sitting in the corner by the fire. The woman was clearing the table.

" You're not working yet, Joe," said Magee. " I see there's a big ship coming in to-morrow, perhaps you'll have a bit of luck, eh ? "

" He doesn't care if he never works," said his father.

" Ah now, he's not so bad, he's a good lad, he doesn't

take a drop now and again like that young Donovan, oh
no, he's a good lad is Joe."

His father was looking down at him. There was a
glint in his eye.

" Joe's all right if he'd only bide by his mother and
go to church."

" Oh, Joe, you must bide by your mother, boy," said
Magee—" oh yes, you must bide by your mother, boy."

Joe remained silent. He wanted to get up and walk
out.

But he could not do that. Nor could he seek the
shelter of his own room. He did not want to ask to be
excused. He did not want his father on his track again
over the books. And he still had one or two hidden away
in the room under his bed. So he remained silent, looking into the fire, and listening to the conversation carried
on by the two men.

His grandfather was sitting over his book. He wished
he were like him, old and contented. He thought the
most contented people he had ever seen were parsons and
priests and old men and children. His father was speaking now. Magee was lighting his old briar pipe with a
piece of newspaper which had served as a table-cloth.

" I'm taking him down to the abattoir to-morrow or
the next day," his father was saying—" Mr. Dring
promised he'd find a job for him, although what kind of
work he'll give him I don't know —I don't suppose he
knows himself yet."

" Well, now," said Magee to Joe, " there's a chance
for ye, boy—take it, and I am sure you'll feel happier
working than hanging round the house here all the time
like an old woman."

Still Joe remained silent. He did not want to go to
work at his father's place. He didn't like the men who
worked there. But he could not tell his father that—no, he
would have to go, that was all about it—because he
could not put his hand to anything else. Once, though,
he had tried to get a job on a newspaper but the editor
had laughed at him, and said that all the worlds to be

E

conquered had been conquered long ago, and any way he had no room for a man who had nothing to say. But Joe had lots to say—but he was afraid to say it. Once, when he was listening to the priest in the pulpit, he felt like getting up and shouting out—" Liar ! "

But he suddenly thought to himself—well, perhaps he's right—the poor fellow, perhaps he hates it worse than I do.

" I hear you were nearly killed the other day by a Scotch bull," said Magee.

" Yes," said Mick, " I nearly was, but I hooked the rascal. I made him cough, believe me—there was blood and dirt flying everywhere."

" I never seen the inside of one of those slaughter-houses meself," said Magee, " they say as how they're horrible places to work in—is that so ? " he asked.

" Well, yes, it is true," replied Mick—" but then everybody has to live, you know."

" Well, yes, that's true enough," said Magee, and he winked at Joe.

Joe didn't understand. He wondered why the man had winked at him.

" You'd better go up and see your mother," said his father.

He got up and left the kitchen. He did not reply to his father. He climbed the stairs slowly. His father heard him pause half-way up. He wondered why he had stopped. Then he heard him climb the rest. He turned to Magee.

" I suppose you heard about my son carrying on with that prostitute from Larson's place," he said.

" Indeed I didn't," said Magee.

" Well, that woman is ruining my son—that's all— If ever I set eyes on her I'll swing for her."

Meanwhile Joe was standing outside his mother's room. He was half-afraid to go in. But the woman was coming up the stairs. He knocked at the door and walked in. His mother was lying in the bed, and Joe could discern the child huddled at her side.

" Hello, Joe," she said.

She looked very weak. He crossed over to the bed, bent down and kissed her. Then he backed away a little from the bed. His mother gave him a searching glance. She could see that something was on his mind.

" Won't you look at your little brother, Joe ?" she asked.

" Of course, of course," he said absent-mindedly. He was not thinking of the child. He was not thinking of his mother. He was thinking of someone else. He had recoiled from the bed. What had made him do such a thing ?

She pulled back the clothes and held the baby up to him. He stood looking at it for a minute. What should he do ? He did not want to take it in his arms, but his mother was pleading and holding it up to him. He bent down and lightly kissed it on the cheek. He saw also one of his mother's breasts, with the blue nipple. He saw her take the child beside her and give it the breast. He burst out laughing. It seemed so comical to him.

" What are you laughing at ? " his mother asked. It was so very seldom that he did laugh. He did not answer for a time. He did not know what to say, for in his own mind he really did not know what it was that had made him laugh.

" It is so small," he explained.

The woman from next door came in to tidy the room. This was a good excuse for him to get away. He felt angry at what he had seen. All the suffering she had borne and just for this. The child would grow up just like him, and have to go through the same mill. It seemed so ridiculous to him. He had not learnt yet that the work of creation is the only thing in life. The sight of the child, the hallowed eyes of his mother, the great breast which he had espied through the rent in her nightgown, all these things revolted him. He thought—" Then is this all—good God ! "

He watched his mother feeding the child. And in that action the centuries of life yet to come were revealed to him. It seemed that he saw in that child the birth of a nation. When the woman came over to re-make the bed he gave a last glance at his mother and left the room. He heard her cough a little and in his heart he felt sorry for her. But suddenly there arose in his mind all the things she believed in, all the things which she wished her son to live for.

He was half-way down the stairs when the woman came out of the room and called to him.

" Your mother wants you for a minute," she said.

He returned to the bedroom.

" What is it you want ? " he asked abruptly.

" I want you to go to confession to-night," she said.

There was a pleading in her voice. He could not understand the change in her. He fought with all his strength to resist the thing. But he could not. She was looking at him out of her great eyes. What should he say ?

" You will, won't you ? " she was saying, and trying to reach out her hand to take his own. He was stupefied. He could not refuse. When he saw the suffering revealed in that face he was lost. He was beaten.

" Yes, I'll go," he said, and was leaving the room when she called after him.

" And offer up your communion for the baby, won't you ? "

" Yes," he said.

When he re-entered the kitchen, only Anthony was there. That gentleman looked up and said that his father had gone out for a drink with Mr. Magee and would be back in a few minutes.

" Tell him I have gone out myself for a bit of a walk," said Joe.

" Shall I say you won't be long ? " asked the old man, looking up from his book.

" Just say I've gone for a walk, that's all."

He left the house and made his way towards the beach. It lay about a quarter of a mile from the house. A gentle breeze was coming up from the river. It fanned his face. It cooled him. The night was drawing in. Above him the clouds rolled on in the direction of the hills far over the river. Joe reached the bottom of the road which led to the beach. There were a number of people sitting about on the sands. He made for an old wooden boat which was lying bottom up a hundred yards to his right. He sat beneath the shelter of it, and gazed far out to sea. He saw how beautiful and fresh the scene was before him, and knew he had but to turn his back on this to find himself staring into the depths of a city. A ship was sailing up the river. He watched its wash long after it had passed him. He wished that he was on such a boat and sailing away to some other part of the world, away for ever. He wanted to be alone with his thoughts, for a long time. A tall man was coming up the beach. Joe could see that he had been paddling in the water. As he passed him he took stock of his bulky body and big feet. The man looked at him and said as he passed—

"Water's fine for paddling in, son, are you going down there?"

"No," said Joe, "I have to be at work."

That was a lie. He marvelled how easily it was for him to have a lie spring to his lips. But he did not want to be bothered answering questions. He was tired. He was glad to be out in the open air, away from everybody. But suddenly he thought of the promise he had made to his mother. He gnashed his teeth and cursed himself for being such a fool. But what else could he have done? If he had refused, he might have made his mother worse. At the back of his mind there floated the idea that he ought to have stood for his principles. If in his heart he did not want to go to confession, he should have said so. If he had been a man, he would have said to his mother—

"No—I no longer believe in God."

But he could not say that. He was bound by duty to protect his mother. He was between the devil and the deep sea. To whom could he look for help, for guidance? No one! True there was Jane, but then she would simply say to him—

"Well, you are a man, you can make up your mind as easy as anybody."

"Ah yes," he thought, "that is all very well, but I have to sink my own principles in order to uphold those of my parents. In any case I might as well go through with it. They cannot live for ever."

But again he thought of the priest, of the confessional box, of the prayers to be said, of the penance, of the communion, what good had they ever done him? What good had they ever done his mother—or his father? Their religion had not made him rich—they were always close to the workhouse. He knew that the church could build a new altar whenever it liked, and he knew that the roof in his own home wanted repairing—had not the midwife condemned it in her own scathing way? Again, he knew his mother was in arrears with the rent. Would the landlord let her have a week's grace? No, he would not—and he thought of the priest calling each Sunday for collection for the new high altar, and for the building of a bigger wing for the priests. They were all right! But supposing his mother said to the priest—"Well, father, I am behind in my rent, and if I don't find three pounds ten to-morrow, I will be thrown out neck and crop, and me with a new-born infant on my hands." What would Father Harley say to that?

Would he put his hand down into his fat pocket, smile and say—"Well now, Martha, I am sorry to hear that, here is money for the landlord?"

He would not! He would just tell her to be of good courage, to remember that our Blessed Lord's mother had the same trials and suffering to contend with, forgetting the twentieth century when civilisation was engulfed by its own greed and ferocity.

And all these things passed kaleidoscopically across Joe's mind as he rapped his fingers upon the sides of the old wooden boat. Then the young woman he loved, came into his mind.

Supposing he had said to the priest—

"Well, father, I love this woman with all my heart and soul, and if I cannot love her I will kill myself!"

What would he have said in reply? He pondered over this for a long time. But there was only one answer. The priest would say—

"If you truly love this woman, you must give her up, you must cut your heart out—after all, what are your sufferings compared with those of our Redeemer?"

Yes, that was it. It did not matter how much one loved or suffered, how often one's soul passed through the furnace, there was always the same answer. It did not matter because there was no suffering or agony comparable with that of Christ or the mother of Christ. It did not matter because it is the law of life that a man shall suffer.

* * * * * * *

And he visualised the congregation sitting there, dumb, their faces grey with the fear of hunger and the fear of hell. For were there not amongst that congregation women who could not give milk to their children?— were there not men there who had had to fight like wolves, with claws and teeth and blood, in order to exist? Yes, yes, it was all true. They were, and there it was! and the priest dinning hell and purgatory into their ears, and the half light of the old church thick with the smell of flowers and incense, and the slow monotonous droning. And the people sitting there silent like a flock of crows, and outside the fresh wind coming up from the river, waiting for them, hovering ever over the big roof of the church, waiting to catch them full in the face and say, "Hey ho! yonder goes life and death, each comparing their own ways. Take that and that!" And they would get it full in their dry faces, and it would refresh them, after the long hour spent in the church, and all would hurry home to their firesides, and to their children, and their duties. And in a flash they would be faced with reality. Would not all that talk of an hour ago seem dead and dry as dust, in the facing of life, despotic and cruel? Ah, he thought, how many of them ask themselves that question? How many realise that their hearts are foul? How many realise that at the bottom of the well of life there was no hope? How many realise that this God to whom they pray aloud sits enthroned amidst the clouds, a sugar stick in one hand and a lash in the other? But they did not think, because they were too much occupied with living. And he thought of his own mother, and of the newly-born child. He recalled her feeding it from the breast, and noticed how it had gurgled as the sap of life had coursed down its young throat. And then he remembered the money that they owed. Supposing his mother said to the landlord—

"Well, sir, I am very sorry, but I have not the money to give you this week, my husband has not been working very often, and I have a grown-up son who cannot get work. Will you wait just another week?"

Would he answer in the face of their suffering—"Yes, I will"? He would not, because life is life, and sympathy is a skin's thickness. He would say—

"I am sorry, but I cannot wait—I want my money."

And then suppose she recalled the words of the priest and said to him, her great hallowed eyes looking into his own—

"In the name of Christ, sir, it will be paid next week."

He would laugh. He would say to her as he fingered his pencil—

"My dear woman, we all have to live, Christ himself had to abide by the laws of His time, and in any case this is strictly an affair between you and me. Christ has nothing to do with the rents in our time."

Yes, that is what he would say. Because in our age we recognise that even Christ was non-sympathetic towards His own Mother, and the landlord being a man of common sense, and being well up in the events of the day, would realise that Christ was a man, as human as he, and that if He had found Himself under the same conditions would have stood His ground.

"Yes," thought Joe, "that is it, one might as well probe these things."

The night crept on. He sat there turning over these thoughts in his mind, examining them, weighing each in the balance against his own reason. And he knew that now he could never believe, for to believe was to be lost, was to fall back, and be trodden upon by those who were storming the heights holding aloft the light of pure reason. And in his heart he said to himself—

" I cannot, I will not believe."

And a voice seemed to whisper into his ear—

" Behold thou hast not even established within thyself the fount of thine own reason."

The wind was blowing about his ears. Far out over the river he could see the red and white flash of the Rock-light. It swept across the face of the waters, illuminating them, throwing off the colour of a dragon's blood. He listened to the gentle murmur of the water.

No moon had shown as yet. He sat staring far out, and as if in a mirage he saw the land of his heart's desire. But the black hul. of a ship passed him and blotted out his vision. Across on the other side of the river he could hear the crashing of hammers, and knew by the red glare in the sky that the slaves of steel were jumping here and there, their fingers like dancing gnomes as again and again they flashed about the white ingots. And then his glance fell to the sand at his feet. He picked up a handful and let it trickle slowly through his fingers. He watched it as it made a little heap at his feet. He laughed to himself, and rose and stretched himself. He heard the church clock in the distance strike nine. He had sat there for two hours ! The sounds seemed to hit the air, to tremble for a moment and suddenly to sail across the waters. He turned and looked towards the city. It was ablaze with light. He saw the pavements aflood with life, figures hurrying here and there, helter-skelter, each seeming unaware of his own fate. He walked slowly up the beach. It was deserted. Except for an occasional figure passing down to work where ships were being broken up, there was not a soul to stir the strange and profound silence of that place. When he reached the top of the road, he turned as of habit to his right and continued on his way towards home. Ahead of him he saw a crowd. Crowds were an everyday affair, and usually it was only over a dog fight or a drunken brawl. As he approached he discerned a policeman hurrying to the scene. He quickened his pace and arrived on the fringe of the crowd just as the policeman was emerging from out the packed body of people. He held a young woman by the arm. Some of the crowd were following and giving vent to their opinions in no light language, but the policeman ignored it all, and continued on his way towards the police-station.

" It was that bloody ' Little Judas,' " screamed from a doorway an old woman who was scratching herself to her heart's content.

" It's her own fault anyhow," shouted another ; " what right has she to be pulling up members of the council, she ought to be ashamed of herself, the dirty bitch ! "

" You're such an angel ! " replied another voice.

" I'll angel you if I find you ! " came the retort.

" Serve him right anyway," said another woman. " They think they're everybody because they're on a council and wear a tail-coat on a Sunday."

Joe was standing on the edge of the parapet. The policeman had reached the bottom of the street. He could not see the face of the young woman, and realising now that she was one of those who frequented the street during periods of economic depression, his thoughts immediately turned towards Jane. He left the crowd and half ran down the street in the direction the policeman had taken. He was just in time to see the officer turn into the doorway with the blue lamp shining over it, and a gasp of joy escaped from his lips. It was not Jane. How glad he was ! He could not have suffered such a thing. He hurried along and turned into his own street. When he arrived home he found that all had retired to bed. He entered very quietly and closed the door softly. Then he lighted the gas, went into the back kitchen, put the kettle on, and sat down by the fire to read the evening paper. When the kettle had boiled, he made a pot of tea, sliced some of his mother's home-made bread, and sat down to the table.

Above, all was silent. He wondered if they were all asleep. He wondered if the woman from the next house were sleeping also. Suddenly he heard somebody descending the stairs. The kitchen door opened and his father seeing him said in a voice that made Joe tremble—

" Quick ! run for Dr. Morley, your mother is very ill."

Without another word his father went upstairs again. Joe immediately put on his overcoat, buttoned it up tightly about his neck, took a last gulp of the hot tea, and turned the gas low. He wondered if he should go up and see his mother before he went out. Was she very bad indeed, he asked himself. And if she was dangerously ill he had a right to go and see her. But he put on his cap and left the house. The streets were being flushed by the corporation carts. A stream of lorries passed him on their way down to the beef ship which had just arrived. The doctor's house was nearly five hundred yards away. When he got to the bottom of the street he suddenly ran.

" She must be very ill," he said.

CHAPTER V

LOVELY day ! Lime Street all agog. The feast of the flesh. Plenty of girls. " How are you, dearie ? " Old men with lantern jaws and piercing eyes, wearing out their old bodies. " Now ring your bells more vigorously, my dear man." " Hello, cocky. Bet you have a nice mother, eh, boy ? "

Shop windows piled with food, ready for the gorge. Trams full of people with smiling faces. A bishop with his gaiters on. Young men with lean hungry faces passing down the street. But no money. Sun shining down on the dirty grey wall of the picture house. The bright rays cast upon the wall give it the appearance of having been washed in blood. Up and down go the young ladies.

Joe was there too. He was standing watching the people pass. He was watching for Jane. It was half-past six. He'd have to go at eight o'clock. Confession. His mouth was very dry. He wanted to go and drink a great big glass of ale. He licked his lips. A big policeman standing directing the traffic. Twenty bulls coming down the street, a man behind them waving a stick. Terrible stink. The man shouts. Great eyes like saucers peering at the people. The people laughing. The bulls start to run. Yelling commences. Sticks and stones for the bulls. That's the stuff, that's the stuff! Big bull standing in the corner of the street ; bending down to drink from the puddles. " Stand straight—gerrup, you dirty bastard. Ha ! ha ! " A crack on the nose with a good hard piece of wood for the bull. " Ha ! ha ! that's it. Take that you bloody old ——"

People running and shouting. Six big men sitting on a bull. Two men kicking it. A rope round its neck. Bull frightened of the men standing near. Trembles. " Gerrup there ! " Dragged to its feet. All the bulls collected and driven towards the abattoir. Smell the blood ! Ha! ha ! The food of man. Joe was standing watching all this. He thought of his father taking up a pole-axe and smashing in the head of one of the animals. " Poor b——s," he said. More people coming into the street. The picture places have opened. Line up. See the sheik carrying off the maiden. Ha ! ha ! Line up ! Man playing a fiddle in the doorway of a public-house. An old man playing on two spoons for accompaniment. Much laughter from the crowd when the old man starts to sing. A big man going into the pub. A nice young woman after him. He stares at the young woman. She smiles. She has a pretty face. " Hello, Nelly."

" Hello."

They disappear into the house. Policeman holding up his hands and dropping them again. Man shouting out at the top of his voice—

" This way for the big winner. Threepence each."

Boy standing at the edge of the parapet watching men

who have dirty faces. Only dirty faces. That means they are coming from work.

"Any bread left, sir?"

On walks the dirty face.

Little child sitting on its mother's knee, on a step. Her old breasts are shrivelled up. Child hitting her in the face with his little fist. Christ a long way off. A crowd of men standing listening to a preacher at the top of the street. Angel-face. Come forth if you would be saved.

"Hello, duckie, how's your ma? Coming ——?"

"O friends, I was saved by the blood of Christ. I tell you that you too can be saved."

Big café with dazzling lights. Many tables. The public eating at the trough. Jaws munching for the love of it. Salvation Army man giving out leaflets. A boy aged fifteen running after a woman of thirty.

"Just this once; I have a shilling. Hee, hee!"

More lights in the street. Great arc-lamps outside the picture houses. Newsboys with dirty noses crying out with all their strength—

"Winner of the last race."

Old man with parcel in his hand, bent like a swine, trotting along to work. Watchman at the distillery. Has a nice clean face. Little eyes like a rat, but kind-looking. Has a prominent tooth. Looks at the people crowding the street. Gives a terrible stare at a young woman who winks at him.

"The bitches ought to be burnt."

Wends his way slowly out of the street. Mother with three daughters coming along. All dressed nicely. All stick their noses in the air at the painted ladies. Very respectable.

Big man at the door of the picture house makes way for them.

"This way, madam."

Man coming rolling out of the pub. "Look out there."

"Where is she, anyway?"

"Hello!"

"Hello," said Joe.

He walked out of the street with Jane holding on to his strong young arm.

"Were you waiting long?"

"An hour—have you only just come out of the place now?"

"Yes; is your mother better?"

"She's very bad."

"Let's get out of the crowd."

"Glad I didn't have to wait much longer," said Joe, "it's a horrible place."

"Which way are you going? The nights get dark soon—let's go this way," she said. She took his arm more securely under her own and they walked on out of the crowded street. On towards the park. Joe said he'd like to sit on a bench somewhere and talk for a while.

"I have to be home in an hour you know," he said to her.

"Why?" she asked him.

"Confession—promised my mother—she's very bad, might go off any time. My father says if anything happens to her, it'll be my fault—that's bad for me isn't it?"

"You can't help it, Joe. She shouldn't have had so many children anyway—nobody thanks them for having them."

"Several are in America," said Joe.

"And I don't suppose they send anything home to her to help her?"

"All have forgotten that—once Harry sent a letter—said he would like to send a bit of money each week, but he can't—married you know—got a couple of kids—said he hoped I was working away and helping my mother. Wish I could get a job somewhere, anything at all."

"Well, why don't you go down with your father? He'd surely get you a job at his place," she said.

Eventually they found a seat and sat down.

"I went down with him," Joe replied, "the foreman said there was no work there—if I had been a bit bigger and stronger he might have shown me how to use a pole-axe—but I wouldn't have liked that," he added," it's against my nature."

" Everybody has to live," she said, " even though it's against their nature."

They lapsed into silence. They held each other's hands. They looked long into each other's eyes. Joe suddenly got up. He looked at his watch.

" Why, it's a quarter to eight now," he said. " I must really go, else there'll be the devil of a row when I get home."

She rose too. She seemed just a little disappointed with him. He saw it and wondered what he had done. He drew her to him and kissed her.

" Are you angry with me, Jane ? " he asked her as they rose to go.

" Well, you say you love me, and yet we're only a few minutes with each other before you want to go."

" But I promised my mother, you know," he said, " and she's very ill."

She tossed her head. She loosed her arm from his own. They stopped and looked each other in the face. Joe was trembling. What had he done ?

" Aren't I as good as your mother, Joe ? " she asked him.

" Why of course I love you, Jane—surely you are not going to doubt me ? "

" But will you come and see me to-morrow at my room ? " she insisted.

Joe felt something tugging at his heart. It sent the blood to his face. He gripped her two hands and whispered in her ear—" Yes, yes, yes."

At the bottom of the street they said good-bye. He stood and watched her until she disappeared amongst the crowd of people hurrying to and fro. Then he turned his steps towards home. When he arrived there, it was to find his father walking up and down the kitchen. Joe saw by his face that he was angry. He did not speak but went straight up to his room. When he came down his father took hold of him by the shoulder and bending low over him, until their faces met, he said in a voice which trembled with passion—

" I see you have been with that prostitute again."

Joe remained silent. Why should he answer? If his father had seen him, if anyone in the street had seen him with her, that was enough, there was no need to answer. His father shook him like a rat.

" Why the devil don't you answer me? " he roared.

The roar filled the whole house. Joe thought of his mother lying ill upstairs. He knew that she must have heard that roar. Now somebody was knocking from the room above. His father released his hold and went to the foot of the stairs.

" What's the matter? " he called.

The woman who was nursing his wife shouted down that she wanted no noise because Joe's mother had just fallen asleep. He closed the door and turned to his son. Joe looked at him as if to say—

" What in hell's name is the matter with you now? "

" The next time I catch you with her, I'll strangle both of you with these two hands."

He stuck two huge fists right up under his son's nose.

Joe went white with hate. He knew then, in that moment, that only a miracle had prevented him from knocking his father down.

" Get your prayer-book and hurry off, and don't forget to tell the priest all your carryings on either. D'you hear? " he shouted after him, as his son went through the door. But he was not answered. He went off then to have a bath in the zinc tub. He forgot about Joe and proceeded to undress himself. He put one leg into the tub and proceeded to scrub it with great energy. Meanwhile Joe had reached the church. Inside, the peculiar smell took hold of him. His heart beat violently. He genuflected before the altar, and walked up the aisle. When he got to Father Denny's confessional box, he genuflected again, and went into the seat. He blessed himself and took out his prayer-book. He opened it at the Preparation for Confession. But already he had his sins tabulated. He knew what to do when he finally went into that little brown box, and heard the grille pulled back.

"Well, my child, and how long is it since your last confession?"

He ran them over in his mind again. He wanted to hurry up and get done with them. He was afraid. He wanted to leave the church as soon as he could. Everything within it seemed to frown at him. The very statues, the crucifix itself hanging high over the altar, seemed to waken into life—he could feel their eyes penetrating his soul. He would not escape. A thousand eyes were upon him. They seemed to tear out his soul and lay it open to view upon the altar. He bent his head and shut his eyes. He mumbled to himself. He repeated the various sins.

"Disobeyed my father and mother and my superiors, forty times. Missed Mass seven times. Told lies a hundred times. Harboured unclean thoughts. Scoffed at the name of Christ thirty times." He repeated these over and over again. He could not think of any more. And he thought to himself—

"But perhaps that is all I have really committed. There are so many sins, it is difficult to keep count of them. Ah"—he had suddenly remembered—if he would clear his soul he had to tell the priest that he was going out with a Protestant woman. In addition that she was a very bad woman. The sweat stood out on his brow in tiny drops. He had not thought of that. What was he to do? Supposing he told the priest that—the priest would upbraid him, and tell him to give her up and to make a good holy communion. But supposing that, in spite of the priest, he carried on with her, that would be a terrible sin. And then he remembered that she had asked him to come to her room the next day. Suddenly the confession was shut out of his mind. His heart beat and his hands trembled. Ah yes, he knew—he knew. And as suddenly he was whirled back into reality when a voice at his side said—

"Are you going in next, young man?"

He beheld a very old man looking at him from behind a pair of old spectacles. He blushed and answered that he was not going in yet, he was not ready. The old man gave him a hard stare and then made his way past Joe into the box. Supposing then that he did not tell the priest. That would not be so bad as the other sin. He could easily forget—or he could tell that another time. But again he thought of yet another barrier that had to be surmounted. If I take holy communion, it will be a sacrilege, that is terrible too. " What shall I do ?— what shall I do ? " he muttered. He was filled with a sudden desire to get up and flee from the church. But he could not. A terrible weight seemed to close about him. He could not move. And the statues had become living things and they were watching him. Ah God, yes ! He might be struck dead. He clasped and unclasped his hands. " What must I do ? " How if he made his confession could he dodge going to communion the next morning ? He knew his father would go with him to the first Mass. He often wondered why his father always accompanied him on such occasions. And the idea arose in his mind that he must be watched, that his father must have suspicions. Oh yes, he had forgotten that.

The old man came out. Joe asked himself for the last time—what shall I do ?

He expected one of the statues to walk down to him and answer his question, to advise him, to guide him. There were people on either side of him. He fancied they were watching him. There were a good many too. Perhaps they had not so many sins to confess as he, and perhaps they were in a hurry to be heard. They might have other things to do when they got home—washing the children—cooking the supper. He must go now. He half rose—hesistated, then suddenly walked into the box and closed the door. It was done now. He must go through with it. He heard the slide drawn back. He imagined he saw the red face of the priest, and felt eyes peering out at him.

"In the name of the Father, and of the Son, and of the Holy Ghost, amen."

"Pray, father, give me your blessing, for I have sinned.

"It is two months since my last confession, father.

"I have disobeyed my parents and superiors forty times, father.

"I have missed Mass three times, father.

"I have told lies sixty times, father.

"I have taken our Lord's name in vain twenty times, father—that's all, father."

He stopped to get his breath. He could hear the heavy breathing of the priest and thought that he suffered from asthma.

"Is that all, my child?" said the priest.

"Yes, father."

"Sure, my child?"

"Yes, father."

"How old are you, my child?"

"Twenty, father."

"Well now try, my dear child, not to miss Mass, for you know it is a mortal sin, and the punishment for such a sin is hell for all eternity."

"Yes, father."

"Pray to our Blessed Lady to help you, my child."

"Yes, father."

"For your penance say ten Our Fathers and ten Hail Marys—now make a good act of contrition."

"Yes, father—O my God I am sorry and beg pardon for all my sins, and detest them above all things, because they have crucified my loving Saviour Jesus Christ, and most of all because they offend Thine infinite goodness, and I firmly resolve by the help of Thy grace, never to offend Thee again and carefully to avoid the occasions of sin. In the name of the Father and of the Son and of the Holy Ghost, amen."

"God bless you, my child."

The slide shut back. He was alone. He got up and opened the door of the box leading into the church. An old woman was waiting for him to come out. He passed round the bench, and walked three benches further up towards the high altar in order to say his penance. He blessed himself and commenced to reel off the prayers as quickly as he could. He could not kneel there another minute. The place seemed to be choking him, and he could not forget that the statues might walk down upon him suddenly, the lot of them, they might fall against him and crush him to death—yes they might do that—then he would find himself in hell—or if he was lucky in purgatory, where the fire was not so terrible. He rose from the bench, hurried to the aisle, bowed quickly, just like the grown-up men who had rheumatics and bad feet, then he hurried to the bottom of the church, stopped for an instant at the holy water font, half dipped his hand into it, suddenly pulled it out again and putting on his cap left the church.

The fresh air seemed to revive him. Ah—how glad he was that it was all over—but it was not over yet ! He walked home quickly. His father had gone to bed. He cooked his own supper, and before starting in on it, went upstairs to see how his mother was. He went into the room without knocking. That was a surprise for his mother. He had never done that before. She hastily threw the clothes about her, sat up in the bed and asked him if he had been to confession. He looked across at her and, bending his head slightly, said—

" Yes, I have just come back."

" Which priest did you go to, Joe ? " she asked him, smiling a little, for she was now very happy to know that her son was after all, and in spite of his occasional lapses due to light-headedness, a good Catholic.

" I went to Father Dunny," he answered.

" That's nice now," she said, " he is a lovely priest "— adding suddenly—" Did you tell him about your carrying on with this young woman, Joe ? "

" Yes," he answered, and knew that he lied. But that was the better thing because he did not want to cause her suffering.

"Good-night," he said in a gentle voice.

"Good-night, my son," replied his mother, "good-night and God bless you."

He descended the stairs. He was glad that the ordeal was over. No matter how he manœuvred he could not avoid telling the most barefaced lies. It was not his fault. If he had told the truth, his life and everybody's in the house would have been hell. So he must lie, in order to have peace. Well, he could easily do that. He had served a good apprenticeship. He laughed when he thought of the old man who was in such a terrible hurry to be hurled before his Divine Redeemer. He could not be like that. His soul was not white as that of the old man's. No, his was a black soul—a mushy dirty soul. Ah well! that was not all his fault.

He ate his supper, and after clearing up the table and relaying it for the morning's breakfast, he turned out the gas, locked the doors, and went to his room. He bolted the door, undressed hurriedly, and got into bed.

He lit a cigarette, blew out the candle, and lay back. After smoking for about five minutes, he put the cigarette in the tray and turned over to sleep. He closed his eyes. A thousand different thoughts floated across his mind. He lay thus for twenty minutes, his brain whirling. Then he reached for matches and re-lit the candle.

"I really don't feel tired," he said half aloud, as he lit another cigarette. But the crows were sitting upon his pillow. They would not let him sleep. They pranced about and seemed to be pecking at his conscience. He threw away the cigarette. He blew out the candle and stretched himself. Outside all was still. In the room to his left his father was sleeping the blessed sleep which follows a day's hard toil. And suddenly Joe was conscious of the fact that a pair of eyes, a pair of horrible fiery eyes, were glaring at him out of the darkness. He covered his head with the clothes and laughed. "Imagination," he said. But he could feel them now, they were peering through the clothes; they were burning their way into his very soul. They seemed to read his innermost

thoughts. An icy mist swathed itself about his heart.
He sat up in bed. He felt terribly lonely. He was isolated ;
a victim to the most horrible thoughts. And of a sudden
there would flash up before him the image of the girl he
loved, and for a time the horrible thoughts were buried.
But those eyes !—they were upon him—he could not beat
them off. He was alone—alone with his soul, which by
turns mocked him and spurred him to be courageous.
His soul which had been swirling in the abyss of desire
and revolt. His soul which in the sight of God was black
and for ever damned. He realised this and tried to pray.
But he could not pray. He could only lie there and suffer.
Suddenly the words of the priest flashed across his mind.

"The Mass ! the Mass !—confession and communion
—or ye are damned. Hearken ye unto the word of Christ
—' Depart ye for ever into everlasting fire.' "

He put his hand to his forehead. It was cold and
clammy. He could see deep into the pit of hell. He
could see the devils careering round and round, never
resting, never ceasing, singing their terrible songs. He
could hear the swish of their tails ; the smell of their
horrible bodies was in his nostrils.

"For I say unto you, if you have not grace ye are
damned for ever." Damned ! Was he damned ! God
could see him now. He could read his every thought,
see into his soul and heart and look upon the blackness
therein. He could not hide himself. Whither should he
fly ? Where ? where ? his soul cried within him. Whither
bound ? He knew not. He could not escape from God.
God had him in His power. He might take him at any
moment. "For remember ye know not the day nor the
hour."

God knew that he had lied. God knew that in the very
moment of his supposed penance, he had had wanton
desires. And that these desires were now uppermost in
his mind. And yet he had declared in the sight of God
that he had made a good confession. He had committed
a sacrilege. How terrible a crime in His sight. Yes, yes,
He might suddenly take away his life. He imagined

himself lying stiff and being discovered by his father the
next morning. He imagined the coffin being carried out
to the hearse. He could hear the coachman's rough
voice saying, " Easy on there, 'ead in first."

The cold sweat ran down his forehead. He lit the
candle. He got out of bed and began to pace the floor.
God was torturing him. He would never sleep. He was
finished. He dare not go to communion, for that would
be committing a second sacrilege. He brushed the
thought out of his mind. It was replaced by a panorama
of filthy thoughts and desires ; terrible pictures !—but
balm at that moment to his tortured soul " Yes ! yes ! "
he moaned to himself. Anything—anything to shut out
God. He went to the window and opened it. The fresh
breeze caught him and seemed to revive him. But always
he could feel those eyes upon him, burning into his very
soul. They seemed to engrave themselves upon his heart.
He burst into a flood of tears. He was alone and the
night was long, the air was calm and still. He was afraid.
He wanted to scream out that he was afraid. He wanted
to run far away into the woods, to lose himself, to blot
out all the terrible thoughts laying siege to his tortured
soul. " Jesus, Jesus ! " he wailed, half aloud.

He shut the window and returned to bed. His face was
white and his eyes were filled with fear and hunger. He
tossed about the bed. He muttered strange things to
himself : fragments of prayers coupled with curses,
fragments of promises to his God coupled with filthy oaths.
He was trapped. There was no escape. He seemed to
hear approaching from afar off the waggon of death.
He seemed to hear the beating of wings all about him.
The image of the priest behind the grille thrust itself
before him. He looked into those eyes. The priest was
watching him intently. He seemed to be waiting to
jump at him, to clutch him by the throat and cry—

" You blasphemer ! You cursed one ! You filthy
soul ! You mocker ! "

He could feel the soft relentless hands pressing upon
his windpipe, he could smell the priest's clothes. He heard

the swish of his cassock. They fought. Now he had the priest upon the floor. He was feeling for his throat. And then suddenly a hand appeared between them, a hand like stone—the hand of God. And the terrible eyes of his Redeemer looked into his. God had him now. He was pointing with his finger towards the depths of hell. He could hear the sizzling of the bodies as soon as they reached the flames. And God had him by the arm, and was sentencing him with those terr ble words—

"Depart, ye cursed, into everlasting fire."

He cringed. He was in a fever. He was thrust down. He felt himself hurtling through space. He could smell the fumes of hell. He cried aloud to be saved. To God to have mercy upon him. He saw a devil waiting to meet him. He was in his grasp.

"God ! O, God ! God ! Jesus save me ! Jesus save me ! "

*   *   *   *   *   *

Dawn. There was a loud rapping at Joe's bedroom door. He woke up.

"It's half-past six," shouted his father. Joe rubbed his eyes. He blew his nose vigorously. He rose and dressed hurriedly. When he went into the back kitchen his father was cooking bacon for himself. He washed under the tap, dried himself, and went into the kitchen to finish dressing. His father sat down to the table and poured out his tea. Joe sat down too. He wondered why his father was staring so hard at him ; why the eyes of the little statue seemed so merciless.

"Joe, I thought you were going to communion this morning ? "

"Well, yes, so I am," said Joe blushing a little and rising hurriedly from the table. He sat down by the fire and began twirling his fingers. Now and again he glanced at his father, who was very busy with the last slice of bread upon the plate. Joe fell to wondering what thoughts were passing through his father's mind. Was he saying to himself—" Now I don't believe that fellow has been to confession at all—he's such a terrible liar—

I'll just go myself and see if he goes to the altar rails—
if he does I know he has been there—if he doesn't I'll
have something to say to him immediately I come home."
Or perhaps he was saying—"Well, he wouldn't dare to go to
receive our Blessed Lord, if he hadn't been to the priest :
—that would be a sacrilege." But perhaps he might
be thinking that after all, Joe was not such a bad son,
that all he needed was constant work.

These things were still passing to and fro across Joe's
mind, when his father backed his chair, got up. and
commenced looking for his cap and coat. Joe rose too.
He dare not sit longer. At any minute he expected to
hear the angelus ring seven o'clock. His mother would
be pained if she knew he was not in church before the
first gospel. Together they went off in the direction of
the church. His father, who was coughing loudly, said
as they were passing the big Penny Bazaar—

" I'll just drop in myself and say a few prayers before I
go to work."

That was a warning. Joe knew now that his father
was suspicious of him. He must now do one of two
things. He must go to communion and commit a sacrilege in the sight of God—or he must not go, and must
face the consequences when he returned home. His
mother would not be able to stand more shocks. If she
knew that her son had again lied to her, perhaps she
would die. They got within sight of the church, and
Joe made up his mind.

" Might as well be hung for a sheep as a lamb," he
said to himself.

On entering the church they found that many people
were already there. It was the first Friday of the month.
Some had round their necks red ribbons from which
depended silver medals. They were the members of the
Sodality of the Sacred Hearts. The two walked up the
aisle and into a bench close to the altar rails. Joe felt
that he was trapped. Again he began to suffer from the
terrible fear : the fear of being suddenly called to account
before God in heaven. He knelt down and cast anxious

glances at his father. Suppose that the priest was late.
There would be a chance then because his father would
not be able to stay longer than a quarter after seven
unless he meant deliberately to be late for his work.
But the priest was now coming out, two little altar boys
following with their hands joined together. They mounted
the steps and knelt. Joe who had once or twice served
Mass when he was at school, started to follow the Mass
in the original Latin. But after the " *Suspiciosus dominus
sacrificium de manibus tuis,*" he became lost. His mind
refused to continue. His father bent over and asked him
why he had not brought his prayer-book. Joe whispered
in his ear that he had forgotten it. His father bent over
again and said in a tone which struck Joe as being
intended to hurt :

" You're a bloomin' heathen, that's what you are, my
son—here—take this book."

He pulled an old worn book from his pocket and
handed it to his son. Joe opened it at the " Prayers
before Communion," but he did not read. The printed
words seemed a mere blur before his eyes. His father
nudged him. He stood up for the first gospel. Joe tried
to look at his watch. Was his father never going ? If
only he would go, all would be well. But the old man
stood steadfast until the bell rang for communion. His
quick, interrogative glance forced Joe forward. He was
the last to go. On one side of him was an old man who
made strange noises with his mouth ; on the other side,
a young girl who had black hair hanging from her
shoulders like a cascade of black waters. Joe was praying that he would not shrink when he heard the priest's
voice saying—" *Dominus vobiscum.*" He suddenly thought
of his old friend, the librarian, who had been so
unfortunate as to drop the Sacred Host out of his mouth.
He could hear the priest coming towards him, the swish
of his robes, making a strange music in his ears. He
lifted up the altar cloth in his hands, opened his
mouth, put out his tongue, and closed his eyes. The
priest was in front of him. Joe shivered. He felt the

Host on his tongue, and a sudden impulse made him
close his mouth like a trap. The priest passed on. Joe
knelt there, his whole body shaking, for if ever he was
black in the sight of his God, it was in that moment :
that terrible moment when he felt the Host clinging to
the roof of his mouth. He remembered that he had
been told at school never to allow his teeth to touch the
Host. Now he could not avoid it. He had to get it away
from the roof of his mouth in order to swallow it. Then
he was seized suddenly with a desire to let it remain
there until he could spit it out. Then he realised the horror
of this and after some minutes managed to swallow it.
He rose, genuflected, turned round, and returned to
his bench. When he knelt he found that his father had
gone. He wondered then if his father had noticed him
shaking, wondered if he had noticed how long he had
remained with bowed head at the altar rails long after
the other communicants had gone. The last gospel
came. He stood up, glad in his heart that ordeal was over.
He made his way out of the church and went home.

The next-door neighbour had prepared breakfast for
him. He sat down, and the woman, knowing he had
been to communion, asked him if he had taken a drink of
water before he started breakfast. He immediately rose,
said he had forgotten, and went into the back kitchen.
When he sat down once more, she told him that his
mother was very much better and that she would be
getting up on the morrow. Joe said he was glad to hear
that. Then the woman went on to say that the baby
would be christened on the coming Sunday and his
mother wanted him to persuade one of his friends to
stand as godfather for the child. She could easily have
got somebody herself, but she was wanting to honour
Joe, so would he ask Dick Donovan to come to the
christening on the Sunday.

Joe said he would see him that day. When he finished
his breakfast he went off to the docks to see if
there were any odd jobs knocking about. On the way
he thought he would venture to the abattoir himself and

ask the foreman there could he give him a trial. So he turned in that direction. As soon as he got there he was taken up in the lift to the general office. He was told that there were no vacancies at present. He told them that his father had worked there for a good many years. The clerk pricked up his ears at this and asked him to wait a minute. Then he was taken down into the yard. The clerk had a little talk with the foreman and the latter came over and said to Joe—

" Come down in the morning and I'll see if I can find something for you to do."

Joe thanked him and said he would come down with his father. He hurried home to tell his mother the good news. She would be happy to hear of the promise. So would his father, who had always said that he was not big or strong enough to take a bull and pole-axe it, although he might learn to kill a pig or a sheep.

That evening he awaited the return of his father. As soon as he put his foot inside the door Joe said—

" I was down at your place to-day, the foreman told me to come down in the morning—I said that I'd come down with you."

His father looked across at him and a smile flitted across his face.

" Don't kid me, my son. D'you think I'm daft ? "

Joe laughed and said that he would be as good as any of them if he got a chance. His father laughed again, then he suddenly changed the conversation by saying that he noticed that he looked nervous this morning in the church. " Were you ill, son ? " he asked.

" I felt a little faint, that's all," said Joe. " I was all right after I got home and had some tea."

" How's your mother ? " his father asked as he started to pull off his boots.

" She's coming down to-morrow," said Joe, " so the woman next door tells me."

" I suppose you know the child is being christened on Sunday next," said his father, " and that John Magee is standing godfather for it."

"Oh," said Joe, "I thought mother wanted me to get Dick Donovan to stand for it, although," he concluded hastily, "it doesn't really matter who stands for it, does it?"

"Well no, I knew you couldn't stand for it; you're too wicked, my son, to stand for anything."

His mother would be coming down the next day. Joe did not relish that. How was he going to see Jane? And besides he had promised to go to her room this very night. Well he would have to lie to his father, although it was only a few hours since he had received the Blessed Sacrament. It would be no harm anyway. He would see. He went out and washed himself, and as he was drying himself with the towel, his father asked him why he was washing. Joe did not like that. He felt like telling his father the truth once and for all. But he could not do that. Best to wait until the damage had been done. His father was pinching his arm and saying—

"Why the wash—where are you off to, anyway?"

"Just going for a walk," Joe replied. "I suppose I can do that if I wish."

"I don't mind where you go or what you do my son, but don't let me catch you, or hear of your being seen with that prostitute down the road—that's all."

Joe blushed. He was angry and showed it.

"She's not a prostitute."

"Don't answer me back," said his father harshly—"let me catch you with her or anywhere near her and I'll wring both your necks, believe me."

Joe walked quickly down the street, his hands stuck deep in the pockets of his coat, just the thumbs remaining to view. His head was bent. Anger was stirring in his heart. "Good Lord!" he muttered to himself, "how long? How long?"

Why was not he a man; why did he not stand up to his father and mother and say what he believed in his heart—speak the truth, the whole truth?

"I do not believe—leave me alone—I will go my own way—you go yours—I am sorry that I was brought up to this religion—I hate it, every fibre of my being revolts against it. At times I have felt that I could tear down those statues, those holy pictures. They are all inimical to life. Who cares how you live? To you the one point is to die a happy death. What rot! As if you do not cling to life with all your power—as if you do not love life better than death. I say I do not and will not believe! The landlord will not mend the hole in the roof; we can all die of consumption for all he cares, but you don't mind because he has his name on a brass plate in the front of the high altar because he gives one hundred pounds a year to the church. Bah! you make me sick."

But he could not say that. After all, his mother was a good and pure woman. But she was weak in that she relied too much on faith, which is fickle and unstable as a cork upon water. Oh! when he thought of it all, it made him by turns angry and sad. The tragedies of faith! Was there no escape from this thing? Was he compelled to bear these things through all the years of his life? He remembered how, when he was eleven years old, he had sat in the church and heard, with hundreds of other boys, of the terrors of hell. As if those boys were listening! They were waiting like himself to get out, to be free, to shout and jump and sing in the delight of youth and freedom. And the priest would tell them of how a famous saint had appeared to a girl in a vision, straight from the depths of hell, and how one of her feet had burnt a hole in the wall. And they had laughed to themselves, because their minds would not visualise this thing; to them it was full of humour. Ah yes! how hard it was to throw off this cloak which childhood had seen wrapped about his soul. How often in the night had he not suffered hell in imagination? How often had the sweat run down his forehead as he thought of the angel carrying him before his Maker? How often had he visualised the cruel hard face of God, the God of little boys, the God with the whip in his hand for the little boys and a sugar-stick for the little girls? And how he had hated those Sundays, when his mother had

made him sit down and read the lives of the saints,
when all the other boys were playing in the park or the
street ! And how he had hated those horrible days :
Mass, Sunday-school, benediction—they had filled his
days. And at school the same ! The catechism ! He
could not bring himself to believe that God was so
terrible a person. And his young soul had been des-
troyed, the beautiful flowers from its garden had been
torn up ruthlessly. It was warped, dried up. No, he had
no soul. He did not want a soul. Of what use was a
man's soul, but to torture him all his years ? For when
one faced life, the cruel reality of it, one had to deny
one's soul. How often had he been dragged through the
abyss of desire—how often had he been dragged through
the furnace of suffering, because of the soul grafted upon
him by a cruel and merciless God ? Ah ! well he knew
these things. And the terrible hour once a year when
the priest rubbed the ashes upon his forehead and said
those words which seemed like burning iron upon his
young heart—

"Ashes to ashes—dust to dust."

Why ? Whither ? And what then ? And the confessional box. When he had to enter with his heart beating violently within him, when he had to tell of the sins
he had committed. Dirty mean sins, sins which were
like running sores festering upon the surface of his soul.
And his mother. He used to watch her laying out her
brown habit, the habit of the third order. He would
see the rough cord. And he knew that when she died,
she would be dressed in this, and so would lie in her
coffin. And the coffin would be brought into the church
and the bell would toll. "God ! God !" he had cried,
"do they think of nothing save death ?" Spitting upon
life ! And then he remembered how she had asked him
if he would join the order, because the bishop has made
a new rule whereby both young men and women might
join. He had laughed and asked his mother how he
would look walking up the aisle of the church with his
robe on, and a lighted taper in his hand. But what

made him revolt against it most, was the need for having
his head shaved. The world of his mother was peopled
by saints and angels. He had seen pictures of some of
them painted by great Italian painters. And after seeing
them he had laughed outright, because he could not
believe there were people like them. He had seen that
Mary Magdalene had no hips. And he wondered what
kind of bodies the angels possessed. He had scratched
his head. And his companion who was with him, the
riend who had lent him the books, had said—

"It's very good, but I've never yet seen a woman
without a backside."

Joe had remained silent then. He did not know how
to answer his friend. He was not strong enough in soul
and heart to know that the criticism of his friend was
founded on concrete facts. And when finally they had
left the gallery they had decided that a new school of
painters and sculptors was necessary. Nobody ever entered the gallery. It contained three good pictures
and a hundred rotten ones. That was what Joe told
his friend. And the people who visited it went to praise,
never to be destructive in their criticism. Because destructive criticism was a crime against art. That beautiful
art, warm as the June sun, listless, lifeless. And sometimes when they went they would stand behind people
just to hear what they were saying. And he remembered
how as they were standing near a picture by Goya, a
young lady had said—"How vulgar—and the colours
are atrocious." But Joe knew that they were shocked
by the vulgarity of it all. They did not see that power
lay in the work ; that its vulgarity had made it powerful.
And they had passed on to the portrait of a great man,
who had been famous for his manifesto on post-mortems.
But it was seldom that they were able to spend all
the time they wished in the cathedral, as his friend
called the Art Gallery. Once or twice his friend had
taken him to a concert, and he had been amazed by the
carelessness of the artists, the indifference of the players
to the audience. And sometimes he had laughed aloud

when some person near him was trembling with emotion.

And they would leave the concert disappointed except of course for one thing—there was an old man of about sixty who drank all before him, but who could play the flute like the devil. They always winked at him as they were passing out. But he could handle his flute.

These things flashed across his mind as he walked along in the chilly air of the evening. Then he brushed them from him. For he was now opposite the house of his loved one. When he rang the bell, Larson, the sweep, answered it. This time he asked no questions, but allowed him in, and told him to walk softly up the stairs as his little son was ill. This Joe did and gently knocked upon the door. He did not wait for an answer, but opened it, looked in, saw Jane smile at him from behind a towel, which covered half her face, and closed the door. They did not speak. He walked over and took her hand. They embraced. She plied him with questions. Did he know that there were a good many men from his father's place who were going to get the sack—did he know that she was thinking of leaving the city? He could only stare at her, surprise written on his face. At length she finished her ablutions and came and sat down by him on the bed. She took his hand and felt its warmth. Her own made him shiver. They were as cold as ice. He asked her why she was leaving the city and she said that she thought it was time she struck out a line on her own. He could not understand her. Had she not already struck out a line, which was loathsome to him, but bread and butter to her.

She laughed, pulled his hair and said—

" Why should I not? I have saved enough money to start upon my own, though I don't know what I'll start."

He was full of suggestions. Told her that he would help in whatever she started. He would leave his family and go and live with her. They would both be happy. He was sure of that. His heart told him. But Jane saw that it was impossible for him to leave his family.

G

"You cannot leave your mother; you are entirely dependent upon her, besides they are sure to find you out, and then there would be the devil to pay—and you know, Joe, I do not want your people following me, and sending down some priest or other from your church."

He only laughed.

"Why," he said, "do you really believe that it is impossible for us to be together always? Nothing more ridiculous ever was said."

Then his heart began to thump against his body. A voice was whispering in his ear. "Go on, you fool—you know what you want."

His face was mantled with blood. She saw now that something had taken possession of him. And this voice was taunting him. It was saying—

"Go on, go on, you fool, get what you want—you know what you came for."

He fidgeted upon the edge of the bed. And again the cold horror of being hauled before his Redeemer assailed him. It bit deep into his flesh. This thought solidified itself, it became organic matter in his whirling brain.

"Well and what then?" he thought to himself as he watched the young woman.

Again he heard the voice of the priest. Again he saw and felt those eyes upon him. And Jane was holding up her face to him, she was entreating—he knew it. He could see the hunger in her eyes. But this terrible God had His hand against him. Someone was holding him by the hair over the abyss. The blood rushed to his heart. "I am lost—I am lost," he cried to himself.

"Joe! Joe!" She was calling his name now. He felt her hands stroking his cheek. Felt her hot breath upon his face. She tightened her hold upon him. He could not resist. Again that voice—

"Go on, fool—you know what you want."

And suddenly he found himself saying aloud—

"You know what you want."

She looked at him and smiled. Her lips framed themselves for a kiss. He was in the act of kissing her when her lips pouted, and she struggled to get away from him. But that made him all the more eager. For the voice was beseeching him, to——

The gulf of desire blotted out their thoughts. They did not exist. They were floating in the realms of nothingness. The hurricane of desire swept him off his feet. Everything was blotted out. His mother—God—everything. He felt himself carried away, whirled down upon the surface of waters which roared in his ears. The smell of her cheap scent was in his nostrils. It sickened him. He closed his eyes. All was forgotten. Alone they drifted far down the dark night. On, on. Whither bound ? The last streak of light faded ; the room was enveloped in darkness. A darkness terrible and intense. He was filling the room with himself. He was great, masterly, ferocious, he was a god, he was master of all. And still they were hurled onwards, the waters roaring in the night of the world. Everything was aflame. Everything was burning. Everything was afire with his desire. The world was lighted up by the light of his soul, burning intensely within him. He was riding on top of the world. On, on, never resting. And suddenly out of the chaos, out of the ruins of the abyss he saw—God—he saw—his mother—he saw everything. A wave of pity seemed to sweep over him. Too late ! He could not draw back. He must go on. There must be no turning back. He was lost. He was in the grip of hell. " Hey ! you—hey ! you," shouted the devils.

"Well !" He heard a great voice, a voice of bronze which seemed to strike the earth with a great metallic clang. Again it sounded in his ears. " Well ! " Ah yes, he knew that voice—he could see that face, he saw that arm. That was God ! He had not escaped. He had been seen. He was done. Damned ! Whither now ? He knew not. He must go on. Tears came into his eyes. His soul he now saw in the light of his conscience. It was valueless. It was not even a soul, it was a bastard growth. It was not his own. He had betrayed and had been betrayed. He saw how minute a thing he was in

the mirror. He saw himself crawling upon the surface
of the earth, lost, despised, forever. God had him now.
The network of desire had closed about him. What use
now to live ? What use now to look with pure eyes upon
the beautiful things of the world ? His eyes could not
see these things, for God had robbed him in a night of
his sight ; he could not see his mother. God had him
and would throw him to the devils. Ah, why had he
not taken counsel of his mother ? Why had he not said
to the priest in the confessional box that night—" I am
besieged, father—I am besieged by desire. It is like a
fiery serpent gnawing into my very vitals, father, oh !
father, help me ! "

Why had he not done that. And then and then——.
But what use to think. He opened his eyes. The woman
was resting in his arms. The bed swayed lightly to the
weight. No sound in the house. All was still. No wind
stirred, and the night was suddenly pierced by the moon.
It sent its beams pouring into the room. Light. He did
not want that. Eternal darkness would be his. He kissed
Jane. And with the soft touch of his lips, she too opened
her eyes, and there was in them a brightness, a light
which seemed to be shining upon his face—he felt it, it
seemed to envelop him in a radiant cloud. He seemed
to be exalted. They both fell asleep. The night wore
on.

At home his mother was waiting for him—his father
was sitting in his chair, glancing every now and then at
the clock upon the shelf. And Mick's brow darkened.
Where could Joe be ? He had never stayed out so late
before. But something seemed to tell him what had
befallen his foolish son. He rose and paced the floor.
And once or twice he went to the foot of the stairs and
in answer to his wife's pleading voice, he answered—

" No !—he has not come in yet, and it is nearly midnight."

He went upstairs. He wanted to go to bed—he was
tired after his day's work. But he could not sleep. He
knew that. What then ? He descended into the kitchen

again and paced the floor anew. Now and again he heard a plaintive whine from the child in the room. The house seemed strange and lonely without his son. Terrible thoughts flashed across his mind. Perhaps he had drowned himself. And perhaps—and perhaps— but he could not yet answer that question. He shouted upstairs—

"I'm going out to look for him."

And into the deserted streets he went to look for his son. Without cap or coat. A policeman who passed him thought he was mad or drunk. He seemed to sway a little—then suddenly he collapsed in a heap.

CHAPTER VI

MARTHA ROURKE was sitting on a chair when she saw her husband go past the window. It was but an hour since he had left for his work. She wondered why he was returning so early. When he knocked at the door, she jumped with fright. She saw that he looked ill, his face was ashen grey, the eyes sunken. He sat down and said—

"I'm dead beat. I never felt so weary in my life."

"God help you," said Mrs. Rourke.

He bent his head upon his breast. She saw that he was crying. He was murmuring to himself. She went upstairs to bring down the child. She thought that perhaps it would make him buck up, as she used to say.

"All these things happen together," he said. "I don't know how it is—I am sure there is a curse over the house."

"All what things?" she asked.

"Why, Joe clearing off—and now they've stopped me at the abattoir."

"What!—stopped you—why——?"

He shook his head. He could not answer, for a pain lay under his heart. He wanted to go and lie down somewhere—to sleep—to forget.

But Martha had now risen to her feet. She was plying him with questions.

"You're right," she said at length, "the house is covered by a curse, and it's my son who has brought it. A devil out of hell!—that's what he is."

She put her hand inside her blouse and pulled out a letter, saying—

"Look at this—and then think on the landlord expecting his arrears to-morrow—and the child to be looked after—and wonder how it is that I am not in a madhouse."

She thrust the letter into his hand. He took it and placing it in his pocket said—

"I will read it afterwards. Make me a cup of tea—I do not feel very well—this trouble with Joe is killing me fast—honest to God it is."

She felt sorry for him in that moment. While she went to make him some breakfast, he pulled out the letter. As soon as he saw the signature he knew what it was. It read as follows—

"DEAR SIR,

"I think it nearly time you paid me my money—you know I never received the thirty shillings which you owe me since the time John was confined. Please let me have the money, £4 10s., or I shall have to put you in court."

"Good Christ!—one thing on top of another," he exclaimed.

He heard his wife coming. He put the letter back in his pocket. She saw a change in his expression. She failed to understand. He was hungry, for he had eaten little that morning—he had been worrying all the night about Joe. He had not returned to the house till two in the morning. He finished his meal.

"I am going down to the dock to see if there's any chance down there," he said.

She did not answer him, merely nodded her head. She was wondering how she was going to face the creditors.

As usual it was left to her. Her husband never bothered about such things. It was always the same. The woman had to do the dirty work. Well, she would do it for the last time. She would go out and look for work herself. She could get work. She would do anything—scrub floors—anything. She went into the back kitchen and tidied herself. Before they knew where they were they would be in the workhouse.

" A nice end," she said half aloud, " a nice end for me—a decent, respectable woman—brought up a large family and this is what I get in return. They all desert me. They have sucked and sucked at my old bones until I can stand it no longer." She burst into tears. What was she to do? Uppermost in her mind was Joe. She loved him with a great passionate love, in spite of his failings. She would have given her life for him. " Ah," she thought, " men know little of what a woman has to suffer. Many a time I have gone to my bed hungry because I would not see my children suffer. And the thanks I get! Dagger thrusts in the heart. But I can stand it no longer. I am sure my brain's going."

She started to beat her hands on the wall. And the people in the next house came in to see what was the matter. They thought it was Mick beating his wife or his son. And they found her there, wild-eyed, beating upon the wall with her hands, and calling out " St. Anthony, help me !—Blessed Virgin, look down on me ! "

They got her away from the wall. They tried to pacify her. When they asked her what the trouble was, she merely said—" My heart is broken."

The husband of the woman next door was a Billie— he used to wear a yellow sash on a fine summer's day in July, and he hated Catholics like poison—but he could not hate this suffering woman. His heart went out to her. He tried to console her, told her that her son was just a foolish young man—that he would return home, the best home he had ever had—" and I know it," said the man.

Someone brought her a drop of whisky in a glass. Then they carried her upstairs. The child was lying quiet in the big bed. They laid her beside it.

As Mick was turning the corner into Bruce Street he met John Magee.

"What's the devil's the matter, man?" asked John, as he saw the white haggard face of his friend. Mick told him his trouble. John took his hand. His heart went out to his friend.

"And haven't you seen the lad since yesterday evening?" he asked Mick.

They walked on a little and then Mick told him all.

"The young devil!" exclaimed Magee—"why it was only last night about seven o'clock that I saw him with a young woman in Lime Street."

"You what?" asked Mick.

"I saw him with a young woman in Lime Street," repeated Magee in a loud voice.

"So it's with that Protestant slut he is then—after what I told him—wait—if I catch him I'll strangle him —I'll swing for him."

"Come, come," said Magee, "easy on, man—you can't go doing those things, you know. It would kill your wife, and her just after having a child—oh no, you can't do mad things like that, Mick—why it would be all over the parish before you knew where you were."

"Perhaps it would," replied Mick, "but there are other things which will be all over the parish before long —never mind the doings of that rascal. Would to God I had never seen his face. He's the devil's handyman, that's what he is."

"How old is Joe?" asked Magee.

"Old enough to have better sense. A young Catholic fellow like that running off with a prostitute! God Almighty! for all I know he might be living with her."

"Them's hard words," said Magee, "how do you know she's a prostitute. How do you know what she is? Perhaps she is as good as your son after all."

Mick stared at his friend. He could not believe it. Had he too left him?

"I'm surprised at you, Magee. I thought you were a decent man," replied Mick.

"So I am," said Magee, "as decent as any man living—but I don't like to hear people run down like that. You surely don't know everything about your son and this young woman?"

"My own mind tells me that he is going the wrong way. He ought to realise, in the first place, that he is a Catholic—and that our holy father the Pope does not sanction marriages between Catholics and Protestants, much less prostitutes."

"There you go again—hit a man when he is down," exclaimed Magee.

"I'm going to find out where this woman lives—it is my duty to save my son—anyhow I'll have plenty of time to do that now, because I was finished up at the abattoir this morning."

"Oh hell!" said Magee, "that's real bad. I'm damn sorry to hear that! What's the cause of it? you've been with them such a long time."

"Fifteen years!" said Mick. "But it's not myself I think of—it's the wife, the best woman in the world—and when I think of the way my son has treated her it makes me furious."

They had reached the dock sheds. Magee asked him what he intended doing.

"God knows," he replied.

"I was just going down to Donovan's when I met you; will you come up that far and have a drink?"

"All right," said Mick.

When they got there, Magee took him into the snug parlour. Over the drinks Mick poured out all his troubles. Magee was sorry for him and he meant it. Mick was ɩ beaten man. He seemed helpless. His eyes were staring vacantly. He watched his hand tremble as he ook up his glass. He had never seen him nervous before. He was like a baby! He thought, too, of Martha. How devoted a woman she was ! What a good mother to her children ! He had known her all her life ; he had gone to school with her as a child.

" Look here," said Magee rising up from the stool, " let's both go down and see your missus ; she must be in a bad way, you know, the poor girl."

" All right," he said.

They set off for home. But they found hat Martha had gone out. And upstairs the child was whining for its feed. Magee went up and brought it down.

"You're a fine little man," he said to the child raising it up and down in the air. He drew his chair into the fire and nursed the child while Mick shaved himself.

"She won't be long, I don't suppose," Mick said to him.

" Oh, she'll be here soon, don't worry on that score," replied John Magee.

" She may have gone down with the rent you know, it was due this morning."

" She'll be quite safe, never fear," Magee told him.

Mick cut his chin with the razor. When a knock came to the door, he dropped the razor. " Joe," he thought.

But it was only his wife. She had been down to see the landlord. He was an old skinflint. God forgive her for saying that !—for he was in the third order with herself, but what could a body say, after the way she had been treated. Magee prayed her to sit down.

" I'll be in my grave soon," she said, as she sat down with a bump.

" Come now," said Magee, " don't worry yourself so."

" Ah well ! there's always justice for us poor folks to rely on," she said after a pause. Magee looking up espied a large spot on the ceiling.

" Why now you must have a leak somewhere," he murmured, half smiling at Mick.

" Yes, that swine of a landlord was asked to come and mend the roof a month ago, but God forgive him, he's never put his face near us yet—it's pretty bad too, we have to put the owld tin bath underneath the ceiling in the front room."

" Oh dear !—is it that bad then, Mick ! "

" Yes," said Mick savagely, " the crazy house is a disgrace to him. I often wonder why the missioner didn't make an onslaught on the landlords whilst he was about it—instead of cursing us poor devils because we take a glass of ale now and again."

" Michael ! " said his wife sternly—" do you know what you are saying ? "

" I can't help it, Martha," replied her husband— " it's the confounded worry of everything—I'm sorry anyhow—let that be enough—eh ? "

" And Joe is really a bad lad then," exclaimed Magee, licking his lips.

" Yes, he's gone to the devil since he met these strange friends of his. Says that he has as much right to his freedom as anyone—as if we deny him it—and thinks he can do as he likes—well, he won't do it inside this house, that's all—I am master here," Mick tapped himself on the chest—" and while I am master, I'll have no son of mine casting disgrace on his parents and getting us a bad name in the whole parish. Martha and I, why we're ashamed to walk down to Mass of a Sunday ! He says he is as good a Catholic as they who are running down to church every five minutes. Well, they might do a bit of jangling now and again—everybody does that—but all the same they are Catholics, and attend to their duties. He started by bringing in filthy books to read. He used to hide them under his bedclothes. One night I caught him on the hop, and what do you think he was reading ? "

" What ? " said Magee.

" One of them filthy books by a scoundrel named Zola. But that wasn't all ! He must needs bring in a horrible filthy book, which ought never to have seen the light of day—a book called ' Ulysses ' by a dirty renegade Irishman named Joyce. I tore it up. I did not want my lad's morals ruined. There are plenty of fine Irish writers without a dirty stinker like that. Why there are good books downstairs if you want to read them—

there's ' Handy Andy ' for instance. But he stuck his
nose up at that. ' Look here,' I said to him ' if I see you
with another book like that I'll knock that nose of yours
up on your forehead."

" It's a great pity," said John Magee, again licking
his lips.

When Martha saw him lick his lips for the second time
she went out into the back to make a cup of tea. She
had eaten nothing herself since morning.

" Could you never get him into your place ? " asked Magee.

" I tried till I was sick. But what's the use now ? I'm
sacked, what for I don't know, but here we are, not a
soul working and don't know where to turn for it."

" Why, look here," said Magee, " why don't you ask
Father Dunny ? He's always ready to help anybody in
distress—he's head of the Saint Vincent de Paul Society."

" No thanks," said Martha, " I never begged in my
life. I'm a re pectable woman and I'm the last to think
of going to the society for anything. And anyhow the
poor priests have hardly enough to live on themselves.
Why, there's a big debt to be paid for cleaning and
decorating the high altar—oh no ! the poor priests can
hardly keep *themselves* alive. You know that the State
doesn't keep priests, John," she concluded, as she commenced to set the table.

" It's right bad, that's what it is," went on Magee, " if
I catch sight of your son I'll ask him to come home with
me—I'll give him a talking to, just one man to another
kind of thing."

But suddenly the back kitchen door opened and the
person of whom they were speaking entered the kitchen.
The three stared at him. He stared at them. There was
a scowl on his face, and an air of defiance in his attitude.
His father spoke.

" Well, where have you been all night—with that
confounded prostitute, I suppose ? "

Joe remained silent. This angered his father, who rose
and rushed at him. But Magee pulled Mick away,
saying as he did so—

"You're a proper hot-tempered man, if ever there was one—why don't you let the lad speak?"

They sat down again. Joe was standing at the dresser watching them. He was watching his mother too, and saw tears coming into her eyes.

"What's come over you at all, Joe?" asked Magee, "you used to be such a nice lad."

Joe stood erect, folded his arms across his chest and said defiantly—

"Do not speak to me—from this day I am dead—yes, dead!"

"That'll do," said his mother, "we don't want any of your airs here—we have enough to worry about, without thinking about you and your filthy ways. Here's your father out of work, and me with a child two weeks old to look after, and God knowing when your father will get a job again. Who's going to pay my rent, pay for the food which you are only too ready to gulp from my table? As if you cared how I get it, so long as your belly is filled. You're the talk of the parish, and I can't hold my head up "—(here she burst into tears)—" oo-hoo-oo-hoo!" His father rushed at him, and Magee was too late to stop him. He took his son by the throat and forced him back across the table. The tea things went crashing to the floor; Martha screamed. Magee led her out into the yard.

"Let him have it, perhaps it's the best—you've worry enough, girl, without taking this on your head."

"I never thought I would rear a son like him," said Martha, between sobs, "I never did—oh, I wish I was dead—all I've done for him—sacrificed my own comfort for him many a time, done everything, and this is the result."

"There, there," exclaimed John, "don't take it so hard, girl."

Mick came running out. He was trembling from head to foot.

"John, John, run for the priest! I think I've killed him."

"Jesus, Mary and Joseph!" exclaimed Martha, "I knew it—I saw it coming—I knew he would come to a bad end."

She ran into the house and found her son lying stretched on the floor. There was a deep gash in his throat and blood stained his clothes.

"My son! my poor, poor son!" she screamed frantically, as she kissed him, smothering her face in his hair.

Mick had fled. And Magee was now knocking at the door, with Father Harley at his heels. When they entered, Magee had to lift Martha off her son's body.

"Has he cut his throat?" asked the priest—he had turned suddenly white.

"His father done it, father, his father," sobbed Martha, from the couch, where Magee had laid her.

"Glory be to God! if I ever think these things would come into my life. And what in God's name have I done to earn it? Since I was thirteen I have had to earn my own living. Never took a farthing from anybody. Reared a large family, and buried several—my God, when I think of it." She buried her face in the cushions and sobbed. Great sobs which seemed to find echo in the heart of Magee, in the heart of the priest who was now bathing the wound in the boy's throat.

"His father has fled, I think," said Magee, in answer to the priest's question. He went out to search for him. He found him outside sitting with his head resting between his hands. When he heard Magee approach he looked up and Magee started back. His eyes were glaring, the saliva was trickling down his chin. His collar was torn and his face was covered with blood.

"Mick! Mick!" said John gently, "it's only me, why don't you come in? The boy's all right, he's not hurt, come in now, there's a good man, everything's all right. What did you hit him with?"

"I picked up the bread knife."

"Well that's a foolish thing to do now, don't you know that?" went on Magee. "Oh, you're an excitable man, if there was one, indeed! indeed!"

When they re-entered the kitchen Joe had been carried upstairs by the priest, and Martha had fallen asleep from sheer exhaustion on the sofa. Magee helped Mick into his chair. He patted him on the back and told him that everything would be all right, not to worry, he had been in worse scrapes when he was as young. Mick did not answer. He saw a movement on the part of Martha, and he thought she was going to fall off the sofa. He fetched two overcoats and laid them over her. Her bosom rose and fell like a sea. Now and again a convulsive sob broke from her and Magee thought the best thing he could do would be to go up and see how the lad was. When he went into the room in which Joe usually slept, he found him lying very still, covered with a white sheet. The priest was on his knees. Joe must be very bad then. Magee immediately got down on his knees, and recited with the priest the prayers for the dying. There was a strange silence about the house now. The priest rose to his feet, took a last look at the figure on the bed, and turned to leave the room. Magee asked him if he thought the lad was fatally wounded. The priest looked at John and wondered if he were some relation, and if the row had been caused through him. Magee told him all about the foolish young man, who neglected his duties. He said slowly—

" You know, father, I think he's just a foolish, headstrong young man."

The priest smiled and said—

" I have heard about him. I think it is impossible to do anything with him."

" But think then, father, of his immortal soul, what of that ?—it is your duty to save him, father, forgive me for speaking like that you know, but I am sorry for the young man—he has got into this woman's hands, yes, that's what it is."

" My dear man, as you know, all our life is devoted to trying to bring back to God the millions who have deserted Him—don't you know that the Catholic religion is gaining world-wide strength ? "

" I am sorry for that young man, father," said Magee.

The priest took his departure and said he would call in again and see Joe.

" That'll be for the best, father, I'm sure," were the parting words of Magee, as he saw the priest out of the door. Then he went upstairs to see Joe. He found him awake. He looked very weak. Magee went to speak to him, but he waved him away with an arm that dropped heavily to his side. But Magee would not be denied. He had much to say to him. He wanted to be his friend. He wanted to talk with him straight from the heart—to show the young man that he loved him—that he was his friend if in a moment of bitterness he had lost the friendship of his parents. Taking no heed to the arm that again motioned him out of the room, he stood his ground and drew a chair to the bed.

" Are you feeling a little better, Joe ? " he asked and he laid his hand on the young man's shoulder.

" A little," said Joe, and lapsed into silence again.

" Tell me what's the trouble—do you really love the girl ? "

" Yes," replied Joe.

" But look here, child, you can't go on like that—you know your father and mother being good Catholics expect you to be the same, and besides, Joe, the church wouldn't marry you—mixed marriages are a curse, my child. And then you can't do rash things like that, Joe, until you can stand on your feet. Why can't you get a job and settle down for a bit—you'll forget all about this young woman—for the right one will come along, you'll see, yes, indeed you will. Now tell me, isn't that a good bit of advice to give you ? "

" I love this girl—and will never love another," replied Joe.

" There, there," said Magee, " don't speak too much, child, you must be pretty weak. Don't think ill of your father, boy ; he did it in a fit of temper—he'll get over that, all right, you see if he don't."

" I have finished with my father for ever," said Joe.

" Come, come," said Magee, " don't say things like that—why, your father loves you."

" Nevertheless I am finished with him. As soon as I am well I am leaving here."

" Now you must try and be a man. Don't do a thing like that ! Your father will be in soon and I am sure you'll make it up between you—just try now."

" I said I have finished with him—and also with my mother—to me they are no longer parents—but people —that is all."

Magee saw that Joe was speaking with great emotion. But he dared not ask further questions. He saw that the young man was not fit to be questioned. He got up and said good-bye.

Joe half smiled at him and watched his big form disappear through the doorway. Someone else was mounting the stairs. Who could that be ? But it was only the doctor. He had been sent by the priest. He dressed the gash in the throat and remarked that it was a good job that the wound wasn't deeper or his father might have been standing in the dock charged with murder.

" He will be one day," said Joe, looking up in the doctor's face.

" Never say things like that, young man," entreated the doctor.

He bandaged up the throat and asked Joe if he would like a job in his office.

" No, I am going away altogether soon, thank you all the same," replied Joe.

" I wish you luck," said the doctor—adding, " Why here's the man we're looking for—it's your father."

Mick stood at the end of the bed. He did not speak, but waited for the doctor to be gone. And when that gentleman had taken his departure, he spoke.

" Joe—I want you to forgive me—I know I have a terrible temper—and I am afraid, that with all the other things happening so suddenly, your mother having another baby, and me out of work, and people tearing down the door for money—well, it put me in a bad mood,

H

and I am sorry, lad—but you know that you deserved
it—now, didn't you ? "

Joe did not answer. He lay there staring up at the
ceiling. His father was speaking again. He did not want
to listen to him. He wished he were gone. He did not
want to see anybody at that moment, only Jane. His
father said—

" Joe, don't take it to heart, lad," and sobbed a little.

Joe rose a little in the bed. " God's curse on you," he
shouted.

*   *   *   *   *   *   *

" Into the river ! " thought Mick.

For that one needed a stout heart — a strong soul.
What then ?

And was not his soul strong enough ? Was not his
heart strong enough ? Could he not fight against the
wind ? Had he not the courage to face the reality of
things ?

He had nearly killed his son. His wife was ill. There
were mouths to feed. Yes, he must fight. But how ?
Ah, that was the thing. How one had to fight ! He was
tramping along the pavements. He had fled from the
house. It stifled him. And now he was faced with disaster.
Oh, if only he could find money. Yes, that was it—
that was what was worrying him. Money. MONEY.
Money for the midwife, money for the landlord—money
for food, for the church. Oh yes. But now he wanted
five pounds. Yes, that was a lot of money. And he must
have that five pounds or the family would be thrown
into the street. The house was not their own. He had to
look for money. Ah ! and when he looked around there
seemed to be no shortage of it—save for him. " Five
pounds "—" five pounds "—he kept repeating to himself. Yes, if only he could find five pounds in the
gutter. Perhaps someone would drop the money. He
would pick it up and run off with it to the landlord. He
could feel the money in his hand—it was burning his
palm. Yes, he knew he would find money. It was the
feast of St. Anthony. He would say three Hail-Mary's

to. St. Anthony. That was the very man who would find it for him. Dear St. Anthony. Send me five pounds. Holy St. Anthony, find me five pounds. Oh dear ! Oh dear ! He was walking in the gutter now. A tramcar passed and splashed mud over his trousers. But he knew it not. He was walking on and on—for he knew he must find this money. And he was praying aloud.

"St. Anthony, send me the money—St. Anthony, find me five pounds." Perhaps a man would be passing at the time and he would hear him praying thus and he would be sorry for him and he would open his cheque-book and he would write down in large letters "Pay the bearer five pounds." Ah, that would be great. That would be a miracle. St. Anthony would do that for him. He knew it. And was not his father-in-law named Anthony ? Yes, he would get the money. A radiance seemed to envelop him. He thought he saw the saint and looked up to him with longing eyes. People were staring after him as he walked along in the gutter. They thought he was a beggar. They thought he was a mad-man—they thought he was drunk. And they all laughed in turn. And he took no notice of their laughs and giggles but walked on because in his heart he knew that he was going to find five pounds.

"Holy St. Anthony, send me some money—until the work comes—St. Anthony pray for us—God in heaven, heed my prayer." He kept muttering incoherently to himself. The darkness was drawing in. He did not realise that he had been wandering the streets thus for hours. And in his soul a flame seemed to burn—it urged him on—and he saw his family, saw them thrown into the street. Saw his son dead—lying stiff on the bed, and knew that he was gone to hell. His mind was unhinged by all the worry that attends those of the abyss. For the abyss is the dark-house of the world—and yet the world knows it not—for it is beyond the sight of men. No light flares in the abyss. No flame burns in the abyss of one's soul. All is dark and gloom. All is silent. Save for the winds which blow, save for the winds that blow them adown the dark roads of life.

For the birthright of the abyss is to suffer isolation—to suffer exile. To suffer and see one's family broken up, blown by the winds of heaven to the four corners of the earth. And did not Mick in his heart know this? Did he not often think on his sons who were away, of the sons whom he had buried? They were all gone—all vanished! He would not see them more. And his one remaining son, a rebel, a disgrace to him and his wife—a disgrace to his religion. How often had he wished for death! Anything to escape from the abyss. The abyss which even now was watching him—looking into his heart and seeing there chaos stirring, stirred by the flame of desire. The desire for what? St. Anthony knew. It was money he wanted. Money to stop the landlord, who wore a brown habit with a rope round it on every third Sunday of the month—a man who had prayed every day of his life to have a happy death. A man who could not fix the roofs of his houses. A man who had no children—who did not know what to do with himself most of the time.

"But there's justice for the poor," he thought as he walked on. He found that he had reached the dockside. He did not realise that he had walked that distance. He must turn back. They would be wondering what had become of him. Martha would be wondering, because she was his wife and they had shared their joys and sorrows together for more than thirty years. But his son —no! Had he not cursed him? "Father in heaven, look down and guide him," he said to himself. He straightened himself, and saw that his clothes were covered with mud. He wondered how he had become so dirty. And when he looked about him he found he was standing in the gutter and that one or two people were even then staring at the gaunt-looking man who was standing in the drizzling rain looking about him as if he were lost. A man walked off the side walk, and took hold of his arm.

"Are you ill?" he asked him in a gentle tone.

"No, no—I'm quite all right, thank you," he replied. "I am going home now," he added.

He wandered home by way of the church. There he would go and pray to St. Anthony to help him in his distress.

And when he arrived there and walked right up to the front bench right in front of the high altar, he saw that Martha was there also. How long she had been there, he could not tell. He went into the same bench. And she saw him.

"Mick," she whispered, "where have you been—I thought you'd met with an accident?"

"How is Joe?" he asked in a whisper.

"He is a little better now—thanks be to God."

"Have you a penny in your pocket," he asked her, "I wanted to burn a candle to St. Anthony—it is his feast day to-day, and I want to burn it for a special intention."

She fumbled in the pocket of her skirt and extracting a penny gave it him, saying as she did so—

"I know, I know, Mick, dear—it's that Joe will get better—poor Joe—but perhaps he will be a better son in future. Let's both pray to Almighty God and His Blessed Mother that he will."

She watched him leave the bench and approach the shrine of St. Anthony before which stood a large stand full of candles, some newly lighted, some half burned. She heard him drop the penny in the box—saw him take up a candle in his hand, bless himself, light it from one of the others and place it in the holder. She saw him kneel and bow to the saint. Then he came back to where she was kneeling and as he moved up to her he said—

"Fancy you being here too—I did not expect to find you—thought you would be looking after Joe."

"Joe is sound asleep," she said.

He saw she had lying on the open page of her prayer-book a copy of a prayer to St. Gerard Majella.

"Are you praying to St. Gerard?" he asked.

"St. Gerard is the great saint for curing illness," she told him.

"I was praying to St. Anthony," he said and lapsed into silence.

A priest came out of the vestry. It was the priest who had lectured Joe on that memorable Sunday. Martha had a sudden wish to go to him and tell him of her troubles. A minute or so later a woman came out to dress the altar with flowers. Martha knew her well. When they were both young women they had been in the Children of Mary together. In her imagination she could see herself placing fresh flowers in the big brass vases. She saw herself walking with a great company of young women wearing her white lace veil, and the blue ribbon and silver medal of the Blessed Virgin.

And in her heart she wished for a return of those days—those days filled with all the brightness of youth—those days which were filled with the scent of flowers, the music of Magee's fiddle, and the memory of her husband singing the Irish song which John played on his fiddle at the celebration of the tenth year of their marriage. She looked across at her husband. His face was tilted a little. He was staring before him. His hands were joined together ; she saw how they trembled. Her heart was full of pity for him. His gaunt face filled her with compassion. She could hear him reciting the prayers half aloud. And when she looked behind her she saw that the church was empty save for herself and husband. A bell suddenly rang. She nudged her husband.

" The angelus, Mick," she said, and they both stood up and recited it aloud.

" The angel of the Lord declared unto Mary," broke from her husband's lips.

" And was conceived by the Holy Ghost," replied Martha in a loud voice.

When they had finished they knelt down again. Martha began to fidget in the bench.

" I think we had better go home," she said, " best not to leave Joe lying there by himself—he might wake up suddenly and want a drink or something."

They got up, genuflected together, walked down the wide middle aisle, stopped to dip their hands into the holy water, and making the sign of the cross, left the church. The street lamps were being lighted and the streets were full of workers scurrying home. To one or two people Mick and Martha nodded—they were members of the congregation.

When they returned to the house they found that their son was still asleep. Together they stole silently into the room. Together they stood over his bed. Then they turned silently away. As they were closing the door Martha said to her husband—

" Don't you think it best to wake him up—he might want a drink or something—it's not good for people to sleep so long."

" He'll wake up soon—anyway we can go to bed—if we hear him in the night one of us can go and attend to him."

They went down into the kitchen. The fire had gone out, and the place was cold. Mick started to light it but Martha told him not to bother.

" Did you notice that the ceiling was damp in Joe's room as well ? " asked Mick.

" I didn't notice," replied Martha—" although I shouldn't be surprised, the whole place is damp—and considering the weather we're having, you'd think that landlord would shift himself a bit."

" He's a hard old customer," said Mick " but he's neither worse nor better than the rest of them—did you go down to see Mrs. ——".

" I saw her this morning," said Martha, " she says she doesn't mind waiting a little."

" That's a bit better anyhow—things don't look so bad as they did. By the way, don't you think it would be a good thing to get Joe away to sea ? "

" The very thing," said Martha, " but would he go— that's the question ? "

" Of course he'd go—what does he think he is at all— a working man's son wanting to choose his own jobs ? "

" He's not very strong, you know," continued Martha " and I believe the ships' doctors are very strict."

" Strict or not, he can go to sea if he wants, but he's

too damn lazy. Ever since he got in with that friend of his who's been lending him books, well—I don't know what's come over him, I don't indeed."

"Let's go to bed—it's no use keeping this thing up for the whole of the night. You ought to be glad that you didn't kill the child."

"I will kill him one of these days—if he isn't going to follow his beautiful religion he can just get out of here —but he's wise, he knows jolly well that so long as his old mother is content to wait on him—so long as his old father is content to slave for him, he won't have to move hand or foot."

"Not so hard on the lad, Mick; he'll change; it's this cursed woman who's put strange ideas into his head —ideas about running away from home."

"Well, let's get to bed, anyway." Mick turned out the gas and lit the candle. When they got into their room the moon was just coming out from behind a sheaf of clouds.

"We won't need this candle," said Mick and thereon blew it out. He was in bed before Martha had started to undress.

She was standing near the door, listening for sounds from the next room, but all was quiet.

"It's a mighty long sleep he's having" said Mick covering himself up with the red quilt—"a damned long one—I wish I could sleep as well as he."

"Sure he was always a great sleeper, Mick," said Martha—"always."

She got into bed beside him. They fell to silence. Mick was staring at the wall opposite him—Martha was looking out of the window.

"You'd better shut that window" she said, "it might be raining during the night."

He got out of bed and shut it. Then he heard a yawn coming from the next room.

"I think Joe's awake," he said—"did you hear the great yawn he gave? He must have had a great sleep."

Martha immediately went into Joe's room. She lit a

candle and placed it on the shelf before the little altar.

" How are you, child ? " she asked as she went to the side of the bed.

" I am all right," said Joe.

" I'll make you a cup of tea, eh ? "

She left the room before he could answer. He heard her crawling down the stairs. He thought his mother must be bad on her feet. It took her such a long time to reach the bottom. Often he had counted the seconds it took her to descend the twenty-two rickety wooden stairs.

He could hear her pottering about in the kitchen. She was making tea for him. His mother was a good woman —if—oh ! if only she would let him do as he wished as far as his religion was concerned. He did not want to remain a Catholic, because it was no more than a scheme to keep poor people and rich people apart.

His features were greatly changed. His face was thin and haggard, and his eyes seemed to have gone to the back of his head ; his hands were white, they had never been so white and soft. That was because he was ill. And underneath his eyes great rings told of the havoc played with his young body. He lay still. He heard his mother crawling up the stairs again. She had not been long. His mother was a good cook. He often thought what a good doctor she would have made if she had had the chance. But then if that had been the case he might not have been there. Well, to him it seemed as if that would have been a good thing. For a Catholic life was a thing to be avoided. One had to try and seek the internal rather than the external. One had to hide oneself away from the world. All the people he had known, all the people he had seen at confession and communion despised life. They were looking forward to heaven. That was the great city. That was their home. They must shun this world, for all that it contained was harmful to their souls. So the priest told them. And he warned them of the folly of trying to get the best out of this life, because in so doing they were liable to lose their souls. The world was such a bad place. If they lost heaven they lost everything. And again they had said to their brethren : " Behold in the high heavens the son of God—He awaits you there, he awaits you with loving arms."

Most of the people thought it would be best to try to keep in His good books for heaven mattered—earth was nothing. So they prayed day after day, week after week, down all the years of their dull lives—prayed that they might be good Christians and die happy deaths. And after their morning prayers, and after their evening prayers, and after the angelus and the grace before and after meals, they prayed to God and His Blessed Son to help them die happy deaths. Only death mattered. Life was nothing. The wonder and mystery of the human tree, with its life force in the world—this did not interest them. Only death mattered—only death counted—for death was the beginning of life. Thus Joe lying on the bed pondered on these things, and applied them to the case of his own mother and father. Did they truly believe in these things ? He thought of the newly-born child, of the belief that if it died it would have entered heaven straight away. But if it had not been baptised it would have lost heaven, through no fault of its own—it would have gone to some place called Limbo. Joe remembered reading about Limbo in his catechism at school. He often wondered where Limbo lay, but he could never find out. Once he had asked another boy a little older than himself where the place was and that worthy had replied—

" I think Limbo lies about two thousand miles east of the Equator."

He had not laughed. For at that time he had believed. But now he knew that it was a lie. Because he had searched the map of the world and could not find the place. Once he had asked his mother if heaven really existed. That had made her suspicious of him. She told him that no one had the right to put such a question. God knew where heaven was because He reigned there.

He had told the priests ; but they were told not to tell
their flocks. Had they done so, some of the more am-
bitious sheep would doubtless have separated themselves from the lamentable planet on which they suffered.
He knew then that his mother and father were no wiser
than he. And from that time Joe had distrusted priests.
His friend had taught him a little about astronomy, and
that had convinced him that Limbo was non-existent.
How could there be a place called Limbo ? And how
were they to know where all these children passed the
remainder of their lives ? Then he had lent Joe books
and Joe had begun to doubt a number of things in
which he had profoundly believed. A little later Joe
had come across Jane and had learnt all about life and
had seen with his own eyes that the world was the heaven.

It was only when the room door opened and his
mother entered with some tea and bread on a wooden
tray that his irritating memories were lost. He sat up in
bed whilst she placed the pillow at the bottom of his
back. He had a terrible thirst. He drank the tea at a
gulp. Martha went down and brought up the teapot.

" You have a great thirst, Joe," she said smiling.

He watched her standing there in her red petticoat,
and marvelled at her strong arms bare to the shoulder,
and the firm legs. Then he took more tea. He could not
eat the bread. He asked his mother to get him a cigarette
out of his pocket. This she did and when he had lit it,
he said that he was quite comfortable. His mother bent
down to kiss him good-night. He turned his face a little
because he could not suffer her to kiss him on the lips.
Then she left the room. He lay back and once more a
train of thoughts passed across his mind.

They were thoughts that sent a glow throughout his
body. Thoughts that made his blood tingle. Thoughts
that spurred him on to live because in living lay the key
to those thoughts. He imagined himself again in Lime
Street watching the street-walkers. He imagined himself
going up to one of them. He could see her face. It was
small and oval shaped, and she had a dimple in her

cheek, and she smiled at him showing a perfect set of false teeth.

In imagination he accompanied her to her room. He watched her disrobe, and felt a pang of desire suddenly surge up in him, blotting out earth and God—everything.

And he felt her soft arms clinging to his body, felt the thrill of her kiss, and suffered himself to be drawn down to the abyss.

These thoughts served to counteract other things. They dispelled the terrors of hell and blotted out the hard cruel face of the God of the Catholics. And the next morning he would wake weak and miserable, and a feeling of disgust would come over him and in his anger he would fling the woman from him upon the floor of her room. Then he would be sorry for what he had done. He would see her lying on the floor. She, the instrument of his pleasure, was repulsive to him ! And he would smite his breast and say to himself—" You ! you !—you are not a man ! "

He would lift her up from the floor and with tears in his eyes beg her pardon. For was not Jane, the woman he loved, one of this unfortunate band ? Did he not love her with his whole heart and soul ? Had he not promised to stand by her if she gave up the life she was leading ? Had he not vowed to do any mortal thing for her ? And here in imagination he was spitting upon one of her sisters of the streets. When he should have bent down and kissed her feet. Did they not know what it was to suffer ? Despised and dejected—outcasts in a world of pariahs and parasites—were they not entitled to say a word ? Did he not see in them the whole of womanhood exalted and sanctified ? As holy as the blessed Virgin herself. And in the light of his conscience he examined these things, and found their value. Again the amative desires would return to him, making of his whole body a wild and raging furnace. And he asked himself—

" How do the priests live? How can they live ? "

For to him it seemed an utter impossibility that they should shun these things. It was spitting in the face of life. It was condoning selfishness. It was despising womanhood. The saviours of the race. He could see again his mother's breast as she fed her child, see the child clawing eagerly at it, for he knew well that it was lying at the fountain of life and sustenance. And how happy he had seemed as he imbibed the sap from his mother's body ! How great it was to give life and force to the world ! Energy and force, boundless and un-limited, to a world that was dry as dust, people, with white-livered humanitarians, who buried themselves in their corners. People who did not see in the abyss —the abyss of the civilisations they glorified—did not see in this abyss the noble seed which was to regenerate mankind. Could not they see that the winds of the abyss blew always ; that they carried in the lightness of their wings the torch of life ? Could they not see that all human work was reflected in the abyss ! And yet they suffered themselves to be hidden away from it—because their souls were too weak and shallow to withstand the mighty winds which burst with great gusts out of the teeming chaos of life.

And he was one of the abyss. He could feel in his very bones the beating of its great heart. He could feel the strength of its soul in his blood. And he felt in that moment a pride in that he belonged to it. It was the heart from which all life was fed and sustained. It was the soul from which all drew strength. The God of the abyss was the only God in that he was the God of divine truth. Truth is like a great eagle. It soars above. It hangs suspended over men, watchful for their safety, knowing their divine duty. For in that duty lay the life and hope of the world.

What were a few artists or scientists compared with these noble souls who faced life fearlessly ? What were these people who were incapable of contacts with life ? They were but the hollow echoes of the great symphony of life which soared up to the high heavens. The great symphony of love and duty. The souls in the abyss were the souls who carried the torch—were the souls that held aloft the eternal flame as they sped on their way down the night of the world. And Joe thinking on these things was suddenly made happy by knowing that Jane too was of the abyss. Always the abyss was calling aloud—

" Come eat—take thou of my body—drink from me, for in me dost thou see the sap of eternal life. In me thou dost see Truth. Ride on my heart, for I am as strong as a lion. Eat, eat, if ye would live." That was the abyss. And Joe was a part of it. He was one of the veins in its great heart. " Come, brother, let us together seek God." That was the abyss.

CHAPTER VII

LARSON coming down the stairs one morning met Jane going up to her room. He stopped her.

" I haven't seen your friend lately," he said, as he flicked some hairs off his coat.

" My friend—I have no friend, Mr. Larson."

Larson laughed. He barred her path.

" Why, the young chap with the down on his chin, whom I let in the other morning. You know well enough —wasn't he with you the other night ? "

" Oh ! " exclaimed Jane—"why, have you seen him lately ? "

" No ; I was wondering what had become of him— he seemed a nice young chap."

" Perhaps he has become a good boy once more," she said. " You know he could not live with his people at home—they are very good-living Catholics, and he is a bit of a rebel."

" Oh, so that's the trouble ! " exclaimed Larson.

He made room for her to pass and she went up to her room.

It was nearly a week since she had seen him. She felt lonely without his company. She knew now that she had fallen deeply in love with the Very Bad Catholic young man. She thought of visiting him, but she soon put that idea out of her mind. As soon as his parents learned who she was, she would be bundled out into the street without ceremony. And she knew in her heart that she must see him. In spite of the fact that he was some years younger than she, she knew that she loved him, no other man in her life was like him. They were all liars. But this one—he was truth itself. She had yet to learn of the lies that were festering on Joe's soul. Why had she not kept him in her room? Nobody would have known of his being there except perhaps the landlord and Larson, and they wouldn't mind. All they wanted was to be left alone—the sweep to look after his little child— the landlord to collect his rents. He was a very exacting man was the landlord. The police had him on their list. He was known to be harbouring queer types. But they closed their eyes to a good many things, especially the sergeant on the beat. It would have been so easy. A nice young woman could hide all the sins of the world, and nobody would know.

Jane was tidying her room when the landlord came up. He was a long thin man, with a practically hairless face. He had a head which used to wobble from side to side. It used to wobble constantly ; sometimes at a dangerous angle. He knocked at the door and went in in response to Jane's " Come in."

He found her brushing beneath her bed. He smiled. She got to her feet and looked at him.

" I have something nice to tell you," he said, and walked further into the room. He sat down on the chair, the only one which the room contained.

She tidied her hair which was hanging loosely about her shoulders, then turned to her landlord—

" Well, what is it you want to say? I'm busy, I've a guest coming this week."

" Now that is coincidental," he said, " I have also a guest coming this week—in fact it was about him that I wanted to speak to you."

" Well, what about him ? " she asked.

" He is a very nice young man I will say," said the landlord, " I am sure you would like him."

Jane did not understand. She wondered what was going on in the big man's mind

" I suppose you have seen good and bad men in your time, Jane," he said.

" I have seen saints and angels and some devils," she said slowly.

" Well now, I can put you wise to a good bit of business—listen. This young friend of mine—well—he is a young parson, and his people are very respectable, very respectable indeed. I was talking to him the other night. And of course he asked me a lot of questions. Now if I tell you straight out, you won't mind, will you ? "

" Go on," said Jane. She was blushing now.

" Well, he said something like this—' I am hungering for a woman, Sam. As you know, I dare not mention such a thing amongst my people, and I want to get away for a few days for a good-time. I have money, and I wish to spend it in a bit of excitement.' He went on to say that he had some trouble with his people, and would be glad to get away for a day or two. And of course, being a business man I suggested that he should come and stay with you. I hope you take it in the right spirit, Jane—he's a nice young man, you know."

For some minutes she did not speak. She did not know what to make of such a speech. At last she was able to say—

" Well, you needn't have bothered at all, because from this day I'm on the straight. Besides, what about Redmond ? She's more his style, I'm sure."

" Come," said the landlord, " you know as well as I do that that Redmond one wouldn't touch a parson with a barge pole, no matter what the colour of his money."

" All the more reason why I shouldn't take him in— the idea ! I have something else to interest me at the moment."

She went on tidying the room, the while the landlord stared at her.

"Needn't be so smart and clever anyways," he said, "if you're going to come those highty-tighty ways, I can only say as how this house is too hot for you."

He smiled and showed two rows of big brown teeth. He thought he was on safe ground.

"You can't put me out of the house, so there—I pay my rent and that's all about it—suppose I went to the head constable and told him one or two things about his precious policemen, you'd look pretty sick, wouldn't you?"

"Don't come that with me," he roared, "or you can pack your bag pretty smart, see."

He strode out, banging the door behind him. Jane was angry with him. She was angry with everybody. The idea of a parson wanting to come and stay with her because years of respectability had developed in him a passion to be unconventional for once in his life! She stamped her foot on the floor. Probably when he came and was in bed with her he would start his infernal argument on respectability. She had had some of that.

"I'll just put Redmond wise," she said to herself and left the room to search for her. But she found that that lady had gone out shopping. She met Larson coming in for dinner. She burst into tears. She had to tell him everything. She told him that she loved the young man of whom he had spoken that morning. And Larson, knowing and understanding everything, consoled her, and in the end promised her that he would look for Joe. She described him and when she left him, knew that in that whole building she had at least one friend. The old man's death had been a shock to her. She had not seen his body, she had not seen him carried out to be buried by the parish, but she suffered in her room, knowing that he was gone for ever, that he would never return. She had suffered silently. She had told no one, because if one has to suffer—and suffering is the law of life—one has to suffer to oneself. And now that she had told the sweep of the suggestion of the landlord, she knew that he would protect her. She knew that the landlord would bring the parson to the place. No doubt he would come to the place dressed like the last young man whose people were respectable. He would come dressed like a dock-labourer.

Well, he could come. He would get no favours from her. She did not want his filthy money. She had in her mind the occurrence in Lime Street the day that the cathedral was being blessed by a party of bishops. She had watched a bishop walking along the street, and some woman had had the nerve to stop him. He thought she was soliciting and gave her in charge of the police, when really she was only asking a few coppers to get bread for her children. And she had hated every parson ever since. It was Joe she wanted. Joe and no other. She had saved a little money. What was to stop them going away and starting a little business for themselves? Nobody need ever know—although she would tell Larson, because he was such a kind man and understood everything and everybody. Perhaps she would be able to get her clothes out of the place with his help. Perhaps, through him, she would find the young man she loved.

But she must go out. She had not been out for two whole days. And perhaps she might even come across Joe. So after having a little dinner, she washed and dressed herself. The landlord who was standing at the door as she passed out, winked at her, and said—

" I hope you're not vexed with me, Jane ? "

" Don't speak to me," she said—" you dirty, filthy beast."

The loud laughter of the landlord was still ringing in her ears when she reached the top of the dirty, dingy little street. She felt in her bag for her money. She wanted to buy something, something which would please and surprise him. She had noticed that he wore a very poor coat—perhaps it was one of his father's. She had kept it in mind, as she was determined to buy him a new suit out of her savings. She walked on towards the shopping district. The road was full of puddles, and she had to dodge the cars and trams. At last she stopped by a big tailoring establishment and her eyes lighted on a fine blue serge suit which was priced at three guineas. She wanted to go in there and then, and buy it. But she was doubtful as to what was Joe's size. Then she had an idea that he would not be pleased with her, because he didn't believe in women who bought things for men. She stood thinking and staring at the suit in the window. One or two men passing by stared hard at her—perhaps she was just a common prostitute—perhaps she was going to smash the window in. She went into the shop and asked to be allowed to see the suit. The man got it out of the window, and immediately began to praise a different suit, which was five guineas. But Jane wanted the suit from the window or nothing.

" I suppose you will change it if it doesn't fit him——"

" Oh, yes, anything to oblige," the man said as he proceeded to wrap the suit up in a large sheet of brown paper. When she left the shop she forgot that she wanted tea and sugar and some cakes. She decided to return at once and leave the suit in her room, because she could not be bothered carrying it about underneath her arm. It was not until she was halfway home that she noticed that someone was following her. She turned round to find the very person of whom she had been dreaming and wondering—wondering why he had not come to see her. Now he stood before her. She could see that he had been ill. His face was haggard and drawn, and his eyes were weary.

" Why, hello," she exclaimed, a bright smile lighting up her face—" I thought you had forgotten me."

He related to her all that had happened. She looked at him in astonishment.

" He tried to cut your throat ? " she repeated.

" Yes," replied Joe, " and he nearly did it, but I've finished with him—he doesn't speak to me now—nor I to him—it is better for both of us."

He did not tell of his sleepless nights, the struggles

which his body was subject to—he did not tell her of his agony of mind—of what step he was going to take. He could not do that. They walked down the street arm in arm. When they were a few hundred yards from the house where she had her room—she said—

" Let us separate—you follow up and ask for me at the house."

He stopped and watched her walk ahead of him. He wondered why she should do this. Instantly there came to his mind the thought that perhaps already she was harbouring a man—already she was offering herself to some man after the promise she had given him. He was seized with an impulse to turn his back on her and walk home. But he knew he could not do that. If he did he would be alone for ever. No, it was best for him to do as he was told, not to have suspicions of his friends. He knew that she was the only being who awoke in him the urge to live—the urge to do something. He followed slowly, saw her disappear into the house. He waited for a few minutes. Then he walked straight up to the door. When he knocked it was opened by Larson.

He was surprised when the sweep held out his hand, exclaiming—

" Hello ! I was wondering what had become of you," he leaned forward and whispered into his ear—"Jane has been watching and waiting for you."

Joe smiled. It sent a thrill through his whole being when he dwelt on the fact. She watching and waiting for him—expecting him to come and see her. And he had not arrived. Had not seen her for a week. He was glad. His heart was made happy by the thought of it. He half ran up the stairs and nearly knocked down Larson's youngster, who was playing with some tin soldiers. He picked the child up, kissed it, and sat it down again on the floor. Then he went to the room door and knocked. She opened it, smiled at him ; and he entered. When he saw that she had laid a table, and had a big brown paper parcel on the bed, he knew that she had been very busy.

" Shopping day to-day ? " he asked.

" A special shopping day, Joe," she replied.

She took his head in her two hands and drawing it down upon her breast, whispered into his ear—

" I have something nice here for you."

He raised his head and looked into her eyes. They were radiant. Her smile pleased him. It made him forget the unpleasant things which had been rankling in his mind for the past few days.

" I'm so glad you've come," she said.

They sat down together. When he looked at this young woman who was five or six years older than himself he found himself asking questions—

" Did he really love this woman? Did he understand that she loved him with a great passion?" And yet his conscience was against such a thing. For in his soul lay the result of years of blind fidelity to a religion which demanded a goodness and an heroic faith. It was one or the other. He must decide. He must ask himself if either of those things demanded a complete surrender of oneself. For he was not strong enough as yet to decide. To say, " Well, it shall be this—or it shall be that."

Chaos was stirring in his soul. It played havoc with his world. He could not make head nor tail of the fundamental things—the scheme of existence. He was pondering on these things when he felt her face near to his own. He was capable of being loved—he was capable of sacrificing himself for an ideal—he was capable of suffering.

" Joe," she was saying in that soft voice of hers, " would you come away with me if I were to leave here to-morrow?"

He was startled by the question. He could find no answer to it. He heard her ask him for the second time— then he said to her—" Go away, why?"

" I'm sick of this kind of a life," she said, " and this morning Larson the sweep said that if we loved each other it would be best to go away together. And he also said that he would help us to get away safely, without fear of being followed."

As yet he could find no answer to her question. He

had not expected it. And he knew what it demanded from him. A duty. A double duty. But he could not obey both. Was there no other way ? " Why could she not wait a little longer ?" he asked himself. "Besides, I've no prospects—what can I do, and I'm not going to live on a woman."

" Jane," he said, " I could not go with you, even though I love you, even though I know that you would do anything for me—couldn't you wait a little longer ? If I left now it would kill my mother."

An idea had suddenly struck him. Would she turn a Catholic for him ? Ah, but had he not already in her face renounced his religion. Had he not already told her of the havoc which had visited him—had he not already suffered with it. Had he not already seen that it was false, because it was inimical to life itself. Yet he found himself asking her this question. She looked at him as if he had taken leave of his senses.

" No," she said, with an air of finality.

" Not even though I loved you with a great devotion ? "

" No," was all she said.

Then he was sorry that he had asked her. No, it could never be. Truly he was on the rack. For faith had eaten into his soul. He could not shake it off. And now the moment had come when he could have cried aloud— " Free—at last I am free," and he was afraid, mortally afraid. Afraid of what ? Could he answer that question ? Was it the massive face of this God engraved upon his soul which was hindering him ? Was he beaten ? Was he again to endure that suffering ? Was he to be the victim of doubt and fear ; was he to suffer as the others weaker than he, simpler than he ; was he to be as them, grey with fear of hell—hoping for heaven ? Was he not a slave to a thing which he could throw off in his hour of victory ? Could he not have a heart strong enough to kill this serpent which was eating into his life ?

" Joe, I did not know—I did not know," she said, and her hands dropped from his shoulders. He did not look at her. His head was bent, he was staring at the floor.

He could no longer look her in the face. He could no
longer hope. For between them lay a gulf. And neither
would surrender. His was the world of angels and saints
and devils and hell and purgatory and Limbo. Hers was
the world of reality. And he could not accept that. He
could not understand the wonderful stoicism that exalted
her. He could not see that she of all women was the most
worthy of his love. He could not see these things because
the huge idol which he and his had worshipped for
centuries stood in his path. It blocked his way. It seemed
to him, like one of those huge prehistoric beasts. Where
then, how then, could he solve the riddle of his life ? From
where, from whom, could he expect guidance and help ?
God hated him—he knew that, therefore an appeal to
Him was useless. He could not appeal to the devil,
because though he had a vague belief in life everlasting,
he could not bring himself to believe in hell. And yet
had the devil occupied a place in his being, a place such
as this God of his now occupied, he would have asked
his help, his guidance, for after all he was of earth, and
he understood the weaknesses of the humanities.

"Is this the end then ? "

He looked up at her. Tears were coming into his
eyes. What could he say? She was waiting for his
answer. She too was suffering. She had not expected
this. Her breast was heaving tumultuously. What could
he say to her ? Was it then the end ? She, of whom he
had dreamed—she, of whom he had hoped. She was
going away.

"But Jane," he said in a pleading tone, "why are
you going away ? "

"I am going away because I want to live. This is a
dead-house. I thought when you said you loved me, that
you were greater than all men. Only a good and noble
man could sacrifice himself to one like me. I who have
suffered the embraces and curses of other men. You
loved me. And I returned that love. To me you were
everything—you were a god. You filled my heart and
soul. My heart has been heavy ; but what is a heavy

heart to a woman? I thought you were a god; but I see you are only a man. I thought you were equal with Christ; but you are not worth the kiss of Judas. Do you not understand? I thought that you had truth on your lips!"

She burst into tears. Hot scalding tears that ran down her cheeks. She was stunned. She thought he had loved her. She thought he was an idol. The blood mounted to her face. She shivered. Her breasts seemed to be pulling her down, seemed like two pillars of marble—cold, lifeless. They were pulling her down into the abyss. And for her there was no escape.

Joe would have taken her in his arms but she pushed him away. She had finished with him. Her idol was but clay.

Joe was stunned. He had not expected such an outburst. Did he not know that she was human? His soul seemed to revolt; his heart seemed to beat violently within him. A voice was crying in his ear—

"Wretch thou art! Thou hast wrecked thine own soul. Thy heart is but dust. Thou art foul!"

What could he say? Was not the voice of conscience beseeching him to take the right path? Which way? Which way? He knew not. He thought of his mother, of his father, of the priest who had confirmed him; he thought of the priest who had heard his last confession. He thought of God who suffered him to exist upon the face of the world.

His mother and father had lived; he had yet to live; she too had yet to live. He must answer.

He found himself standing over her inert form and saying in a soft gentle voice—

"Forgive me. I was weak, I am sorry. You know that I love you."

"Go away—go away," she said, without raising her head to look at him.

"I am damned!" he screamed aloud—"damned for ever! Jesus! O Jesus!"

A silence fell. A strange silence which seemed to fill

the whole room. A terrible silence. An awe. And in
the offing lay chaos and destruction. In the offing were
the abyss and desolation. His brain—how it had stood it
he could not understand. Weighed down by woe, which
sleepeth not, weighed down by poverty, by fear, and by
faith. He recalled the words of God ; he remembered
hearing the priest quoting those words—thus—" O ye of
little faith."

" A lie ! A lie ! " he screamed, " a dirty, damned and
bloody lie ! "

He was beside himself with grief. This then was the
end. Hope had vanished. He saw now quite clearly ;
he peered far down into the well of life. And saw—
nothing. He was praying in his heart. He was mumbling
prayers which he had uttered in childhood. He was
saying "O God, if thou art—if thou art—help and guide me."

But only the echo of his own voice answered him. He
wrung his hands.

" Jane, Jane," he was saying, as he knelt down by the
side of the bed—" Jane."

" Go," she said, and raised her tear-stained face to his
—" go, and come no more."

Her words bit like iron into his soul. He turned, and
picking up his cap left the room. As he descended into
the kitchen which Larson occupied, he came face to face
with him. Larson, smiling, said—

" Well, Joe, I am glad to see you've come again. That
poor young woman up above was crying her heart out,
after you left the other morning. She thought you were
never going to come back. I hope that you will both be
happy." He held out his hand, but Joe rudely walked
past him and into the street. Larson stared after him. He
followed to the door and watched the youthful figure
walking up the street. He thought he saw the figure
stagger. He was going to run after him and bring him
back but something held him. Something made him
walk up the stairs and knock at the young woman's door.
Something made him enter. He found Jane lying stretched
on the floor.

CHAPTER VIII

THE tall young man who was hurrying down the road in the direction of the city, suddenly stopped, looked round and smiled.

"Why, hello ! " he said, " I thought you were dead or gone abroad."

Joe smiled, and held out his hand, which the other shook warmly.

It was the friend who had lent Joe the books, and this friend was a Socialist.

" I have some books of yours," said Joe, " I ought to have returned them long ago—although I might say that ' Ulysses ' is burnt, and no more."

" Good Lord, man, how did you manage that ? I'll never be able to get another copy for love nor money. Who burnt it ? "

" You can guess, can't you ? " replied Joe, as they walked on.

They changed the topic of conversation. Hugh said he was going to the club. Did he know they had a club, a select one of their own ? They were only six members. Would Joe like to join and make it seven ?

" The Seven Deadly Sins," laughed Joe, " all right I'll come along, where is this club ? "

" A friend of mine who is a bit of a sculptor has par- titioned off one of his rooms, and we generally have talks there—he has a pretty decent library and there is a piano."

" Do you play ? " Joe asked.

" I never play, my dear man," said Hugh—" because there are cleverer people in this world than myself."

" What do you do then ? " Joe continued.

" I have three meals a day and eight hours' sleep, and a rascally boss takes away from me the rest of my time."

They were nearing the house now.

" What are the other chaps ? " asked Joe, who was very interested.

He had first met Hugh in the free library when that gentleman had been pouring over a volume of the " Tales " of Ariosto. And they had become friends. Hugh had opened up another world for Joe. And another hell. The hell of conscience.

When they reached the house Hugh ran up the steps and rang the bell. A young man came to the door. Within, Joe could hear a piano.

" Come in," said the young man, opening wide the door.

" This," said Hugh pointing to Joe, " this is a young friend of mine who at present is living on the fat of the land, has nothing to do but read and is a very good conversationalist."

" Pleased to see you," said the young man whose name was Raynor, and who, as Hugh afterwards told him, worked on the cotton exchange as a clerk.

They were taken through the dimly lighted hall into a room where the piano was being played. Hugh introduced Joe to the three young men who were sitting by a fire listening to the man at the piano go through the finale of Beethoven's B flat Sonata.

" I'll join you in a minute," said Raynor, " make yourselves comfortable."

He disappeared, leaving the two men to pass the time as best they might. Hugh drew chairs to the fire. Joe felt somewhat out of place among these young men, whose clothes stamped them as well-to-do. There was a large red volume lying on the mantelshelf over Joe's head. Joe reached for it. He settled back in his chair and glanced casually through its pages. Raynor, who had come in quietly, smiled and asked him what he thought of Tolstoi. The book was " Anna Karenina."

Joe replied that his opinion was of no interest or value to anybody. Raynor laughed and thumped him in the back.

" Come along, let's hear what you have to say about the Russian microbe."

" I do not like the book," said Joe definitely.

The two young men who were leaning over the fire immediately sat up. This was what they had never heard before. A young man did not like Tolstoi ! Well ! well !

" I do not like his work," Joe was saying, as he toyed with the pages of the book—" because he condemns evil, which I defend ; he extols pity, which is superfluous."

" What ? " exclaimed Raynor.

" I merely said," Joe went on, " that evil is a necessity, and pity is superfluous. Our civilisation could not exist five minutes after the elimination of evil ! "

" You surprise me," said a young man with very red hair—" personally I always thought that the book itself was his greatest work."

" Probably it is his greatest work," replied Joe. " I merely said that I had certain opinions about it."

They all laughed. Then Hugh said—

" Now, Joe, I'm going to ask you a question " ; he turned to the others and said : " this young man as an ex-Roman Catholic can perhaps best answer the question" —he looked across at Joe and continued—

" Joe—do you believe in the infallibility of the Pope ? "

" No," said Joe. " I do not believe in the infallibility of anybody. Even Christ was not infallible."

Hugh told them about Joe's running after a young woman down in the back quarter of the town.

" Inspired by the famous Raskolnikov ? " said Raynor.

" I have not heard of him," said Joe, " who is he ? "

" Oh, he was a bit of a prig, then he suddenly changed and fell in love with a woman off the streets. He kissed her feet—he was sorry for her."

" That does not say that I am a follower of him—he had pity for this woman, perhaps he thought it was love, they are so akin," replied Joe.

" Have you no pity in you then ? " asked Raynor.

" That depends," said Joe ; " listen—would you take pity on your mother if she was very ill—or on your father when you saw that he was getting too old to work and he had a hump on his back ? "

Raynor did not reply for some time—then he said—

"Of course I would—of course I would."

"Well I would not," said Joe—"because pity there is superfluous. I do not pity this woman of whom you speak—I love her—if I pitied her I could not love her, do you understand?

"I hate pity and praise evil, because evil is the most potent force in our lives. When you come across a man who says to you—'Isn't this prostitution question exciting everybody at present; I pity the unfortunate victims of our civilisation'—take no notice of him, for you know he is a liar. It is much easier to lie than to tell the truth. All evil is necessary. Consider: it stimulates the best art, brings forth the highest genius. It is a great power, I tell you—why will not people realise it?"

He looked across at the others. They were all smiling. He wondered what they were smiling at. Was it at him, or was it at his ideas? Raynor went across to the piano. Joe listened to the playing for a long time, then asked—

"What is it about?"

They told him with one voice that it was a Nocturne by a man named Chopin.

"Did they give him a pension when he got old?" he asked.

They told him that Chopin had died in Majorca, after living with a woman who wrote novels under the name of a man.

"Of course, of course," said Joe. "I thought there was a woman in it, it was so pretty—have you ever played any of Beethoven's sonatas?"

Raynor turned round again to the keyboard and played the "Sonata Pathétique" for him. When he had finished Joe said—

"There is no woman in that."

"You're a terror on the women," remarked Hugh, "why the devil don't you go and get married?"

"That question is as ridiculous as the nocturne you recently played," replied Joe.

"Have you ever seen a woman, Joe?" Raynor asked as he got up from the piano.

"Of course ; seen hundreds of them."

"I do not mean in that casual way," continued Raynor. They all laughed.

"I would like to know what some of your ambitions are, anyhow ? " said Joe.

"My greatest ambition," said Raynor, "is to violate a nice young lady."

"That's not much," said Joe, "that's everybody's hope, old and young, though the older the better."

"Life is a funny thing," remarked Raynor later—"a deuced funny thing."

"Why funny ? " asked Joe.

"Well the apes and rascals always get the best of things."

"Apes and rascals," said Joe, "who may they be ? "

"Have you ever read 'The Decameron'? " said Raynor.

"No, I haven't as yet, but if it's interesting I might try and get it."

"When you've read that you'll understand what I mean," concluded Raynor.

"Oh, by the way," said Hugh, crossing to Raynor, "you must show my friend the figure of Mary Magdalene which Lars has done."

They all rose and went into an inner room. It was bare, save for an easel, and in the middle of the floor was a figure heavily draped with a white sheet. Hugh pulled off the sheet, saying—

"This is an example of the new force permeating modern sculpture."

Joe went closer and examined carefully the huge figure. A smile flitted across his face.

"Well," said Hugh, taking hold of him by the arm— "what do you think of it ? "

"If that's a saint, I wonder what an archangel's really like."

"The Italian painters and sculptors never thought out a figure like that."

" Her backside is too prominent," said Joe ; " that's all there is the matter."

" My dear young man," said Raynor, " that is exactly the point—but with the advance of civilisation did you not notice that the human anatomy is altering accordingly ? "

" Perhaps it is," said Joe, and turned away from the figure.

The atmosphere weighed upon him. He wanted to go out, to get away, back to his room—he wanted to be alone. He heard a clock outside strike and looked at his watch. He turned to Hugh.

" I'll be going—I'm pleased to meet your friends, explain to them, won't you, that I am a stranger to these things."

He left the house and set off homewards.

As he was crossing the tram-lines, he saw a young woman coming towards him. It was dark, he could not see her face, nor she his.

She said to him—" Coming with me ? "

" I haven't a cent," replied Joe.

He knew he had heard that voice somewhere before. He pulled the woman's fur down from her neck, and staggered back.

" Jane."

" Joe."

They stood looking into each other's eyes, the while an infuriated tram-driver was ringing his bell and cursing them to all eternity.

" We'd better get on to the footpath," said Joe.

They walked on to the side-walk.

" Well," he said.

" I didn't know it was you," she replied, " anyway less said soonest mended."

She was turning away when he caught her arm.

" But you said you had no money," she protested, and tried to get away from him. He was astounded. So this was the woman then who said she would go straight.

" I know I said I had no money."

"Well, then that's enough," she said. "Good-night."

He watched her walk away. He dug his finger-nails into the palms of his hands. He wanted to run after her, to strip her naked before the people and to tell them what she was. Then his rage left him, for he knew that he had had his chance. But he must see her. He could not let her go. He must explain. He followed behind her, dodging into a corner of a shop door whenever she stopped to question a man.

She turned out of the street, Joe still following her. Then she stopped before a house with a long flight of steps. Joe stopped too. He saw her ring the bell, and disappear inside. He stood like one in a trance. All kinds of thoughts were flashing through his mind. Had she left her room? Was she living here now? Had she become the mistress of some man? He turned on his heel.

He hurried home. When he got in, his mother was waiting for him.

"Where were you, Joe?" she asked.

"For a long walk."

He sat down and asked what was for supper. His mother frowned.

"That's a nice question to ask," she said, "and you knowing that your father hasn't done a stroke of work this two weeks, and you idle nearly three months—a nice question indeed—what d'you think there is—bread and dripping, and plenty of salt out there in the back if you want it. There's tea on the hob there, the milk is in the cupboard, but there's no sugar—your father will have to do without for his breakfast."

"Oh, well, it doesn't matter," remarked Joe. "Has he gone to bed?"

"Of course he's gone to bed—where you should have been long ago, instead of landing in here at half-past eleven at night, and asking your poor old mother what's for supper. I don't really know how I'm able to put down stuff at all for you—I'm up to my eyes in debt. I'll have to sell that chest of drawers to-morrow."

"Well, well, go to bed then, and let's have my bit of

supper in peace. For the love of Christ, go ! There is always some row or other—as if I haven't listened to enough sermons already."

"You have listened to none—you could do with a sermon now and again—from the priest, young man. I will let your father know how you speak to me, and he'll flatten you with his fist—you dirty mean bastard."

It was the first time she had ever used such a word towards her son. But her temper had got the better of her.

"Thanks," said Joe ; "it's the bastard who gets it in the neck all the time."

She left the kitchen, without saying good-night. "As soon as she goes upstairs," thought Joe, "she will tell him "—meaning his father—" and he will come down and start an infernal row just because I'm cute enough to look after my own business. Well let it come, if there's to be a row, there'll be one, and that's all about it."

He was glad that she had called him that. That was what he wanted. The sooner a rift between them the better. His father came downstairs.

"Haven't I told you before about giving cheek to your mother ? " he asked.

"She called me a bastard," replied Joe.

"Well, I've already told you, if you are going to try to ride the high horse you can get out of here, I'm not having any rebels here, don't forget that."

"Rebels ? Who's talking about rebels ? " said Joe. "Why don't you leave me alone—you're trying to get me to be a good Catholic, yet you won't let me alone for a single moment, and you've got my mother the same way. Perhaps it would be better if I did get out of your sight."

He rose as if to leave the house, when his father stopped him, saying—

"All right, no airs, sit down, and don't be so clever next time ; do you know that with one thing and another you've got me as bad as yourself—what you want to do is to go to the mission to-morrow night—it's the last night ; a good sermon wouldn't do you any harm.

K

" Joe, I ask you will you try and go, it'll alter your views, and the grace of God will make you a better man, do for my sake, although more for your mother's sake."

" Leave me in peace, that's all I ask. I expect I'll go, d'you think I never go to Mass ? "

" I hope you do, Joe," said his father. " I hope you do, by the grace of God."

" Well, why d'you follow me every time I go out ? D'you think I really miss it ? "

" See, it's nearly midnight, go up to bed and try and lead a better life, not for my sake, mind you, but for your mother's—if she thought you hadn't made your Easter Duty she would drop dead. She's a good-living mother, although half the time she hasn't a penny to bless herself with—think of that—many a time when you sit down to your dinner, do you ever ask yourself if your mother has had any ? No, you think only of your own belly—self, self, self, all the time. I'll agree I lose my temper sometimes, but wouldn't it make any man lose his temper ? Here's your mother doesn't know where to turn to pay the landlord ; doesn't know how she's going to put the next meal on the table—and you turn round and treat her like a dog. Just think a little more of others and not so much of yourself, and you'll get on a lot better than you do."

Joe sat with his head downcast. He could not look his father in the face. He was on the verge of tears.

He'd have to decide to-morrow. That he was finished with religion, or that he was going to lead a good Catholic life once more. It had to be one of the two. But he was going to find out a few things first. He was not going to surrender without a struggle. He must lie no more. He must speak the truth.

When he got up the next morning his mother was smiling. He wondered why.

" Your father says that you promised last night that you would go to the mission. Joe, I am glad indeed to learn that you are going to be a good Catholic once more

—you know you were the one who had the most faith when you were a child. D'you remember the day you made your first communion, and you wanted to be a priest ? "

She hurried to get him his breakfast, still smiling, but she did not know of the chaos stirring in her son's soul. She did not know the thoughts that were stored in his mind. He sat down and tried to avoid looking at her.

" That is a fine man, that Brother John," she was saying to him as he stirred his tea, " a truly fine man—now he could help you, Joe, why don't you go to confession to him to-morrow night, after the sermon and benediction ; he'd help you, my son, and you could get those rosary beads blessed. Joe, do try and lead a good life, for the sake of your own soul. It does not matter if we starve, son, so long as we remain faithful to our beautiful religion."

He could not speak. What answer could he give to such a question ?

" I didn't promise anything," said Joe suddenly, looking across at his mother to see how she would take it.

He noticed the change in her at once, and he added quickly—" I'll see, yes, I'll see—I'm not such a bad one, you know, mother."

" You have some funny ideas, my son," was all she said. She left the kitchen and Joe could hear her washing up the dishes.

" I'm going to try and go to sea," Joe shouted.

She came to the kitchen door holding a dish-cloth in her hand.

" That's the best thing, Joe ; go away to sea ; get out of this terrible atmosphere which is making you lose your soul. Get away and I'll be glad, for believe me, child, that young woman who you were carrying on with is no good to you."

" Why do you keep bringing in that woman ? Can't you leave her out of it for once ? It has nothing to do with what we were talking about—nothing at all."

" But her influence, son," she said, speaking in slow measured tones, and banging her fist on the table to accompany her words—" her influence is that of the devil himself."

Joe went up to his room then. He sat down and wrote a letter to his friend Hugh.

" DEAR HUGH,

" I must write and tell you that I am going to-night to have a talk with one of the priests. If he wins, I am going to turn over a new leaf, but if he cannot answer my question, I am finished for ever with my mother. It is terrible to be living in an atmosphere of doubt. Every time I come in something fresh has happened. The walls are plastered with holy pictures, and some of the pictures you have given me have been torn out of their frames to make way for St. Theresa, St. Anthony, St. Margaret, St. Joseph, Our Lord at the Last Supper, and I can count I don't know how many in my own room, and as fast as I take them down they are put up again. I think they are both going mad. They have been at me again about going to confession and holy communion. What can I do ? I don't believe in these things and if they knew the truth they would drop dead. Anyway I am going to see the priest, then I'm going along to find Jane. I'll let you know how I get on. *Semper fidelis*.

JOE."

He put the letter in an envelope, sealed and addressed it, then went down in to the kitchen. He asked his mother for a few coppers to go down on the car to the landing-stage, but she said she had none.

" Oh, well it doesn't matter," he said, and went off with the letter in his pocket.

" I'll have to send it without a stamp," he said to himself.

He walked off quickly in the direction of the priest's house which lay just behind the church. After he had been there he intended to look for Jane. He was without a friend to help or advise him. Hugh was too busy to

give him any advice, and besides he wanted the girl's
advice. They were dependent on each other for their
happiness.

When he reached the priest's house he stood outside
for a few minutes making up his mind finally as to what
questions he should put to him. He kept scratching his
head and a young servant cleaning the windows of the
bedrooms above was sitting on the window-sill watching
him and giggling to herself. He looked up and saw her,
but did not smile when she smiled at him. He went up
the steps and rang the bell.

"I wish to see a priest—anyone will do," he said, and
entered the house.

*   *   *   *   *   *   *

The room was a pleasant little room. It had red paper
on the walls. There was a picture on the wall of a man
who had white whiskers. He had a merry twinkle in his
eye. The carpet on the floor was green. Red and green.
Lovely contrast. A nice little room, but no bed in it. The
priest was a fat man. He had a head of black hair, and
little eyes that peered at you from beneath bushy eye-
brows. They were like two pinheads of fire. He walked
up and down the room. The window was open. The
floor creaked beneath his weight.

"H'm! h'm!" he muttered as he walked up and
down. "Do I believe in God? Wait!"

Joe sat silent. He did not look up into the face of the
fat man.

"Do I believe in God?—ha, ha! just wait a minute,"
said the priest.

Joe was fidgeting on the chair. The priest was watching him playing with his cap, swinging it from one hand
to another.

"You're the son of Michael Rourke, and your mother
is named Martha, yes?" He kept on walking up and
down, his cassock swinging from one side to the other.
His hands were stuck in his trousers pockets. He stood
by the window and looked out at the sun which was

hanging above him, throwing its golden rays down upon the cross which was fixed at the top of the church belfry. A lot of people were walking up and down in the roadway. Trams were rushing along at a terrible speed. A man was shouting out the price of potatoes. The priest turned from the window and looked at Joe.

Joe watched the priest out of the corner of his eye. The priest stopped walking up and down the floor because he was fat, and he got tired quickly, and he used to sweat like a horse.

He looked at the picture hanging on the wall over Joe's head.

" Do I believe in God—do I believe in God—do I believe in God ? " He kept saying to himself.

" Yes," said Joe, rising to his feet, " do you believe in God ? "

" My dear young man, do you realise what you are asking ? " said the priest with a slight frown on his face.

" Yes," answered Joe, " I asked you a question—can you answer it ? "

The priest's face was mantled with blood. He walked over to the young man and squeezed his arm, so tightly that Joe winced.

" Why do you ask that ? " said the priest.

" Well, life is such a funny thing—a man is born, why ? He gets pulled this way and that, why ? He dies, why ? Same thing. Suppose I believed in God, and I died to-morrow, what would happen ? " he asked.

" When a man dies his soul appears for judgment before his Maker."

" That's the point I want to know—how can my soul appear before my Maker ? "

The priest looked hard at him, squared himself up, and said—

" How old are you, and where were you reared ? Were you always a Catholic ? "

" Yes," replied Joe—" but you have not answered my question, father," he added. " Listen, do you know the man who owns our house and all the other houses at the back of the river ? "

" Yes," said the priest.

" He is a rich man—he has his name on a brass plate in one of the benches near the middle aisle in the church —he gives a lot of money to the societies."

" Well," asked the priest, " what next ? "

" Is he a good man ? " asked Joe.

" A good-living Catholic," replied the priest.

" But he does not believe in God," asserted Joe, standing up.

" Why not ? " asked the priest.

" I know he doesn't, that's all," said Joe, " you come and have a look at our house."

" I believe in God," said the priest, " because in the first place nature herself is the first proof that God exists—secondly I believe in God because God's only Son has sacrificed Himself in order that we may attain salvation."

" Do you believe in the Holy Eucharist ? " asked the priest of Joe.

" No," replied Joe—" nor in heaven or hell !—What do you say to that ? "

" I am convinced that you are a fool, and that your questions might just as well be put to the local comedian —he is best fitted to answer them."

" My mother is afraid to die," said Joe—" why is that ? My father is fearful of hell—why is that ? "

" If your mother is afraid to die," said the priest, " it is because she has not learned to love God ; if your father is fearful of hell it is because his conscience is the devil's conscience."

" But my mother goes to communion three times a week ; she is in the third order of St. Francis—how can she not love God ? " asked Joe.

" She is afraid of death—she knows not God, even though she go to communion three times a week."

" Would you tell her that to her face ? " asked Joe, who coloured slightly.

He was sorry that he had brought his mother and father into it. But he had to because they were the cause of his unhappiness, his doubt.

A bell rang out in the corridor. The priest went to the door, opened it and looked out. Then he closed it again.

" Well ? " asked Joe, impatient for an answer.

The door was opened again, and the servant standing on the threshold said—

" Dinner, father."

" All right," he replied. The door closed again. The two were now looking each other in the eye. There was a bit of a smile playing about the priest's lips. He was looking at Joe as if to say—" You think you are a mighty clever chap, but wait—just you wait, young fellow."

" Why is God cruel to sinners—what is a sinner anyway ? " asked Joe.

" God is not cruel, my son," said the priest, " it is only those on earth and in hell who are cruel."

" But why if I died before I was baptised, would I be sent to Limbo—where is Limbo ? I want to know very much, because I had a brother who died without being baptised."

" The guilt of original sin is on every man's soul," said the priest, " therefore he has to be baptised in order to appear clean before the eyes of God."

" But it is not a man's fault if he is born—it is an accident. How can any man be responsible for his existence unless he knew he was going to exist ? "

" God alone can answer that—that is proof of our great faith—in that we are content to wait until the day of judgment, hoping always that God will clear up the mystery of our existence."

" But it is not a mystery," replied Joe—" because we know how man is born and therefore——"

" Therefore what ? "

" Man's existence is no mystery," continued Joe, " it is only God's existence which is the mystery. We know we exist, but not that God exists—that is why I asked you did you believe in God—it is a question which is on every man's lips."

" Not on Catholics'! " said the priest, seeming anxious to be rid of his visitor.

" Why not on Catholics' as well as others ? " asked Joe.

" Catholics have faith, a wonderful faith, a faith that is as strong as the rock it was first founded on—a Catholic asks not questions—and expects to answer none that comes within that circle."

" But I am a Catholic," continued Joe ; " if I knew that God *was*, I would be happy, but I know nothing— but that I am alive, and that life is a very hard thing to get through, and that it is unfortunate to be poor, because only the poor work."

" Well, well," said the priest, " you are a funny young man—one of these days your question will be answered. I believe in God because I am a Catholic, not because I am a priest—because I am a Catholic—understand that. I do not doubt. I never doubt."

" Then you won't help me ? " said Joe rising to his feet and walking towards the door.

" Have faith, the spirit of God is in you, my child— heed not—one day God will manifest himself within you. That is all.   Christ be with you."

The priest walked out of the room. He left Joe wonder- ing why he had come. Had he made a fool of himself? Would the priest even now be laughing at him—would he be telling his friends at the dinner table about the young man who wanted to know if he, the priest, believed in God ? Next Sunday he would speak in the pulpit in the course of his sermon about a certain young man who doubted the existence of God, though his parents were Catholics. Ah !—but wait—— He had fallen into the trap. He said his mother had not the grace of God in her. That was a lie. Could not a person have the grace of God, and yet be afraid to die ? Oh yes, he had him there. He would tell his mother that. See what she would have to say about it. And his father too—he was a good

Catholic, but he had not the grace of God because he too was afraid to die. That was strange. He was glad he had caught the priest. Perhaps he would speak about that also on the Sunday. He hoped he would. He left the house and walked in the direction of the city. For now he was satisfied that the priest believed no more than he did. Now he would go and see Jane. She would be waiting for him perhaps—perhaps. Yes, and perhaps she had gone away. What if she had ? He would be left alone for good. " No, no, she will not go, I know that," said Joe to himself as he walked on into the town. At the bottom of Lime Street there was a car-jam. He managed to get through the crowd and at length came to the house where he had last seen Jane. He walked up to the door and pulled hard at the bell. An old woman came to the door. She asked him what he wanted. He asked if Jane were living there. When the woman heard him mention the name, she looked hard at him, as if to say—" I hope you have money too, like the old man."

" Wait a minute," said the old woman, and disappeared inside the house. She was back in a few minutes. She asked him to come right in. She showed him into a large room, which was beautifully furnished. Joe stared with evident astonishment as he beheld the beautiful things. He thought—" This is a rich man's place, or I'll be damned, but what is Jane doing here anyway ? "

Jane suddenly walked into the room. He looked at her, but did not smile.

" Sit down," she said, motioning him to a big cushioned arm-chair. He sat down and waited patiently for her to say something. But she was silent too. He was wondering now if he had any right to come and see her.

" Jane," he said, " I've come to tell you that I am sorry that I made a fool of myself the other day—sorry from the bottom of my heart."

" It is too late now," she replied and sat down opposite him.

" Too late," gasped Joe, " what do you mean—what's happened ? "

" Oh now, don't come that sort of thing; he's an old man of course, but he's got plenty of money, and that's what I'm after—I've finished with romance and that kind of thing, money is what I am out for, and if ever you can put me on to a good thing—well, I'll be glad. Of course all old men are the same, they get a liking for filth and young women when they pass fifty, but they are soft-hearted when it comes to tapping their pockets."

" Jane," he exclaimed—" Jane ! "

He was staggered. Her cruelty knew no bounds. He felt like going across and stangling her. Was this the same woman whom he had loved and who had loved him—was this the same young woman who had promised to live a good and clean life for his sake ?

He could not speak. He could not look her in the face. He was trembling all over. He got up and walked slowly past her. His face was white. Then he turned and gave her one look and turned the handle of the door.

But suddenly she had to run to him, put her back to the door, and confronted him. She pressed closer to him. He could feel the rise and fall of her breast against his body. She was looking into his eyes. Like a cat she suddenly clung to him and burst into tears. He could not understand. He tried to fling her off. Her mouth was seeking his own. But he was disgusted. He wanted to spit in her face—to strangle this thing which was clinging leech-like to his body. But suddenly he was powerless. The old desire was stirring in his blood. He could not get away from her. But he managed to fling her off. She lay sprawling at his feet, holding on to one of his legs. He looked down at her tear-stained face.

He could see the blue nipple of a breast through the opening of her dress. If he stayed another moment he was lost. Lost to what ? He must answer that question for himself. Ah yes, he knew. He would be left alone for ever, and he would be in the hands of this cruel Catholic God, this God whose breasts were like stone, and who suffered people to burn everlastingly. " No, no, I will not." He lifted her up in his arms.

" Tell me the truth," he said, and held her fast.

" You know the truth, my darling, my strong one, you know already."

" But what are you doing here ? " he asked.

Then she told him that she left her rooms because she had had a row with the landlord, and she had shifted into better rooms down near the town. And one night as she was walking along Lime Street an old man had stopped her and asked her some questions. And she had gone home with him, but it was all right, nothing had happened. " He is about sixty-five," she said, " and has lots of money, he wanted to put a thousand pounds into the bank in my name. He's in London now on some business or other, and he's coming back to-night."

Joe started up when he heard that. He was coming back to-night.

" Are you going to remain here then ? " asked Joe. He made a move as if he were going, but she prevented him.

" No, not if you want me," she said.

He did not know what to do. He must make up his mind quickly,

" You must get another room somewhere before the night comes," he said, " and to-morrow I will come and stay with you altogether."

She held him closer and kissed him.

" I knew, Joe, I knew," said she again and again.

" Well, I'll have to go home first though," he was saying, as he slipped from her embrace, " then I'll get a few of my things together and come back to-morrow without fail. You have made me very happy. I have lots of plans for the future."

She saw him to the front door. She watched his big form as it shot across the road and boarded a tramcar. Then she went into the house again. But she started to pack all her things immediately.

She would return to her old rooms, the landlord would be sorry for what he had said to her, and she would be glad to get back amongst friends. And then there was Tim Larson's child. She loved him with a passionate devotion. And again Tim would be glad to see her and when he saw Joe he would be delighted. He was going to give Joe a job going round with him sweeping the chimneys. She hastily gathered all her clothes together. She was wondering what the old man would have to say when he returned and found she had gone. But still there were plenty of young girls for old men like him. He had the money, he could choose when and where he wished. But no old man should now wear his old soul out with her. She was happy. The one person whom she loved had come back to her. Her eyes were bright as she wrote out a message to the old man, and left it on the dressing table in her room. Then she went out into the street and called a taxi. Soon she was whirling along in the direction of her old rooms. And when she arrived the first person she saw standing at the door was Larson.

"Hello," he said, "so you've come back."

"Who's come back?" said the landlord, poking his head out of the door. "Oh, it's you, is it?" he exclaimed, "well now, your room is still empty and the young parson has gone back to his people—so you can got right up and settle down again ; of course," he added, "the old terms for new tenants—one week's rent in advance."

She took out some money from her bag and paid him. Then Larson carried her box up to the room. When he was leaving the room she stopped him.

"Where is little Bobby?" she asked.

"Oh, he's as right as rain, I'll send him up to you," he said.

"Have you never come across your friend, Joe?" he asked her.

"Yes, I only found him to-day by a lucky chance, he is coming to-morrow."

"It will be all right," said Larson, "so long as his people don't follow him about, I believe they're terrors."

She laughed. "Send Bobby up then," she said, as she closed the door behind him. She commenced to unpack her things. Then she arranged the furniture, it had all

been altered by the landlord. Soon she would have it
as cosy as of old.

She could now blot out for ever all that terrible past.
Life for her would begin anew. Together they would
face the hard road, loving each other with a great and
lasting love. And Joe would start work and they would
go away and be happy. And no one should come to mar
their happiness. They would go far out of the city, away
where only strangers dwelt. And the fetters of fear and
doubt would fall away for ever from Joe's soul. Everything would blossom anew.

Bobby came running into the room. She picked him
up in her arms. He talked to her of all the things he had
seen since she went away—he told her all the news about
the young man who came to stay in the house, and had
been living in her room.

" And he wore his collar back to front," cried Bobby.

She hugged him close. The child had always found a
corner in her heart. She was glad to see him again.
Many a time she had sat with him on her knee in the yard
on the old wooden bench, listening to the wonderful
tales of the old man who was no more. She brought his
figure into her mind, and she could see him now, wiping
his eyes—those eyes which seemed to be ever running
with tears. For he had seen much and known much and
heard much. And his words were full of wisdom for the
young woman whom life had singled out for sorrow.
But after sorrow, joy. And there was joy in her heart as
she looked forward to the future.

There was joy in every human being—joy for all, but
one had to suffer first in order to have joy. She had
suffered too. But the bright days were not far off. They
were in the offing, waiting for her, holding happiness in
store for them both. She sat down and crushed the child
to her heart. And she thought many things, and the
things vanished and were no more. Her eyes were wet.
Just then Larson came into the room. He smiled. He
was going to take the child down now for a wash, and
he had to go to bed too, for it was late for a youngster to

be up. After they had gone she went to open the window, and stood looking out upon the same scene. And she thought of the wonderful devotion of the sweep, who had to live alone, and keep his child. And he was like a mother, everything was for Bobby. He watched over him as jealously as a cat over her kittens. She could hear him screaming now, and knew that Larson was washing him in the old wash-tub. She wanted to go down and do it instead of the sweep. She heard Fresh Redmond's voice. She was singing. She had evidently had a good time. And below standing at the door was the long landlord, with his pipe in his mouth. And she could hear him greeting the passers-by. He knew such a lot of people. She once thought that he must know every person in the town. Certainly he knew all the policemen. The inspectors too. And he knew a lot of tram drivers, and money-lenders and pugilists and racing men, all kinds of people like that. He used to sit by his fire reading out all the winners of the races. And in the next room Fresh Redmond would be trying to get a wink of sleep. And she would shout to him—

"Why the devil don't you read to yourself—if you want to read, don't start off as if you were going to give a sermon." There had been great scenes when the young parson arrived. Fresh Redmond wanted to have him all to herself as soon as she heard that he had money. But the landlord went out and brought in a nice young woman from Pitt Street; she gave him all he wanted very cheap. But his bank roll had diminished, though he had gone away happy in the thought that he had lived. Of course it was always so easy to batten on the tenderloin. The ladies who married feeble old men used to come into the abyss too, and they would pinch a nice strong husband, leaving some poor woman to sorrow and grief. It was so easy. Money was the handle which turned the organ and made the monkey dance. And this young parson had made the monkey dance. He would go back wearing that wonderful look and having about him that wonderful demeanour which characterises only parsons, and respectable ones at that.

Larson came up to her room, bringing the child with him. She was having something to eat when he entered, and she immediately asked him to join her in her little picnic.

She handed the child a cake, then, turning, said to Larson—

" I wish I had a child like that."

Larson looked at her and smiled.

" You may have some day," he said, " there's a good time for everyone in life."

" But not for me, that is impossible—I could never have a child," she replied.

He understood and was sorry for her. But he told her that she would be happy, and that being happy was every-thing. She listened to him talking and allowed her tea to become cold. She was going to go down into the kitchen to get some more hot water, when Larson picked up the jug and went off himself. She was looking at the child sitting on the chair, and a sigh escaped her lips.

" If only his people would agree, but they are such terrible people," she was saying to herself, when Larson came back with the hot water.

She made him have a cup of tea with her.

" Did you ever find out," she asked, " where our old friend was buried ? "

" Yes," he said, " the parish buried him in St. Cuth-bert's Churchyard. I was thinking of going there some Sunday and taking a few flowers with me, he thought a lot of the child here, he was his best friend."

" Yes, I loved the old man very much, and it was very hard for him to die like that—did he have no relations at all ? " she asked.

" They say he had one or two brothers living in America, but there was no means of communicating with them. The poor chap, he was buried without a friend to follow him to the grave."

" He seemed to have been a well-educated man," said Jane.

"Yes, he was a clever man, though he came down in the world through no fault of his own. I think he lost his business or something like that. A bank failed and he lost his money, I forget which, I remember him speaking about it to me a long time ago."

"All the children in the street knew him and loved him," she went on, "he used to look upon me as a daughter."

"He was a very good-living man—he would not harm a fly—it is a tragedy to be old," said Larson.

"I hope I never live to be as old as him anyway, not if I have to pass my life here—one might as well be dead."

"Well, life is hard for some and easy for others. I don't know how it comes about but some people get all the happiness, whilst others get nothing. This is a bad place to live in if one is old and feeble, and has no money."

"There is always the workhouse left for the poor—it's a Godsend too at times, especially for those who have no friends."

"Yes," said Larson, "but how many live to go there? It kills one's soul to have to go at all, but think when one has not even a living friend."

"It is very hard indeed," said Jane; "very hard, and very cruel."

Then he told her of how he had come to live in the same house with her. How his wife had been killed by a train, and there had only been enough money to bury her decently. And he had been left with the child—had sold up his home to go and live in a room. And he told her of how the authorities had tried to take his child from him, and how he had fought like a tiger and won the day against them.

"You know," he said, "these people on the Guardians think they are Jesus Christ, but they are only rascals, trying to see how much they can get out of life without doing anything. When you see them wearing their white shirt fronts you think they are going to perform miracles, and all they do is talk, talk, talk."

"They're all twisters, the lot of them," said Jane.

L

She poured out another cup of tea for him. Then she pulled down the blind and lit the gas. She had a good look at Larson then.

He looked to be a man of about forty-five, and he had thin features, a nose slightly Hebrew in shape, and a black moustache. He always wore a black shirt with a collar to it, and a blue tie. He had black curly hair, and one curl always hung mischieviously over his right eye. He was a man whom you would take to have been abroad, for his skin was browned by hot suns.

A clock struck below. Larson jumped up and picked up the child.

"By God, it's late," he said.

She bid him good-night, kissed the child full on the lips and then began to make her bed. She noticed that the little statue of the Virgin Mary was no longer there. She was glad to lie down and stretch her limbs. The night fell. All was still. Only the murmur of the river could be heard.

CHAPTER IX

"Now what have I to do?" thought Joe. "Well, in the first place I must just sit down to breakfast as usual, then say—'I am going away—forever.' Yes, that is the only thing. It will be best to make this statement after my father has gone out—it will avoid a row, and he won't miss me, perhaps he will even be glad that I have gone. Yes, that is the best. It must be done. The whole truth must be told. Am I not a man? Have I no mind of my own?"

He paced up and down his room. Below he heard a door banging. It startled him. It was like some devil hammering away in the entrails of the earth. He saw his face in the mirror. He looked hard at the pale features, and thought—"Yes, you, you, you have to tell the truth, my fine one."

"Words are terrible things, terrible," he was saying to himself; "yes, the words only, not their meaning. Yes,

yes, of course, this is the result of being brought up the wrong way. Well, this is the finish. I know now that I could never have lived this life. Because I am not free. I am tied down. I am fettered. Yes, there will be an end to it once and for all." He thought of his interview of the day before and said to himself—

" Even allowing for one's faith, can one still be happy in the knowledge that there is a fitting end to our scheme of things, I wonder ? Now he said that faith was the great thing—well, what then ? My mother has faith, perhaps greater than he, and yet, she is afraid. Of what ? Of Death perhaps. Of meeting with God perhaps. Or even of hell and purgatory. Even so, she had the grace of God. She would die a happy death. It was in the book. It could not be denied. But why were these people always thinking of Death? Why not think of Life, which was more profound, more magnificent than Death? Ah, why?" He could not understand. He was a prey to the forces which were doing battle for his soul. He was conscious of the turmoil going on within himself. A dog barked below in the yard. He ran to the window and opened it. A gust of wind came and he felt it slimy upon his face. All was noise and bustle and roar. A vast concourse of sound filled the air. It seemed as if the world had suddenly flung itself in his face. Oh yes, he understood. The world was calling to him. It was calling to him, and saying—

" It is not in the graves of the living that life will be found."

Yes, that was it. He looked out upon house-tops and bricks and slates which stretched for miles and miles, far down to the very banks of the river. It was like a calm sea. It neither rose nor fell. It was a thing that moved not. He closed the window. Then he looked at his watch. He thought, " Now she will have found her way back to Larson's place. Well, that is very good, but if I go to her, she will have to leave the town. It would not be a healthy place for either of us. We would not be able to walk abroad at night, or in the light of day because

people would know. Yes, that was it—people would know.
He knew he was hemmed in by the stout walls of con-
vention and tradition. Had he not the strength to knock
down that wall? He must assert himself. What were
people anyhow? They were like himself, swayed by
great passions and by trivial emotions which were but a
cloak for those who wished to bury forever within themselves that warm torrent which is at the seat of every
man's soul—that torrent which rages, and which is
held back only after great battles with oneself. For
civilisation imposes a restraint upon these passions. And
nice people have no passion, only a luke-warm emotion,
which rises and flows at will. They knew that life was no
kid-glove matter, and consequently they brought all the
forces of restraint to hold them in check. Joe was being
held in by these. What would his mother say when he
told her? What would everybody say? They would all
be astonished. They would hold up their own heads a
little higher, because that is the proper thing to do when
these things arise in one's life. And all the decent people
going to and coming from communion and confession
would be talking about him. They would gather in little
knots outside the church door, and they would be busy
with their tongues, "about that idiot, that devil, that
dirty, mean son of his mother, who had spat forsooth upon
his religion, and who was *actually* living with a woman of
the streets." Hands would go to head, tears would
come into eyes. "It is terrible for his mother," they
would say. And they would all go home and have their
dinners, and over the table they would bring in Joe, and
they would analyse his soul, they would dissect him : he
would lie there calmly whilst they went through the
process. And they would foretell his future. They were
such wonderful people. They could see a long way
ahead of them ; yet they could not see their own souls,
only the souls of others. And they would say—

"He will come to a bad end, he will end in gaol, or
on the gallows : God look down on his poor mother ! "

And if he met any one of them in the street (which

God forbid), they would stick their noses in the air and walk past—haw—haw—they were nice respectable people. Their souls were clean as a new pin. They were not afraid of meeting their God. He could see into their souls and know that they were clean, and in accordance with all true Catholic principles. Yes, yes.

He heard his father come in. He went to the door of the room. He opened it and listened. He wanted to hear their conversation. Perhaps they would be talking about him. Then he closed the door. For it seemed to him as if the thoughts in his mind had actually become living things. He could see these beings stepping about the room. They were following him everywhere. When he closed down the window, they closed down the window also. When he retreated to the bed, they followed him there and sat down with him. He must not let them escape. Supposing his mother were to come up and suddenly open the door—or his father. Then it would all be plain. They would know his thoughts, for they were living there in that room. He must keep a guard on himself—until to-morrow ; yes, until the morning. It would all come out then. He was a prey to doubt, dark conflicting doubts which seemed to drum a tattoo upon his heart. He paced up and down the room. He did not hear a voice calling to him from below. He did not hear a footstep outside his room door, nor the voice which was saying—" Are you deaf, did you not hear me calling you down to your supper, what there is of it ? "

But he did not hear that. He was still pacing up and down when the door was flung open and his father came into the room. He started as if shot. " Are you deaf or are you mad ? " asked his father.

He could only stare at him with wild eyes, which seemed to be probing a course down into his father's soul. He did not move.

" Joe," said his father, " are you coming down or not ? "

" Yes, yes," he said ; " yes, I am coming down."

He was filled with a terrible fear that his father had

understood something. Perhaps he knew now. Yes, even now. What then? Must he speak out now? Perhaps that would be the best. He waited until his father had gone before he began to gather together the lost strands of his thought. And these things which were in the room, living beings, he must gather them also. He could not allow them freedom. That was dangerous. When he went to the door the things followed him. He could hear their footsteps following him down the stairs. Could he not drive them off? He must get a hold of them, hide them, kill them. When he went into the kitchen and sat down he knew that they were sitting at table with him. When he raised his cup to drink they drank also. He was agitated. He knew his father was watching him. And now his mother was watching too. Perhaps they would think he had gone mad.

" Here's some cold meat," his mother was saying, " it s out of your father's sandwiches, he did not get started this morning, and brought his bread home with him."

He picked up some cold meat from the plate mechanically. He plastered his bread with mustard.

" More tea," said his father.

He could not answer him, but watched him filling up his cup. He could not look at their faces. They seemed to be watching and waiting, waiting for a chance to steal his thoughts. He knew it. He could see it in their eyes. Had they read his mind? Supposing they had, what must they now be thinking?

" The landlord is going to turn us out of here next Monday if the rent arrears are not paid," his mother said.

He kept on pulling at the piece of bread in his hand. It seemed now as if he had at last got hold of one of those beings and was strangling it to death.

" Well, there's nothing left for us but the workhouse," said his father.

" It's hard on me, you know," his mother was saying. " I've struggled all my life to live a good, clean respectable existence, and have remained faithful to my religion—it is hard, yes, very hard indeed."

She put her apron to her face and bent her head down.

" Well, never mind," his father was saying, patting his wife on the shoulder, " there'll be a good time for us just now, perhaps ; by some means we may be able to keep the landlord from putting us out."

Joe took notice of their conversation. He was too much occupied in watching those thoughts of his which seemed to be roaming all over the kitchen. He heard his mother sobbing, and his father saying encouraging things.

" Joe, if you were a decent son, you would go and get a job somewhere, instead of fooling about as you do ; think of your poor mother, what she has to face—good Lord, man, why it's terrible—it's not so easy for me to get work now, you know."

But he seemed not to have heard them. He rose from the table and stood by the fireplace. His father rose too and walked over to him.

" What's the matter with you ? " he asked angrily.

He did not like being treated so by his son, and he hated the thought of his son treating his mother like that —but not to have answered either of them—that was terrible. Joe was staring into the empty grate.

He said to himself, " The morning will see this over."

He looked across at his mother sitting in the chair. Was he sorry for her ? What had brought chaos into his life ? Was it she ? Who had tried most between them to make his life happy ? He could find no answer to his questions. " Ah well—to-morrow," he muttered.

" I have a job for you to-morrow, Father Dunny wants a young feller like you to do his garden. There's plenty of work there, lots of old trees that want cutting down, and the soil needs turning over."

" Will he pay for it ? " asked Joe. " How much d'you think he would pay ? "

" Do you expect payment off a priest ? " asked his mother, letting fall her apron, " a nice Catholic you are, expecting good men of God, as poor as church mice, to pay you for what you should be glad to do. Indeed!" she ended with a curl of her lips.

"Well, I suppose the lad'll want something for his pocket, you can't expect a young man like him to go about forever without a penny in his pocket."

"I never had a penny in my pocket," she said in icy tones.

"Confound it," said Mick, "neither did I, haven't I been working since ever I was able to stand, and I haven't had a penny half the time to get a glass of beer; what the hell are you talking about!"

"I don't want any of your cursing and swearing," said Martha, "a nice example to set your son indeed."

"Well, shut up then about the damn money, you are at me all the time about it—is it my fault if he can't get a job, haven't I done my share? Other men are able to sit down in their arm-chairs at my age, but I have to keep going like an old horse all the time," said Mick.

Joe was used to that. He had heard so many rows in his life that it was a matter of common occurrence, like the weather.

He knew his father was right, anyway she was always getting on to him. He wondered what his mother told the priest when she went to confession. He would have liked to hear what she did tell the priest. Perhaps she did not tell half her sins, like himself—what—why that was just the reason she was afraid to die.

He wanted to turn round and say to his mother there and then—"If you had all the half-crowns you gave for Masses—if you had all the shillings you have given for the Church building—if you had all the threepences you paid at eleven o'clock Mass—if you had all the pennies you put on the plate and in St. Anthony's bread-box—if you had all the money you spent on holy pictures and lives of saints and holy water fonts and foreign missions, you would be a rich woman."

But he could not say that. His father would be against him right away. But who knew better than he about these things? Didn't she have men coming to the door collecting sixpences for holy pictures ? Why ! wasn't the house like a picture gallery, and what with the flowers she bought for the altar and the blessed candles and the St. Vincent de Paul people, why, he thought she would have been rich, and would not be waiting like a stuck pig for the landlord to come and pitch her out into the street. Well, perhaps he would tell her all these things to-morrow. Yes, that would be a good idea. She was his mother, agreed ; but she had a right to hear him just the same. And for that matter so had his father. But his mother would tell him all about it. Once he went away he would not come back. Oh no, he knew what to do. The world was a big place, there was plenty to do in it, only you had to get your bearings first, then you could forge ahead with a will and a way.

"Well, I'm not going to do any garden unless I get paid for it," said Joe.

His mother looked at him and said—" Well, don't go at all, you might have the cheek to ask the priest to pay you, you might even ask him how much he is going to give you—don't go, for God's sake, don't go—I don't want disgracing, any other young man would be glad to do it for the priest—they have little enough help as it is—why do you know some of them poor priests hardly have a penny to call their own, and half the time they are hungry —don't you laugh at me, you hound of hell "—for Joe could not help smiling—had he not seen the fat priest yesterday—did he not smell the cooked joint as he was passing out of the vestry—" one of these days you'll be struck dead for your blasphemy—God forbid it, but you are looking for it," she concluded.

"Well, I'm going to bed," said Joe. "Good-night."

He did not hear their good-nights, so he closed the kitchen door silently and walked up to his room as if he was being followed by some demon or other. He stopped at the top of the stairs. He could hear his mother say— "And why shouldn't he do it for nothing ? He would get the grace of God if he turned his hand to a few other things like that—what about Donovan's son, he's a credit to his family, to his mother and father—there he is every Sunday going round collecting with the priest—d'you think he's ashamed of his religion? Not he—he's proud of it—like any Catholic should be."

" Oh well, give me a bloody rest," he heard his father say—" if he won't go and do the garden he won't go and that's all about it."

" I think you are getting as bad as him," she said.

" You would drive any man to distraction," he said rising and going into the back kitchen to wash himself.

She got up and went upstairs. She was conscious of a terrible weight pulling at her heart. She climbed the stairs slowly, even counting them to herself. She went into the room and closed the door. Joe in his room was standing listening against the wall. He was expecting to hear his mother begin weeping, she generally hid herself away when she wanted to have a good cry. He marvelled at the ease with which the tears flowed. He wondered if all women were the same. He was thinking of that time when Jane too had burst into tears. Perhaps it was easier for women to weep than for men. He knew that they suffered silently, and were more capable of suffering than men. This set up a new phase of thought. He said to himself—" Well, she will be able to bear it—she has borne other things, she will bear this," and then savagely, " that's what they are for : suffering and pain, what else ? —she is trying to lean on me when I am leaning on her with all the weight of my body and hungry heart. But it is not satisfied. She cannot supply that for which I seek. No, there is another way. Jane alone can make me happy." He did not undress, but lay on the bed thinking. His father came up and he heard him close the door of the room with a loud bang. He was in one of those tempers which could arise as easily as tears from his mother's eyes. Well, to-morrow there would be plenty, no doubt.

He woke early, got up, dressed, and began to pack some of his clothes into an old suit-case. He went down into the kitchen, looked at his mother who was reading the morning paper, but did not speak. He went out, washed, and then had his breakfast. His heart was throbbing like an engine. His head was whirling round— his thoughts were all scattered, he could not gather them together. But he must set them in order. He must not get confused. He must brace himself up, be calm and collected, he must not fail—his mother might faint, or have a fit, she might even have a heart attack and die. That did not matter, he had to say what was in his mind. And now for an excuse. He had not long to wait. His mother put a loaf down on the table.

" Has father gone to work ? " asked Joe.

" He's gone to look for it," she replied. " A nice row you started last night ; your father's in a queer temper this morning—he soon changed his opinion when I told him a few things, and all I have to with my few shillings a week—he's going to do the garden himself for Father Dunny ; imagine an old man like your father going out to bend his back, which is bent enough already, while a young man like you can afford to walk about as if you were a duke."

" I am not worrying about Father Dunny," said Joe— " let me have a bit of breakfast and give me a bit of peace."

" You ungrateful swine," said his mother—" if Father Dunny got to know that."

" To hell with Father Dunny," screamed Joe, " let me have a bit of peace, it's the likes of crows like him who are the cause of all the misery in the world."

" Joe !" exclaimed his mother.

" I mean what I say," replied Joe with heat. " I am a Catholic no longer, but a man at last."

She laughed. And when she spoke there was a veiled sarcasm about her words.

" My God," she said at length, " my son, my son—I knew, I knew there was a curse on this house—yes, I knew—Glory be to God and His blessed mother, O look down on me."

" Yes, there is a curse," said Joe, " the curse of this and

this and this." He had risen from his chair—he was tearing the pictures off the wall. A statue was near him, on the shelf, and a lamp was burning to the Sacred Heart. He lifted the statue up and sent it crashing to the floor.

"Jesus!" screamed his mother. "O Jesus, you will be struck dead for that—you will, you devil from hell—struck dead."

She got up and flew at him. He felt the smell of her body and recoiled. He was conscious of a physical disgust descending on him like a blanket. She had her two hands on his face and was trying to scratch him. She was trying to get at his throat. He laughed aloud. But she crushed his head against her breast. He could feel the huge breasts rising and falling as if a sea were near to him. He could hear the sounds of the waters.

"Get off me," he screamed—"get off—Ugh!" He could not stand that smell.

"You filthy beast!" she exclaimed.

He wanted all his strength now. He scrambled to his feet and flung her from him. It was done now. Everything was ended. Yes, he was free. But at what a cost. He looked at her lying upon the floor, her huge figure huddled up like a bundle of rags. And that smell was in his nostrils. Ugh!

"Joe, Joe, my son," she sobbed aloud.

But his cruelty knew no bounds. All that he had suffered, all those nights when doubt and desire and fear had laid hold of him, and had dragged his soul through a hundred hells, all this came back to him now.

He laughed aloud and said—

"Ha, ha!—up the Pope, and a big spit for Billie—ha, ha, ha!"

He rushed upstairs and came down with the suit-case in his hand.

"You see," he said, "I am quite in earnest, I am going away for good."

"You have broken my heart," said his mother, "I will never live through it." She was on her feet now.

"No, no," she was saying, "I will never live through

it, through the shame and disgrace and curse which is upon me and upon this house. I am damned by my own children. I am only an old bundle of rags, and I will remember your words and will take them with me to the grave—and what of your poor father, a poor beast of burden slaving away with only a step to the workhouse. Think of that, think of that—but I know you have no heart."

"And, God!" Joe was saying, "he has broken mine too—I will not tell you what I have suffered because you will not understand. I am going away because I am the devil's friend, and he has no place here. I know. I went to Father Dunny the other day. And I had a talk with him, and he could not answer my question when I asked him if he believed in God—no, but you see that is why I would not go to do his garden, because he knows now what I am. If you did not spend so much money on these useless things, and if you did not strangle yourself to pay the priest and pay your threepence every Sunday to go to the Mass, you would not be shaking and quivering for fear you would be turned out of the house. Whose fault is it if he does? Not mine anyway. It is not my fault if I cannot get work, it is the fault of the crows who will take money off the likes of the landlord, because they know he is rich; but let any of them ever follow and try to bring me back and I'll tear them to pieces, the rogues; they nearly ruined my life with their tales of hell and all the rest of the horrors which only a big fat Catholic could invent. Oh yes, I know all about it, I have seen a few things, I did not go about with my eyes closed. All the times you thought I had gone to confession and communion I had lied, because I had to lie to save myself, and out of consideration for you—but I will lie no longer. I hate your religion, and only forgive you in knowing that my birth, like everyone else's, is an accident. But many a time I have wished I was dead. Many a time I have been eaten into by the fever of Desire, and to whom could I go for help? How could I tell you that I a grown man was hungry for women? Hungry after years of prison.

Hungry after the prison of doubt with my soul urging me on to destruction, with my heart stifling under the load of doubt and fear. Well, I was a hungry young man—I, your son, and I knew what you did not know—I knew that I was a man. And behind all the hocus-pocus of confessions and communions and goings to Mass and reading about saints, at the back of all that I was thirsting for air, thirsting to be free. You would never ask me how I was—you never said once to me, ' Well, Joe, I know you are a man now, and that certain things will have come into your mind, and don't let me stop you, boy, but see that you get some good Catholic girl.' You never said that. But you thought I was all right so long as I was attending my Easter Duty, as if that ever did me any good ! And I am going away now to this woman because I love her, and because I know that you would never allow her face inside this house. How could you ? Why, you would tear her heart from her body. You know you would because she is not running down to the church every five minutes like yourself and all the rest of the old hags in the Third Order of St. Francis, precious lot of saints they are—is Mrs. —— a saint—when she can send you a dirty note and tell you she's going to put you into court if you don't pay the money you owe her? Is the landlord a saint ? Although he's got money to burn he won't put a slate on this roof, but on a Sunday you will smile at him and he will smile at you, and you'll be good friends. But you never see his claws beneath his gloves, and he wears a brown habit, but he has the snarl of a wolf if you don't pay your rent, he can put down five thousand pounds to help build a cathedral, but he can't put a slate on a roof. Do you think I believe in a religion like that ? No, not at all. I hate it. Hate it. There, there, I have said enough, I am only making myself ill."

"You will remember that at the last day—you will tremble before the sight of God—He will never forget, and I will never forget—for even after I am dead, my soul will follow you about, will torment you as you have tormented me—a fitting ending to my life."

"We are born and die in pain," said Joe—"that is nothing new."

"You will live in hell—that's where you will live," she said.

"And you, of course," he said grinning, "you will go to heaven—the unfortunate victim of your precious son —the poor martyr, the poor bleeding victim—some of you mothers imagine you are Jesus Christ or Mary Magdalenes."

She dragged herself to her feet. Near her lay a large piece of the statue. She lifted it up and threw it at her son. It missed him, smashed against the door and fell in a shower of fine dust to the floor.

Joe picked up his cap, and said—

"Good-bye, I am sorry that I have caused this scene. Very sorry."

His mother was lying stretched upon the floor.

"I am very sorry," he said and, turning, left the house.

He did not know that his mother was dead. He did not know. For Death, compassionate as ever, had not forgotten the most insignificant of her children.

* * * * * * *

There was Raynor and Hugh and a man named Rimson—this latter was a little man with a bald head and eyes like a fish. He coughed because he had a bad cold. He wore a black coat and grey trousers, and a pair of brown shoes. A fly settled on his bald head. He flicked it off with a finger and thumb. Raynor was humming to himself. They were sitting together in The Restaurant. Hugh had a white scarf round his neck. There was a glass of beer at his elbow. The air was thick with smoke.

Hugh said—

"Did you hear about Joe, he's cleared off from home —his mother died with the shock of it. The doctor said she had been ailing a long time."

"And he's cleared off," said Raynor—"well, the rotten prig."

"Oh come," said Hugh, "that's a bit hard on the fellow I must say—you must remember he's had a rotten home life—and it was only right that he should get out like he did."

"And kill his mother—his best friend?" said Raynor.

"And kill his mother," replied Hugh.

"Well, I don't give a God damn, he's a dirty rotten prig—if he was my brother and he did that to my mother, I'd kill him," said Raynor.

Rimson said—

"He's living at the other end of the town, isn't he, with a woman?"

"Well, what about it?" said Hugh. "They love each other."

"Yes, I suppose they do—while they're in bed," said Raynor.

"Don't you believe in a man loving a woman, Raynor, old man?" asked Hugh.

Raynor did not reply. He looked across at Rimson and said—

"How many years have you been married, Jack?"

"Seven years," said Rimson.

"Do you still love your wife?" Raynor went on. "Because it might help us better to see the case of this young prig who has killed his mother."

"Yes, I still love my wife," replied Rimson, and he coloured a little.

"Look here," said Raynor, turning to Hugh,—"do you believe any man should love his mother?"

Hugh hesitated. He did not know exactly what to say. He was in the position of having no parents to love. But at length he spoke.

"Now, what answer can I give you?" said Hugh. "Let us see—here is this young man runs off with a woman, renounces his religion, and his mother dies as a result of the shock. He could not love this woman and yet love her, his mother, because that was impossible. You see, his mother hated the woman because she was not a Catholic, and he hated his mother because she wasn't a freethinker or a Protestant or something like that. If you will study the thing from the right angle you will be able to see how akin love is to hate."

" Well, I love my mother," said Raynor, " and no man can say that I do not show her respect."

" You are in a better position to say that than my friend was—all I say is that I hope he will be happy, because if he isn't after this, well, I shall think the man is mad, that's all."

" His father swears he'll kill him as soon as he puts his hand on him," said Rimson, " but that's a fat lot of use, isn't it ? Fancy a father murdering his son, and a son killing his mother—it's like putting a bad egg in a milk pudding, the wholesome with the unwholesome. That's the worst feature of family life. The parents think they own the children, think they have a right over their bodies and souls. If a child rebels it's the result of a thing like that. What else could you expect, anyway ? "

" Is he going to the funeral ? " asked Raynor.

" I don't know, they took his mother into the church—the priest was after Joe, but they couldn't find him, neither his father nor the priest. But they hope that he will come somehow for the funeral."

" Where is this woman staying ? " Raynor asked. " Because I would like to go and see Joe, perhaps he might come back with me—it would be pretty rotten if he didn't follow his mother to the grave."

" Rimson here, he knows," said Hugh.

Rimson told him the best way to the place, and himself rose to go. Hugh stopped him and asked him to have another glass of beer. But he was " not having any more, thanks." He said good-night and disappeared from view.

" You're pretty hard on that young man," said Hugh as he came and sat down by Raynor.

" Not a bit—if he wanted to throw off his religion he could have done so without creating all the fuss he did ; why the people next door reckon he started smashing up the things in the house."

" Well now, that is the result of being tied up too long —it is like a dog on a chain—when it gets free it goes mad, becomes excessive in its desire for vengeance on him who tied it up. It is the same with Joe. He was tied up too much. And it might have been expected anyway from a chap like him—he has a hot temper. He swears he'll kill the first priest who comes after him."

" But the priests wouldn't bother their heads about him —not they—mind you he'll have to turn up sooner or later."

" Raynor, my dear chap, your University education has not done you much good ; I should have thought that a chap of your education and attainments would take a broader view of the case than you do—you're just as much a prig as he is, Raynor," said Hugh, as he filled his glass from the bottle.

Raynor jumped to his feet, blushing slightly.

" Sit down, sit down, don't go acting like a fool," said Hugh, grinning.

" I'm a prig?" said Raynor. "How long have you had that opinion of me ? "

" I've always had it," replied Hugh, still grinning ; " all University people are prigs, the damned lot of them."

" Oh ! " said Raynor and sat down again. He drained his glass. The colour had not left his face. It left a mark, as if he had been struck a blow. He was still blushing when Hugh got up and said he was going down to the Labour meeting.

" All Labour people are prigs too," said Raynor.

" Just so," said Hugh, " but they're damn good prigs, believe me.

" I work in the Insurance," went on Hugh ; " the other day one of our head bosses died—he was a good man and knew his business—he had worked his way up from the bottom."

" Well ? " said Raynor.

" Well, we got a man in his place yesterday, and he doesn't understand a damn thing about insurance, but

he could quote you miles of Horace, and in the original—
and he's a rotten prig too," concluded Hugh.

"You're pretty rough on the universities," said
Raynor; "why don't you go and take a course there,
you'd be able to study the people properly then, instead
of calling them down as you do. There are good and
bad everywhere."

"I realise that," said Hugh, "but I prefer either the
all good or the all bad; at present I'm flying the latter
flag, and it's good enough for me, anyhow."

"But you always seemed to me to be very contented.
This is quite a change from the attitude you generally
adopt."

"My dear man," Hugh was laughing now, "I am
quite convinced that Universities are a waste of time—
money—and good brains. They've educated a hell of a
lot of people; I'll admit that—but they haven't turned
out a good man yet."

"Bosh! Fiddlesticks," said Raynor excitedly, "just
look at So-and-So, and So-and-So, why they are at the
top of their professions."

"Agreed," said Hugh, "but they don't count much to
us, they never come along our way, you know—if they do,
then it's while we are asleep. They are all the same," he
went on, "they turn them out like a box of matches, and
they're all climbing over one another to get to the top of
the hill. But when they do get there what happens?
—well, they stick, that's all—like fly-catchers."

"It's the same everywhere," said Raynor; "everybody has to stick to his job, no matter what it is."

"Yes, but you come talking to me about a young man
being a prig. Now if you had been in his position, you
might have been a bigger prig than he—do you understand? Joe's a chap who appreciates his belly before his
soul. You appreciate your soul and your fine mind
before your belly. On the one hand he gets down to the
bed-rock of existence—on the other hand you think that
he or anyone like him is inferior to you because his belly
is his master. Well now, I must tell you that you have a

lot to learn before you commence running down people whom you only know five minutes. I stand by him, because I believe he's right. Now supposing that thing had happened to one of your friends—how would he have gone on about it? Well, in the first place he would never have rebelled, because that is the last thing that people like you think about—besides one has to allow for society and consider it and its value, to you as an individual; you know that they would have to stand by society—because it made them, do you understand?"

"Well, go on," said Raynor, "let's hear the monkey talk."

"Supposing this young man was let loose in the society you live with—what would happen? You know what would happen. There is no need to think it over at all. Why, he'd have people wanting to string him up for no more reason than that he is a healthy young man with appetite, and wanting that appetite satisfied. Why, he'd pull down the house about your ears, man," said Hugh.

"He's a queer chap altogether," remarked Raynor; "anyhow I'm not going to sit here listening to his bad and good points, I'm going home."

He got up and began putting on his gloves. Hugh was looking at him closely. He had refined features, but one could discern just beneath the surface that brutality and arrogance, so much admired in well-bred men. Hugh saw it in Raynor. He bid his friend good-bye, and saw him off. Then he returned and put on his own overcoat and pulled the collar well up about his neck, for it was raining heavily outside.

Would Raynor go looking for Joe? He promised him a lively time if ever he became familiar with the young man who was a prig and who had killed his mother. Then he let himself out, passed the bar-tender, bid her good-night, and shot down the steps in search of a bus to take him to the Labour Hall. He jumped into one that was full, and had to stand on the top-deck whilst the rain poured down and drenched him, covering his coat with a kind of silvery dust, running down behind his collar and making him feel very uncomfortable. And the bus sped along, throwing up spouts of mud and water as it whirled along, rocking like a cork on the water.

* * * * * * *

It was a wild black day when they buried Martha. The bell tolled and they carried her into the church and out again. Mick was there, and John Magee and two relations had come from London, and there was the woman next door, and Father Dunny sprinkled the holy water on the coffin. He rode in the coach preceding the hearse. The wind was blowing devilish hard. At the church door there were a lot of papas and mamas and babies. Raynor was there too, so was Hugh. Raynor had been trying to find Joe, but he was lost. A big woman picked up her child who was playing with horse-dung in the gutter and smacked its bottom.

Hugh laughed. Raynor asked him what he was laughing at. Hugh merely said—" I am laughing at that woman smacking the child, of course."

" The bottom of the child is the seat of emotion, and the hand that smacks is like Aaron's Rod," said Raynor, and he laughed too and showed his big front teeth, which were like horses' teeth. Once one of his friends had ridiculed his big teeth. He advised him to have them drawn and get false ones. (One must have nice little pearly teeth, you know.)

There were eight men carrying the coffin. The coffin bumped and bumped, because the pall-bearers were the best they could get. The man leading by the head on the right of the coffin had his cap sideways on his head. He looked as if he were drunk. They pushed the coffin in, the coachman saying in a deep voice, which seemed to have come out of the bowels of the earth, " Easy there, my hearties—easy there."

Father Dunny came out and got into the carriage. Then the hearse moved slowly away. The mourners were coming out. They were wearing their brown habits, while John Magee had one that was too short for him. He

looked like a Roman Gladiator. Mick was coming down
the pathway. And his eyes were red, and his mouth was
hanging loose like that of a cow after it has finished
chewing the cud. Then they all got in, and the coaches
moved away. A lot of people stood looking on. " Lord
have mercy on her," said a woman with a scab over her
right eye.

" Ah well, she's better off—she did not live to see her
son reap the reward of his wickedness."

" O-hoo," said a woman with a face like a piece of
parchment—" she was a good friend to me—she was—
Oo-hoo-oo-hoo."

" I'll smack your ——, you b——," said the woman to
the child who was playing in the gutter again with the
horse-muck.

The cortège was just turning into the main road. It
looked like a long black snake as it wound its way out of
the street. The crowd dwindled. No more excitement
until the bell tolled again. Hubbub of voices talking about
the poor. Hubbub of voices condemning the son to hell.
Hubbub of voices criticising Mick's shabby black coat
and vest. Woman wearing a green shawl blowing her
nose with great energy and saying as she drew the flat
of her hand across her nostrils—

" Did you notice John Magee? He looked like John the
Baptist—ha, ha ! "

Policeman coming down the road. He has a big head
and a huge red neck, like a sad gash in a bull's belly.
Very red neck—red hair growing on it. Has a bulbous
nose. Sniffs as he walks along. Watches the crowd going
home. Looks at them and brushes his coat with his hand
at the same time. Very tall. Stands outside the urinal.
Takes off his helmet and brushes back his hair. Has grey
eyes. Looks at a woman passing with her skirt whipped
up about her. She's been scrubbing a step. Winks at
her. She smiles, looks down at herself and finds her blouse
blowing open to the wind. Blushes and walks away. Man
walking about watching everyone, has a squint in his eye.
Picks up bits of cigarettes as he walks along. Policeman

pats his chest. Has flat feet. Priest comes out of the church, looks up and down the road. Walks up and down the pathway saying his office. Looks at the garden which Mick has been straightening up. Wind blowing bits of twigs under his feet. Dodges them as if they were bugs. Has a nice kind face. *Gloria tibi, domine.* Keeps muttering to himself as he walks up and down. *Suspiciosus dominus sacrificium de manibus tuis.*

Old man going into the church. Priest raises his eyes from the book and nods to the old man. Priest goes inside. The angelus rings. Then hooters blow and whistles shriek. The cemetery is cold. The coffin is an oak one. It smells like rum. It has on the brass plate : Aged forty-nine years. R.I.P. The priest is mumbling over the grave. Mick is twiddling his thumbs and crying as well. A few people stand near and look as if they had lost their souls. The coffin is lowered into the grave. Mick throws some sand on it and it makes a noise as it rattles on the brass plate. John Magee throws some. The woman next door throws some too. They all file back to the church. Then the coaches roll along. They all get in with sad anxious faces, like a business man who has just put through a big deal. The coaches roll out of the church-yard. They stop at the house. They all walk in. More papas and mammas at the door. More babies and bare bottoms. The door is closed. The blind shoots up. Smell of whisky and roast meat. Big table borrowed from the shop that sells fresh ribs. Covered with a white cloth. A large woman with a red face washing dishes in the little back kitchen. Coachmen come in, blowing their hands. Look like Tyburn martyrs.

" The dirty bitch."

" He was a nice lad."

" Pass the salt John, please."

" Now don't be shy there."

" Do your heart good that indeed."

" Mary Maginty's joined the Children of Mary."

" Yes, Paddy has a rash on his belly."

" It's fearful cold to-day."

" The graveyard's nearly full up."

" D'you take sugar in your tea, Bridget ? "

" The mission was a fine one—wasn't it ? "

" Oh ! did he get married yesterday ? "

" She'll take it all out of him though."

" Big bull, he is just the same."

" Likes his glass of beer."

" Did you hear about Corby's one ? "

" What's that, Annie, more bread ?—Here you are."

" She's a Tartar."

" He has a hard heart, believe me."

" Well, Mrs. O'Toole, is your health all right ? "

" That's right."

" Step over the stool there—that's you "

" Seven o'clock Mass on Monday it is."

" I laid him out."

" He looked like a saint."

" Heart disease."

" Dr. Rogerson was in the cruel war."

" He has a wooden leg."

" Likes the women, doesn't he ? "

" All right, Mick, I'll help Annie with the dishes afterwards."

" Are you going to the sermon on Monday night ? "

" He's a very clever man, beautiful priest."

" Why am I a Catholic ? "

" Father Dunny has made things hum since he came to our parish."

" He boozes like a fish even though he wears a sash."

" It's not like it was, is it ? "

" Are you there, Annie ? "

" Take your coat off, Mrs. O'Toole—that's right."

" The devil take you, John Magee."

" Aha now—you're a cute boyo."

" Have a slice."

" Yes, they sell lovely tea—two shillings a pound."

" She's a cute little bastard."

" Oh ! it's lovely—is that the new medal ? "

" Indulgence for a happy death."

" Lovely—lovely."

" Let's see it."

" Paddy has one on his neck."

" The landlord gave another thousand pounds to-day."

" Lovely man, isn't he ? "

" You're a great tea drinker now, aren't you ? "

" Take a drop—that's it—do you good."

" Is your leg still bad, John ? "

" Ah !—well."

" The meeting is postponed till Wednesday."

" Excuse me, ladies."

" His heart's broken."

" Someone at the door."

" Why don't you blow your nose ? "

" Following me everywhere."

" Mrs. Riley wants her black coat, she's waiting for it."

" Did you ever ? "

" Go to hell and wash yourself."

" Good-night, Bridget."

" Good-night, Annie."

" Good-night—good-night."

" The devil it's cold, it is."

" There now."

" Stop it, you bad man."

" Deaf and dumb."

" Thinks he's clever."

" Good-night and God bless you, Mick."

" Say a thimbleful for me now."

" He's back again."

" She's coming herself."

" The divil she is—she's in a bloody hurry."

" Good-night—good-night everybody—mind yourself, Annie, he's a divil of a man."

CHAPTER X

WHEN Joe arrived at the house where he knew Jane had returned, Larson again opened the door, but this time there was no smile for him. He merely said in dull level tones—" She is in her room."

Joe looked at him and wondered. He had been so friendly the last time they had met—and now—he rushed upstairs and into the room. He flung the bag on the floor. Her eyes were bright as she came towards him.

" You have come at last," she said, reaching his cheek and kissing it.

" Yes," said Joe, " I have come—yes, I have come."

" Sit down, dear," she said to him and brought out the little cosy rocking chair. He sat down. He was like a man in a dream. His hands were twitching nervously. She thought he was ill and brought him a glassful of water from the big white jug on the table. He drank it and handed back the glass.

" Oh !—my God ! " he gasped.

She was at his side in an instant. She had buried her head on his breast. " What is the matter ? Quick, tell me, has something happened ? "

" It was terrible," said Joe, "I left her lying in a fit on the floor. I became a madman. I tore the pictures off the walls—smashed down the altar, vilified her, my mother, hated her as I never hated her in my life—I think I've killed her."

" But you have come, dear—aren't you happy now ? Tell me."

" I am ashamed," was all he said.

" Of what ? " she asked.

" Of myself."

There was a silence then, broken only by the sound of slow hammering down in the yard. It sounded like the measured tread of brazen-footed Fate. Then he spoke again, and the words came slow, calm and dignified. they rose and fell with a kind of awe, they floated in the air like bats in the blackness of night. And then they fell from his lips like a torrent, hurling themselves forward as with a divine frenzy—and he was speaking more quickly, with the speed of fear. She tried to calm him. But he was looking straight ahead of him. He seemed to be gazing into a void, beyond which the beings of his thoughts wandered to and fro, like tormented spirits in a land where death is known not ; they lived in a land of calm and bright sun. And he did not feel the warmth of her body against his own—the quick beating of her heart —the soft touch of her lips against his.

" I think I have gone mad," he said at length.

He rose slowly, she clinging to him with all the strength of her body, and he stood there looking ahead of him, with a strange light in his eyes, like a god of ages long past. And his lips were trembling. He could not shut out these thoughts. His hands hung listlessly by his side, and his breathing was slow and steady.

He was speaking again. And she was looking up into his face.

" Oh Christ—help me ! Help me ! " he exclaimed frantically.

" Joe, Joe," she was saying, " sit down, sit down—tell me, see I am here, the one you love."

At length he sat down. She let go her hold of him. For suddenly she had become frightened.

" Jane," he said—" will you go and find out for me if my mother is all right ? "

" But how can I do that, Joe?" she replied. " I could never go near the street but I would be recognised—and they would tear me to pieces."

" Jane," he was saying.

" There, there, do not worry so. Perhaps it was only a faint—and your father would be in and he would help her a little—haven't you suffered enough already, won't you be happy here with me ? Tell me."

" I have not finished suffering yet—there will come a time when all that will cease, even now I am not yet free," he said quietly.

" I'll make you some coffee," she said, darting out of the room. And when she returned ten minutes later, he was standing by the window looking far out across the roofs with their air of sameness and monotony. He did not hear her calling to him. She crossed to the window and pulled him away.

"My strong one, come, here is some tea ready for you."

They both sat down but they did not speak much during the meal. She on the one hand was afraid—he, too, was afraid—between them had suddenly risen a barrier, ever so delicate, like the silken tape which the athlete breasts at the last mad minute of the race. They were afraid of each other. Fearing lest either of them should be the first to break the spell—to send their world tottering at their feet. The strong wind was blowing in. A whiff of it entered Joe's nostrils. He started up as if stung. She jumped up and ran to close down the window. She thought he was really ill—feverish.

"Now you must lie down," she said.

He sat on the edge of the bed whilst she removed his boots and his coat and vest. She covered him up with the thick red quilt which she had had for five or six years. She stroked back his thick hair. She was afraid. She did not want to disturb him. He was soon asleep. Then a knock came at the door. Who could it be? Perhaps it was even his mother—or his father—or a priest. She trembled with excitement. The knock was repeated, this time three dull heavy thuds on the door. She went and opened it and peered out.

"My name is Raynor," she heard a voice say—she could not distinguish the young man in the dusk of the landing. She held fast to the door.

"Well, what is it you want?"

"Have you a young man here named Joe Rourke?"

A sudden thought flashed across her mind. She replied with some heat.

"Why—who wants him?"

"I want to speak to him about something very important," said Raynor, and tried to put in his foot between the door and the wall of the room.

"Tell me what it is, and I will tell him as soon as he returns—he has gone for some groceries for me."

" I'll come back again then," he said, " because I want to see him myself "—adding, "are you Jane ? "

" That is my Christian name," she replied.

She shut the door and stood listening to him descending the stairs.

When she looked at Joe he was sleeping, and she could discern on his face a kind of trouble, a weariness. She sat down and commenced to stitch.

The bell of the church rang out. She put away the work and commenced to undress. Joe opened his eyes. He looked at her, and it seemed as if he were looking at her with the eyes of a babe. She smiled and continued undressing. She drew the blind and lit the little gas-jet by the window.

" I am thirsty," he said, " will you get me some water ? "

That morning when he had left his mother, he had not gone to Jane. He had wandered half the day about the docks—had lain on the grass in one of the parks until nearly five o'clock. He had been in an agony of mind.

And though in his heart he knew it was over and done with—he knew that it had cost suffering to both—it had cost something which could never be atoned for, in heaven or on earth. Twice he had been tempted to return, to fall on his knees before his mother, and had wavered. But now as he lay there he knew that he had done the right thing. But at what a cost.

He had left his home—his parents who had worked for him so hard. He had abandoned them as though they were criminals, when really they were only the people who had fed and clothed him and guarded him from the evils of youth. She brought him hot coffee and he drank greedily.

He was looking up at her, looking at her bare arms, at the virgin-like features, marred by the deep purple rings beneath her eyes, and he knew that in her lay forgetfulness, in her lay oblivion, rest, and peace. To her he must cling with all the strength of his body—he was dependent on her now—he was like a helpless child whose mouth has to be guided to the breast of its mother. In the silence of the night they took. All was calm and peace.

He woke up during the night in a fever. She got out of bed and brought him some fresh water. She felt his forehead. It was hot. Yes, he was ill.

She did not go to bed again. She could not excite him more. He was speaking.

" I am ashamed—I am ashamed," and he burst into tears.

She held his head between her two hands and drew his face up to her own. She saw in the depths of his eyes a fear and could not understand. She saw or thought she saw the dark waters of unrest stirring in his soul. And over her own there crept an icy mist. Was she, too, ashamed? Was not the sin her's as well as his own?

" There, there," she was saying, " your mother will be all right—there, there ! "

She kissed him again and again and tried to soothe him. He lay back on the pillow and watched her with half-open eyes pottering about the room.

" Jane," he said, " aren't you getting back again ? "

" It is nearly six o'clock," she said.

They could hear the steady tramp of feet outside. The men were going to their work. And perhaps their own hearts were lightsome and joy filled, and yet here he was, in a fever of doubting and misunderstanding. The siren of a tug-boat rang out in the still air like a threat. All was silent again.

" What must you do, Joe? " she was saying. " Listen, I want to ask you something—why are you ashamed? Why are you so nervous ? You are making yourself ill."

" I think I have killed my mother," was all he said.

" Supposing I had died," she said.

He could not answer that. He did not know what to say. What must he reply?

" If you had died I would have died also," he replied. " Because I love you," he added.

" And your mother ? " she asked.

" She may not be dead—but God help me—if she is——"

" You will have a fever if you excite yourself more—
there, lie down and sleep a little longer."

There was a tired look in his eyes, as if a weariness had
descended upon him like a cloak in the night. He turned
on his side and began staring at the wall. She did not
speak, but commenced to tidy up the room.

" Will the landlord ask questions ? " he asked suddenly,
turning round to look at her, as she arranged the little
chintz curtains of the window.

" He knows, my dear—he knows all about it—he's a
very nice man so long as one pays the rent."

While she was busy arranging the curtains he slipped
out of bed. When she turned round he was lacing his
boots, sitting on the edge of the bed.

" Why up so early ? " she asked, for she was certain that
there was nothing he could do at that hour in the morning
—certain, that he was not contemplating returning
home.

" I am going for a walk," he said—" you don't mind,
do you ?—I won't be very long."

" What about breakfast ? " she said, barring his passage
to the door.

" Oh well—when I come back, I'll only be about half
an hour."

" By the way," she exclaimed suddenly, " there was
somebody looking for you last night——"

" For me—who was it ? "

" He didn't say," she replied—" I really didn't open
the door to him—only a little bit—it was dark on the
landing."

" I wonder if it was my father ? " said Joe, swinging
his cap in his hand.

" I don't think so, by his voice I took him to be a
young man."

" Oh well," he said, " perhaps it was only one of my
friends, although how they got to know I was here, I
can't imagine for a moment—anyway I don't want to
see anybody at present excepting you." He laughed
and was gone.

But when he had left the room and found himself in the street, his light-hearted spirits left him. He stood for some minutes looking either way, wondering what he should do—where he should go.

" I think I'll strike off this way," he said to himself ; " nobody knows me up this district." He set off at a good walking pace. Every now and then he stopped and turned round. He thought he was being followed. The eyes of every man seemed to be upon him. He seemed to know what they were thinking.

" Poor young chap—thinks he can follow the capers of the rich—but he can't lie in bed all day."

If only he could hide somewhere. He was half inclined to go back again, but he had walked a good distance. He stopped by a shop window and looked in. He heard a footstep behind him and jumped. The passing policeman looked queerly at him and thought he was going to smash the window—thought he was drunk.

He stopped a few doors further on.

" I'll watch that chap," he said to himself.

Joe turned away. As he did so he heard a voice hailing him. He knew that voice. He turned round to find Hugh standing behind him. That individual stared at him, as though he had never seen him before in his life.

" By God, you look ill, man," he exclaimed.

" Do I ? " replied Joe, laughing.

" What are you doing up in this direction anyhow ? " he continued—" you're miles away from home."

Hugh was on his way to work. In contrast to Joe he looked clean and fresh : there was about him a perfume of recently applied soap. His face was red with the quick walk. But it gradually lost its colour. They stood talking for a long time. Then Hugh said—

" Why don't you drop in to see us ? We haven't seen you for a long time, and Raynor wants to see you, he was down at your place looking for you the other night."

" Which place ? " asked Joe trembling visibly.

" Why, what other place is there ? We all know about your leaving home—the place where you are stopping. "

They knew, then. But did they know everything? He wanted to ask him if he or any of his friends had seen his mother. It was on his lips, but he could not speak. He was afraid. He cursed inwardly at having bumped into him. He could never go near his friends again. He would not trust them. They seemed to be all spying on him.

"God save me from my friends," was what he kept repeating to himself.

"Well, I'm off," said Hugh, "I'm in a devil of a hurry—don't forget I will be down there to-night if only you will drop in, and don't forget about Raynor, he was at your house the other night—he has news for you—well, good-bye."

"Hang Raynor," muttered Joe as he watched his friend walk away. He stood looking after him for a minute or two, then retraced his steps back to the room. When he got there he found that Jane was out. He ran down the stairs to enquire where she had gone. Larson who was coming in from the yard espied him, did not smile, but in answer to his question merely said—

"She went out to fetch a few groceries, she won't be long."

He left Joe standing wondering why Larson's attitude had so changed of late. He had never seen him like that before. To him he had always seemed to be generous, kind-hearted and jolly, ready to do anybody a good turn. But he could not understand this latest development at all. He went back to the room and sat there waiting for Jane to return. She had made the bed and the room looked quite cosy. "What a great little worker she is," he said to himself. Then she burst into the room, with a parcel under her arm.

"Why, how long have you been here? I only left about twenty minutes ago."

"I have just come in," said Joe, "and as a matter of fact I am sorry that I went out at all."

"Why?" she asked.

"I am meeting people whom I don't want to meet."

N

" Whom did you meet ? "

" A friend."

" Perhaps it was he who called here the other night."

" I don't think so—but I know that there will be people watching for me—trying to get me back to the paternal roof and all that kind of bosh."

" You'd better stay in then for a few days," she said.

" Won't you come away out of this place ? " he asked her, taking her hand.

" Oh come, Joe, what is the matter ? You are all nerves lately."

" But you will come, won't you—with me—into the next town ? I'll get work there ; we will be all right."

" Are you afraid ? " she asked.

" I am," he said.

" But I thought you had broken definitely with your people, surely you are not going to give in now after fighting such a battle ? "

" I am thinking of my mother."

" And what of me ? "

" Of you too," he said—" that is why I want you to come away."

" Well, not just now, Joe, not yet awhile—I have certain things to do."

" How long will that take ? "

" About a week."

" But I want you to come now," he said.

" I can't, Joe—I can't—just yet—have a little patience."

" I have great patience, but I ask you to consider the position I am in."

" If your mother called now, would you go back home with her ? Tell me."

He did not answer.   She plied him again with the question. He said—

" I do not know—I love you and that is why I ask you to come away now."

" Do you consider my case, apart from your mother's ? "

" Yes," he said.

" Well, then, lie low for a few days—you are not unhappy, are you ? You have a bed and food—you have me—are you not happy so ? "

" Yes," he answered, but he pulled himself up then.

She could not understand him. A change had come over him.

" After all," he was saying, " I owe a certain duty to my mother, don't I ? "

" Well yes, you do, but you owe one to me also."

" Are you angry with me ? " he asked her, looking into her eyes.

" I am and I am not—do please, Joe, consider me as well as your mother."

" I am, I am—did I not say so before."

" Well, let that end it, don't let us start quarrelling right at the beginning of our happiness. We depend on each other now for love and happiness."

Someone was knocking at the door—then a voice said—

" The coffee is ready now, Jane, if you want it."

" There now," she said, " here is coffee, we will get our breakfast together."

She busied herself arranging the little table. She put down a large mug for Joe because she knew he was such a thirsty young man. There was toast too, which Larson had made on the fire in the kitchen below.

They ate in silence, looking into each other's faces the while. Each was trying to read the other's thoughts. Each looked but saw nothing. Yet they remained staring the one at the other, each waiting for the other to speak —each wondering what the question would be—each having a question to ask yet fearing to speak.

" Sugar ? " she said, and continued stirring her own tea.

" Thanks," he said and smiled at her.

The ice was broken. Soon the great floe would melt away and they would be able to see into each other's heart and know the secret lying in its bosom. Each would see the doubt, the fear, the hopes lurking within them. Joe dropped his eyes because he could not stand the glare from her own.

She shook him gently.

" Are you falling asleep, Joe ? " she asked.

He blushed and sat up and finished his meal, trying to appear at his ease, when he knew that his mind was in a turmoil. Something was pulling at his heart-strings, playing a tune upon them that revived memories of times now past. He opened the conversation again by asking—

"Does Larson get much work ?—I never seem to see him dirty at all now."

" Well, the work in his line is not very much, because so many of the people are living in rooms, and then lots of people eat out in the cocoa-rooms and restaurants. Then a great many people use nothing but gas."

" And they never have a fire at all," he said.

" Oh yes, they have fires, but they clean their own chimneys, like the landlord here—he always waits until it is raining heavily or it's foggy, then he sets fire to his chimney."

" A good idea," said Joe.

" The police fine you if they catch you at it—but I'm afraid that they will never catch the cute one below stairs. He has them all checked off. Yes."

" He seems to be a queer customer ? "

" I have had this room six years, and I never knew him to do a straight deal yet, but he treats his tenants all right, so long as they pay their rent—he won't have people coming and doing as they like with them. Oh yes, he has his good points as well as his bad," she concluded.

" Our landlord is a holy terror," Joe broke in. " When I left there was water coming in through the roof, running down the walls, but never a man did he send to put a slate on the roof. He sent my mother a notice saying she had to get out in a week if the arrears were not paid."

" That's pretty hard," said Jane.

" He's a big man in the church too, the one I used to go to."

" They generally are," said Jane, smiling broadly.

" Is he married ? " asked Jane.

" Yes, and he had a family of ten all living ; my mother had a child the other week—she's had a lot altogether."

" That's being greedy," replied Jane. " How old is your mother ? "

" I think she is about fifty," said Joe.

" And your father ? "

" Sixty-two."

" Oh ! "

" He doesn't get much work now," said Joe. " He used to work in the abattoir—in fact he worked there for about fifteen years, but last week they sacked seven men. He can't get work at the docks because the union says he has to be a member—well, it costs about five pounds to be that and he hasn't got fivepence, let alone five pounds, but now and again he gets a little odd job as a gardener. The other day my mother wanted to have me go and do the garden in the priest's house, but I didn't go, because it's not worth it—they don't give you much ; my father went and did it up for Father Dunny."

" Where are all the rest of the family then ? " she asked him.

" Oh, they're scattered all over the place."

Jane was looking at him closely as he answered her questions, now and again she noticed that he hung his head—she wondered why.

" I hope you don't think I'm forward by asking you these questions," she said—" but it's only for passing the time, that's all—you speak so little, Joe."

" But you never tell me anything about yourself—I don't know even now whether you have a mother or a father, or aunts or uncles."

She laughed, got up from the chair, and sitting down by him kissed him and put one arm round his neck.

" Sometime I will tell you all my history, and then you'll be able to write a story about it."

" Will it be a long one ? " he asked.

"It depends how much you want to hear about me. I have had a queer kind of history, I'm like a penny that has been shuffled here and there and everywhere."

"Oh, I see," he said.

"Well now, you won't go back home and leave me, will you—not even if your mother came and asked you?"

He could not speak. It had come so suddenly. Had he better not say straight out what was in his mind?

"Would you like to see my mother?"

"But she hates me like poison, she would kill me if she found I had brought you here."

"She's not that bad," said Joe, "she might even learn to love you."

"That could never be, because I do not believe in your religion."

A thought flashed through his mind. His religion. Her religion. It was always the same, the religion cropping up. And now he knew that he could never become reconciled to it. That would never be.

"It is best for us both that she keep away—I do not want her to follow me about. I do not want to see her. If only she would forget this religion, if only she would see my point of view. Why, how great it would be."

"That will never happen, Joe; 'tis better for you to stand by your own soul, than to pay homage to something you do not understand."

Was she right? Did her words contain even the germ of truth? This soul—this huge Catholic soul—bat-like, hovering over him always. Could he never shut it out? Had God done with him? This huge Catholic God with the arms of stone.

CHAPTER XI

"I CAN never again worship God," said Joe as he met Hugh.

"We are all born to live, suffer, smile, struggle, die, that He may live forever."

" That is right," he said—" He will never die—He will exist always—in our minds."

" He is strong though," Hugh replied.

" He can crush mountains," said Joe.

" And thrust bad Catholics into hell for ever and ever," added the other.

" That is another God—that is the Catholic God—but He is more of a butcher than a God," said Joe. " My mother wants me to go to Mass and I will not go."

" Don't you believe in the Mass then ? "

" I do not."

" You do not think then that when you received the Holy Eucharist, that it was the true body of Christ—transubstantiated ? "

" It is merely a piece of bread—the last time I received it I spat it out."

" Were you not afraid of being struck dead ? "

" I am afraid no longer."

" But going to Mass will not be detrimental to you in any way—you could go if only to make things smooth for yourself."

" At school I was taught to believe in a saint who could be in two places at once," Joe laughed.

" Are you afraid of the priest when you do go to confession ? "

" I am not afraid."

" Why then do you let these things worry you ? Every one of us follows some kind of a religion, symbolic or otherwise."

" But I have never benefited by following my religion, according to the words written in the prayer-book."

" Religion has nothing whatever to do with your mother—you can still love her."

" Not while she remains a Catholic."

" Is she a very strict Catholic ? "

" Yes, very strict."

" Supposing I went and had a talk with her."

" It would do no good—only death can efface the evil done—the priests are to blame."

" Not all the priests are to blame—every man has his own will—you can govern or be governed by that will —do you understand ? "

" Yes."

" Fully ? "

" Fully."

" If I went to confession would a priest hear me ? "

" If you were seriously in earnest."

" Do you have to tell everything ? "

" Everything—it is a matter of conscience."

" And supposing you hid a sin, a wilful and mortal sin —what then ? "

" Your confession would be valueless."

" Do you feel in you the benefit of confession—has it any effects on you mentally or physically ? "

" None—the effects to the contrary are purely auto-suggestive to my way of thinking."

" Oh ! "

" Are you compelled to go to Mass ? "

" Yes, under pain of damnation."

" Do you believe in hell then ? "

" That is impossible."

" Why ? "

" The evidence of its existence is not absolute."

" Well ? "

" There is a story of a saint whom God personally directed into hell in order that He could use her afterwards as an instrument to send back to earth with the evidence."

" What then ? "

" It is said she returned, appeared in a vision to a very devout woman, and that one of her feet touching the wall burnt a hole right through it."

" That is very funny indeed."

" That is what we believe."

" You are all nerves, of what are you afraid ? "

" Of God."

" Your God ? "

" Yes."

" Is not that also an instance of suggestive powers ? Does your imagination govern your reason ? Does your reason capitulate to the auto-suggestive processes of your mind ? "

" When I was a child I always suffered from nightmares —it was through reading certain books. I caught that atmosphere from the books, it remained with me—it has become organic in my mind."

" Will not the love of this woman blot out these terrible things from your mind ? "

" No, that can only come with death."

" If you were dying to-morrow, given up by the doctors, would you send for a priest ? "

" I could not answer that—that would depend entirely on my state of mind at the time."

" You have not yet rooted out of your soul that which you have been battling with for so long."

" I am obsessed by fear—I cannot explain it to you now."

" Are you certain that this woman loves you ? "

" I am—the only thing of which I am at this moment certain."

" Are you sure that that also is not a case of the suggestive powers dominating the powers of reason ? "

" We love each other—I have left my home because of that," said Joe in a somewhat exalted voice.

" I am sorry for you."

" Why ? "

" You are the victim of bad training. But what do you intend to do ? "

" I am going out of this town—I shall find work there —we shall be together, I will forget easily and without effort."

" You will not return home then—do you consider the step you are taking ? "

" I do."

" You will not even try ? "

" No, I do not wish to be asked to make my Easter Duty again."

" Are you sorry for your mother ? "

" Only that she is my mother—that is all—well sometimes I am sorry she too is a Catholic."

" She would never change her religion then ? "

" No, that is her life—she lives for that only—externals
are nothing—internals everything."

" Is she easily led—ignorant—has she had a fair school-
ing ? "

" She is not ignorant only in the matters of which I
have been speaking—for instance, I could not ask her to
leave the church for ever."

" That would not be necessary—you go your way—she
will go hers."

" The barrier will remain always—she will follow me—
hunt me out—fall on her knees, beg with her heart full of
sorrow—what can I do ? Must I say yes ; all right, I
will go to Mass—I will be a good Catholic ? "

" You learned that obedience is one of the first laws
of your Church ? "

" Yes—no one disputes what is said, what was and
what will be said—it is accepted."

" Try not to think on these things, but go back to this
woman, and if it is for your own good, then go away
with her."

" It will be hard—like tearing a heart from a body—a
living heart."

" Yes, I recognise that—that is a part of life."

" Try then to forget this thing—it will kill you in the
end—you must decide once and for all—you must say in
your heart—' Which shall it be ? ' and abide by your
decision—there is no other way."

" And if either of these things proved to be wrong ? "

" It is enough ; be it wrong abide by it—because in
doing so you have been actuated by your own reason."

" I am proud to have you for my friend," said Joe,
looking at him with devotion.

" I know, I know," said Hugh, " you are my friend—
any time I am willing to help you, but remember :
think it out before you do anything rash. You see, you

are in an unfortunate position—you understand me ? "

"Fully," said Joe, "I have already decided. We are going away to-morrow—it is for the best—if my God can show me any other path and it is virgin, I will gladly go that way."

"Well then, let's have a drink."

They sat together in Hugh's room at his lodgings. They expected Raynor later. Hugh had not told Joe of his mother's death. He was afraid to do so. He did not wish him to make any decision consequent upon this news—which he knew in his heart he must do—but he would not suffer himself to be the instrument which prompted it.

Raynor would tell him, anyway. It was best perhaps, although he knew that his young friend did not like Raynor at all. Their attitude towards life was entirely different.

He filled Joe's glass and watched his hand tremble as he took up the beer.

"What are you going to try for when you get out of here ? " Hugh asked him.

"What can I do ? " said Joe, "I can only go as a labourer, anyway they are paid as well as the tradesmen these days—I might get work with the corporation there, they are erecting houses and re-laying roads, there will be work of some kind for me. It is one of the first things I shall do, because soon this woman will be dependent on me."

"Have you ever realised," said Hugh, "that that woman could never have children ? "

"What of that," said Joe, "is a child essential to happiness ? It is a pity that a person could not be born say at the age of fifteen or twenty, it would get him over that terrible period in life which I know too well—it does not matter about the children—we do not want any—we live for each other, that is all."

"So long as you realise that, it is all to the good—I just thought I would tell you—again, are you sure that you love each other—it is not a flash in the pan—you have not committed yourself to something from which you may be glad to free yourself in later years ? "

" One does not live for ever," replied Joe, smiling across at Hugh.

The door opened and Raynor came into the room. He was wearing a dark blue suit, a white collar and blue tie. He had just shaved and there was a slight cut on his chin. He came forward smiling, and said to Joe—

" Hello, you blackguard, what's this I've been hearing about you ? Won't do this and won't do that—a pretty mess you have put yourself in anyhow."

Joe laughed aloud and would not answer.

" Sit down and don't give yourself patronising airs, hasn't the man enough to contend with without contending with you ? "

Raynor sat down. Now and again he shot a glance at Joe, and knew that he was watching every move of his eyes. Had Hugh been saying something ?

" Look here, Joe," he said at length, " I want to be your good friend—now listen to me, won't you go back home ? I will come back with you, everything will be all right, not a word will be said, everything's all right— your father will be angry of course, all fathers are like that—we've all been through the same mill——"

" No, you haven't," said Joe in a rasping tone. " What mill have you been through ? "

" Come, come, man, try to look at it from somebody else's point of view beside your own—always be ready to listen to a bit of advice."

" Go on," said Joe.

" I am not a Catholic," said Raynor, " but I was brought up to understand the love of my mother, and to behold the manifold beauties of life—consequently I have learnt from that, that life is as you make it for yourself— it is no use your rebelling against a symbol which has thousands of years of tradition and authority and loyalty behind it—a man has to conform to some of the rules, no matter how much he may be against them."

"What has that to do with me?" said Joe. "What have you to say of the woman?"

"I have never seen this woman, I understand that she was once on the streets. I do not judge a woman from that aspect at all, I am only going to ask you if you really think you could be happy with such a woman, you must remember that they have a terrible past to live down, and that they carry in their hearts a running sore, a perpetual hate against the society which has placed them in that unfortunate position."

"Well?" said Joe. "What about her?"

"Nothing then," said Raynor hastily—"but will you be happy with her? That's all I ask you. I haven't known you five minutes and here I am acting like a father towards you."

"Well, I have just had a talk with him too," said Hugh laughing. "He doesn't want to hear any more, believe me."

"Well, here's my hand on it," said Raynor. "I wish you success, and don't forget to write us whenever you feel you are in a pickle."

"Of course, of course," said Joe, "I am not going away for ever."

"I have something else to tell you, but I will not tell you now, perhaps it is better that you learn it for yourself—I do not wish to destroy your happiness."

"What do you mean?"

"Oh, nothing," replied Raynor, "nothing at all."

Joe could not understand. What was at the back of Raynor's mind—what was he trying to keep from his knowledge? Had something terrible happened? Instantly his thoughts were centred on his mother. But no, surely it was impossible. Then Hugh disturbed him by saying that Raynor was going to play the piano a little in the next room. They all three went into the next room. It was a little larger than the other and the pianoforte, covered with dust, was standing near the wall by the door.

"It's a bad place for a piano," said Raynor, as he lifted the lid.

" Well, you know these people," Hugh was saying ; " they buy a piano, and use it to stand the portraits of their fathers and mothers and sisters and brothers on—a kind of family art gallery."

Joe laughed. Raynor struck a chord.

" It's never been played for months," said Hugh, seeing upon his friend's face an expression of disgust.

" I should think it hasn't," said Raynor—" what will I play for you ? "

" Do you know the Sonata in G of Mozart ? " asked Joe.

" And where pray did you last hear the Sonata in G ? " said Raynor, looking over his shoulder at Joe.

" It just came into my head," said Joe. " I've never heard it played."

" No, I should think you wouldn't have asked me to play it, had you heard it."

" Do you have music ? " said Joe.

Raynor did not answer. He was wondering what had prompted his friend to say such a thing.

He struck the opening chords of the Valse in E flat of Chopin.

" My father used to hum that tune," said Joe.

" Indeed," said Raynor.

" Yes, he was in a Turkish bazaar one day and there were half a dozen Egyptians playing the same tune upon drums or something like drums."

" You fool," said Raynor and shut down the piano.

Raynor was thirty-one years of age. He was a draughtsman in an engineering firm. He had first met Hugh at a Labour meeting, and from that time had been one of Hugh's staunch supporters and companions. Hugh was secretary of a great many things connected with the Labour movement. Sometimes Raynor would help him with the work. Raynor's family was pretty comfortably off. One of those families remarkable only for their strict respectability, onanism, and white-livered humanitarianism. His father was a justice of the peace. " Hungry Raynor," they called him. His mother was one of those women who knew nobody until she married. They were lucky with their friends and acquaintances. By sight they had fifty friends, they knew personally twenty-five. She rarely had them in her house. Usually she visited them. Her husband was a jealous man, and did not believe in having too many people in the house. They had sent their son to study at the University at the age of twenty. He had studied in medicine, but had failed to pass the examinations. He was not so disappointed over this affair as were his people—they were furious, in fact his father went and gave the examiner a good talking to, which made him laugh.

Then he actually got his son into an engineering works, and by dint of perseverance he became a draughtsman.

Hugh was a mere insurance clerk. He had brains, but the brains of clerks were not a valuable asset to the insurance companies at that time. Consequently he had to sit and watch men from the University coming and taking the best of the jobs. It made him angry. One had to have a degree, and all that kind of thing. His parents had died when he was very young. He had lived in the same rooms for a matter of five years from the time he had come down from the small country station. He was a good-living man, did not drink, smoked little, and as a matter of fact drank only when something special was on. He drank with Raynor and Joe, because he knew that they would look upon him as a kind of leper if he refused. He was not interested in women. He was too busy trying to live and trying to do his best for a movement which was growing by leaps and bounds. Joe had first met him at a gathering organised to demonstrate the bad conditions of the slaughter-house men. He had liked him from the very first. And the three were faithful friends bound up in one another.

They knew what was worrying Joe. They knew what had happened to his mother. But they would not tell him. They knew what the consequences would be. And they were always chary of giving advice. Because as soon as a man started giving advice, Joe looked upon him as his enemy. It was a suspicion which had grown upon him, as a result of the happenings of the last twelve months of his life. If Hugh had said to him with all seriousness : "Joe, I do not advise you to live with that woman from the streets," he would have known that Hugh was his enemy. He knew they were all against him having anything to do with such a woman. She was some five or six years older than he. To them she was a kind of leper, something loathsome to be shut out, to be kept apart from all that was clean and healthy in life. Hugh on the one hand did not wholly condemn her. He only wondered why the woman had fallen in love with him, a mere youngster of twenty. If they were going to be happy, that was everything. That was Hugh. Raynor on the other hand was different. He would have said in all seriousness, "I advise you to put this woman out of your life altogether ; you might well catch a disease from her."

As a matter of fact he had already intimated to Joe, that this was something which might eventually happen. But Joe had put him right on that point. He told Raynor that he had slept with the woman. He wondered at Raynor's hostility. He knew what was in his mind, that calm and contented mind which took life so seriously and yet appeared to be never out of order at the worst moments. He had wanted to see the woman, but Joe would never give him a chance to find out where she was living. He little knew that Raynor had found out. He did not know that it was Raynor who had called upon him until Hugh, whom he had met the morning before, informed him. He would have liked to be able to read the thoughts then in his mind.

" Penny for your thoughts," he asked.

" They're not worth that much," Raynor replied.

He was anxious for news of his mother. He was half inclined to slip along now and find out the worst. He knew he had excited her, had made her weep, which was the last thing he wished to do. But he would not face his father. He had a terrible temper, and there was no knowing what he might do if he went back. Of course he would not stay there, he only wanted to see how his mother was after the row. And then the priest would have been too—he knew that—his mother or his father would have brought the priest down, shown him the pictures he had torn off the walls, the smashed statue of the Sacred Heart. No, he could not go back, although he wished someone would bring him some news, as to how they were going on at home. They were in a bad way : he was certain of that. Perhaps they had even been put into the street. He knew his mother was too proud to go to the St. Vincent de Paul society and ask for a little help. "We'll manage somehow," the wonderful slogan would be able to help them hold up their heads in spite of the poverty which was upon them always. They would not think of doing any such thing. All the parish would stare at them, point them out to one another as they went into church. They would say—

"Yes, that's the result of having a son who is too lazy to work, and a dirty good-for-nothing, who despises his beautiful religion."

No, his people would never stand that. They were far too proud.

They had a collecting box at home, and into this they used to drop pennies whenever they had them to spare. That was to help the Foreign Missions. One morning there was no gas to light. And coal there was none. When he had suggested that his mother take a penny from the box to put in the gas she was furious with him. She would not think of such a thing. Never. Never.

"That would be a terrible sin," she had said.

"But you could put it back again as soon as you got a penny."

"I will never touch it," she said.

One day when he had nothing in his pocket, he had broken the seal and taken some coppers out to buy cigarettes. Then he had sealed it up again as well as he could with gum. The box opened at the bottom, and a piece of paper gummed over the lid held in the pennies.

He got a surprise one day, though. He had actually lived to see his mother do the very thing which he had suggested. For there was nothing in the box. And the day came when a little girl, whose mother was the local collector for the Foreign Missions, had come to take the box away to be emptied. His mother was in a flummux. She did not know what to do. But she had a very agile brain, and it was all settled in five minutes thus—

"Just take Miss Morgan in the parlour for a minute, Joe ; I have something which I want to give her mother." She had run upstairs then, got an old copy of "St. Anthony's Annals" out of her drawer in the middle room, brought it down and laid it on the kitchen table. Then she had picked up two clean shirts of Mick's, run to the top of the street, pawned them for two shillings and ninepence, got most of the money in copper and hurried home again. Then she went out to the closet, taking the money and the box with her. And she emptied most of the coppers into the box, one at a time, making as little noise as possible. Then she returned to the kitchen.

"Are you there, Lizzie ? "

Lizzie answered in a squeaky voice.

"Here you are then."

She was in the kitchen.

"Here's the box, I'm sorry to have kept you waiting, but I wanted to give your mother an old copy of the Annals, there is a beautiful story in it about Bernadette."

She had got over that all right. But Joe had known all along that she had been taking pennies from the box. That was how she was able to give the priest a shilling when he called on the Sunday before.

There was a collector in the church, and he was like a bull in both manner and appearance. He always was at the door at eleven o'clock Mass. And you could rarely pass him without giving him the threepence, because sometimes he would stop you and say " Coppers, please." He wasn't supposed to do that and if the priest had found him out there would have been trouble, but he never found out, because the people were afraid of complaining.

But Joe used to walk past and never pay a penny. He hated asking his mother for the money for church on a Sunday—though she used to give him fourpence. But he put only a penny on the plate. He used to spend the rest. One Sunday as he was going in the collector said, taking his arm—" Do you know this is eleven o'clock Mass, man ? "

Joe said he knew and tried to push the man out of his way, but he held on to him saying, " They usually pay threepence at this Mass."

" What for ? " asked Joe angrily, and pushed him aside, to stride up the aisle as if he owned the whole church, congregation and all.

One morning his mother was with him. She paid her threepence and watched her son glide in without paying anything. She whispered to him as they knelt in the bench : " What do you do with the money I give you, if you don't pay ? "

" What d'you think ? " said Joe, " you never ask me if I have a penny to buy a paper or a cigarette."

She watched that he put twopence on the plate though, just after the Elevation. She told his father, when she returned home. He fumed and roared, and said—

" In future you'll go to Mass with me, son, and I'll pay for the two of us ; a nice Catholic you are to begrudge a few coppers to the Church of God."

" They're not my coppers," he had answered.

" No, your poor mother's, who doesn't know half the time how she's going to get them."

" That's not my fault, is it ? " Joe had replied with some heat.

His father had knocked him down then. They had not spoken to each other for a whole week. Then when the priest came with the collector on the Sunday following, his father let on to be as nice as pie with his son, and he watched him while the priest was talking to Martha. The priest used to look queerly at him sometimes, as if he was a bastard growth of some kind. He took the shilling with a smile.

CHAPTER XII

" AND ten o'clock Mass will be said for the repose of the soul of Martha Rourke, lately dead. May her soul and the souls of the departed rest in peace."

" Amen."

" In the name of the Father and of the Son and of the Holy Ghost—Amen."

The fourteenth Sunday after Pentecost. Epistle of the sixteenth chapter and the twenty-fourth verse.

" Brethren, walk in the spirit, and ye shall not fulfil the lusts of the flesh : for the flesh lusteth against the spirit, and the spirit against the flesh ; for these are contrary one to another ; so that you do not the things that you should. But if you are led by the spirit you are not under the law. Now the works of the flesh are manifest ; which are fornication, uncleanness, immodesty, luxury, idolatry, witchcrafts, enmities, contentions, emulations, wraths, quarrels, dissensions, sects, envies, murders, drunkenness, revellings, and such like ; of the which I foretell you, as I have foretold to you, that they who do such things shall not obtain the kingdom of God. But the fruit of the spirit is charity, joy, peace, patience, benignity, goodness, longanimity, mildness, faith, modesty, continency, chastity. Against such there is no law. And they that are Christ's have crucified their flesh with the vices and concupiscences.

" At that time Jesus said to his disciples——"

The congregation rose as one man, and bowing on one knee rose again, they stood whilst the priest continued—

" No man can serve two masters ; for either . . . "

The congregation sat down. The priest coughed. The congregation coughed. The priest looked at them through his spectacles. He did not speak for five minutes. He was looking hard at them. Some returned his stare, others sat with slightly bent heads, many were gazing down at their hands, feeling in their pockets, the church echoed with *Ahems*. Then a silence broken only by the priest's voice—

" My dear brethren——"

Another pause. The priest was watching the fourth bench from his pulpit. He recognised there the father of the man whom he had chosen for his sermon that morning. He watched Mick pull a handkerchief from his pocket and wipe his eyes. One or two people in the same bench eyed him closely, as if he were an escaped convict, a murderer, a depraver of women, a devil incarnate. Venomous and cruel were those glances ; pity, cynicism, and sarcasm too.

" My dear brethren," said the priest, commencing afresh.

He stopped, again looked at the man sitting before him. Then he saw him collapse. Some of the congregation had seen it also. Two collectors looking like guardsmen came hurrying up the aisle. Mick was passed from one to the other until he was able to fall into the arms of the collectors. They carried him down to the bottom of the church, one of the men sprinkled some holy water over his face. Then together they carried him outside into the fresh air. They sat him on a chair. Then they stood looking at him as if he was some strange being from another world.

" Heat," said one.

" Lack of food," said the other.

Mick opened his eyes.

" How d'you feel now, old man ? "

" Will somebody take me home ? " he said in a feeble voice.

Then he collapsed again.

" The man's had no food, that's what it is, packed too tight in that big bench too."

Somebody brought a taxi. They lifted him into it and he was taken home.

" My dear brethren, you all know how our Blessed Lord chastised the rich merchants who came to worship in the temple—you all know how he swept the money changers from the temple with the lash. And how, my dear sisters and brothers in Christ, Almighty God bestowed upon His Son the strength to do these things." Then the preacher became fairly launched : he spoke at great length and with numerous digressions.

Having concluded, he turned and walked down the wooden steps from the pulpit. After the Benediction the huge congregation filed out from the church. At the doors, and at the corners of the three streets adjacent, little knots of women were gathered talking eagerly. The men had hied them off to get refreshment after the longest sermon they had ever listened to by a parish priest. Father Dunny was a poor speaker, they said. He did not throw his voice very well. He did not speak up. He was always yawning, coughing and saying ahem, after every fifty lines. The women were talking about Martha and Mick and Joe. They knew all about it. Of course why should not the whole parish know about such an awful thing ? They had as much right to know and solve these things as anybody. So they argued and argued, and decided this and decided that, said this and that, thought this was right and that was wrong, on one of the coldest days of the year. " Glory be to God, don't stand there all day, my dear," said an old woman. For it was very, very cold. And then the dinner must be got ready.

CHAPTER XIII

THE house with the queer smell is a dead house. No sound issues forth, the days and nights pass comparing their ways, and all is silence. Although the smell is there, and will depart not. And sometimes Magee comes in to have a talk with the man who sits by the fire-place with a black scarf round his neck and a face like that of a man who has been in hell. The man once was Mick, but he might as well be John or Gerard, for not a semblance of Mick remains. Mick's soul, like his body, had changed.

It was a very cheap, dirty soul now. For a man gives up thinking beautiful things when he has seen into the abyss. It is not a nice place. It also stinks. The droppings of every animal under the sun—the smell of every being on the lamentable planet who has suffered the misfortune of having a soul grafted upon his more unfortunate body. The smell of blood, and filth, and urinals. For it must be remembered that the abyss boasts more urinals than any other section of the globe. Of course a man uses them more often than a haw-haw, because a haw-haw looking at a painting of a famous brewery, and seeing the large barrel on the picture will mistake it for the sun, whereas the other man knows that it is beer. Which shows that brewers and not artists are men of departmental import-ance. Yes.

Magee has a cataract coming over his right eye. It gives him a pain sometimes. But he doesn't care. He always has a good word for Mick. Mick doesn't speak much now. He says " Yes " and " No," and nods his head. That demands effort. Once when Magee men-tioned Joe's name Mick's face went white and his eyes rolled, and he said, standing up straight and looking at John—

" Don't you ever mention that lousy bastard's name to me again—see ? "

Magee saw, of course out of his one eye, for it's the devil when you have a cataract over your right eye. Ah yes. Now if it had been over his left. They sometimes laugh. But Mick when he laughs looks like a lunatic, and John looks like an archangel.

" It's a funny damn world," says John.

" Why funny ? " asks Mick.

" Take a penny off an old drunken woman and give to a blind man—ha-ha."

" That's neither one thing nor the other," replied Mick.

" You're a hasty bloody man—give us a chance—that's you," said Magee.

" Take your confounded owld landlord, what does he

do ? Why he batters down your door to get your rent, and then he goes and gives it to the church."

" A man may do what he likes with his money," says Mick.

" And a man may do what he likes with his soul, if it comes to that, hey ? "

" The soul's a damn funny thing, eh, so difficult to understand. I'm getting that way now that I don't give a God damn for anything—'scuse me, you know."

" Did Mary take the kid all right ? "

" Oh yes, it's doing all right is the kid—it's like its mother, but it has the queerest habit of crying only in the daytime, it never cries in the night."

" Well, what of that whether it cries in the day or night ? Sure it wants the breast and that's the holy—all about it."

" You'll have to get out of the house, I suppose then ? " asked Magee.

" Well, I sold a table and a couple of chairs yesterday, and that paid some of the rent, I think that I will go into a room because while there's a bone left in my body I'm not going to the workhouse. Not on your life."

The workhouse is not a nice place. People with no money and their bodies full of fleas go there. It's a nice world though, all the same. The workhouse has big walls like a gaol. The sun shines sometimes, but when it does it only shines on the closets for men. That's a queer place too. And the food you get there is cooked in great pans. That's queer too. The men have no teeth, and the women have nice alabaster-like faces. That's queer too. But the workhouse is queerest of all. There is a smell there. The men work hard and the women do their best. It's such a nice place. The workhouse master has a long face, a black beard hangs thereto—looks like Jesus Christ. Calls the men by their surnames, the women have a matron, stiff as a piece of sugar-cane. " Don't slop your porridge about there, Gurman."

She has a voice like an organ—rich contralto. When Mick goes there the workhouse master will call him by his surname too. He'll have to help wash floors and clean closets, and knives and forks. The prayers are very nice. No decent God would turn his back on them. All hoping to die soon. Very keen indeed on death. Women wear grey shawls and funny bonnets—men wear moleskin trousers, light coloured, heavy reefer coats. Very ugly when dressed. Mick will wear them too. The landlord is on the board of guardians. A famous authority on post-mortems. " Lord have mercy on the poor souls."

Magee wouldn't touch the workhouse with a barge pole.

" Hell of a place," says he.

" Cut you into tiny bloody bits, if you haven't an aunt or uncle to come along and say : ' Wait a while—try a bit more solid stuff next time—his mother was a respectable woman—— ' "

" Did you try for your job back at the abattoir ? " Magee asked him.

" Finished ! " said Mick.

" That's pretty hard now, you know," said Magee.

" Not as hard as my heart, by God, at the present moment," said Mick.

" Well, you did your duty by him, it's up to him to do his by you, isn't it ? "

Voice outside the front door. It's a very small squeaky one too—

" Have you seen Annie anywhere ? "

" She's in the yard beating the carpet."

" Have you seen our Annie anywhere ? Have you seen our Annie anywhere ? "

" She's beating the carpet—she's beating the carpet—she's beating the carpet ; you're the deafest bitch I ever set my eyes on—there now."

" God look sideways on you, you blaspheming devil, Michael Rourke."

" That's a great woman out there now," said Mick, turning his ear towards the window.

" Indeed she is," said Magee—" she's enormous everywhere."

"I think I'll have a little walk," said Magee, and he got up from his chair.

"A nice little walk, you know," he went on and he put the chair back by the wall.

"It's a great day for walking too," said Magee, and he took his hat off the chair. The chair had a high back, and was varnished light brown. It was heavy. Magee put on his hat and turned to the door. He stroked his whiskers.

"An' how much did it cost you to open the grave, Mick, my boy?"

"Four pounds ten," said Mick.

"Well, ta-ta for the time being—keep your heart up now, and don't get too well in with the divil."

The door closed. Mick was alone in the house. He sat staring into the fire. "Dead, dead," he kept muttering, "dead—an' last week she poured out my tea." He kept rubbing his hands one against the other, palm to palm: it set up a friction which tickled and irritated him. Then he dropped his head on his breast and said—"Now if I could get my hands on that fellow—if only I could, God forgive me though," he added hastily; "Yes, God forgive me, for I don't know that I wouldn't lose my temper. It's a divil of a one too. Indeed it is."

The woman next door came in for the loan of the dolly-pegs.

"Well, they're here, Mary, if you want them—really you can have anything you want in this place."

"Will you have a little drop?" she asked him, smiling and showing her two buck teeth—"just a nice little drop now, cheer you up a bit it will."

"I don't mind," said Mick, and he smacked his lips They were thick lips and over the upper one a straggling moustache grew, and it was rough and long and brown, and it was matted like fungus. Mick was proud of his whiskers. He got up and turned to the woman, saying in a very solemn voice—

"Shall I get a glass, Mary?"

" No, no, Mick man, I want you to slip in the back-way, that's the boy."

Mary slipped in the front and Mick slipped in the back.

It was a pleasant little kitchen and there was a warm fire. She said " Sit down " and he sat down. Then she went into the back kitchen and called him out to her. She had her back to the back door. She had a glass in her hand. Another one lay on the table half full of whisky. " There now," she said, " that's yours."

He drank her health and she his. Then she got near to him and he looked at her in a funny way. She looked at him in a queer way too.

" But surely you only kissed your husband an hour ago," said Mick, as she sidled up close to him, and he could feel the rise and fall of her swelling breast against his own.

" Husbands are so very dull," she said.

She was a nice woman, with black hair as black as the sloe, and she had brown eyes and they twinkled merrily now. She was of medium height and her face was oval, and her features were handsome to a degree, marred only by the heavy sensual chin and the two buck teeth.

" Some other time, Mary, not now—the wife's hardly cold in the owld grave."

" Yes, I'm going on Sunday to take a few flowers, and the priest is saying ten o'clock Mass for the repose of her soul—Lord have mercy on her."

" I often wish, Mick, that I had belonged to a religion like yours, it's lovely to have some place to go, to have somebody to whom you can open your heart and ask guidance and help from—it is really."

" Well, what's done can't be helped of course, but there you are, surely you wouldn't like to become a Catholic, Mary ? Why, your husband would strangle you."

" Well yes, it's a bit late now though. Many a morning I have sat in the window there and watched your wife—God rest her soul—I have watched you and her and the poor boy "—Mick winced—" and seen you trotting off down the road, and I've said in my heart—' Ah, if only I could be as happy as they—to be able to go down on your knees and look God in Heaven straight in the face and know He's looking at you, oh it's beautiful.' "

" Well, well, what matter, you can pray too, what's to stop you, but watch your husband he's a devil when he starts."

" Yes," she said, and drained her half glass of whisky. Mick gulped his too.

" I have a little account with God, you know, Mary, a kind of debit and credit account. I have to speak with God about this, you see I've done my duty by Him all these years, and the least I now expect is that He'll do His duty by me. That's not much to ask of anybody— the settlement of a little account."

She pressed a little closer to him.

He did not move from his position.

" Ah well !—Can I ! "

" Not now—not now."

They remained close, breathing each other's breath— looking in each other's eyes, feeling each other's heart beat—wildly.

" Did you ever find out what became of poor Joe ? The foolish boy he was too."

" I never did," replied Mick—" I never want to either —the dirty rascal he was."

" Ah now, don't be fierce to the child, bedad did you never do a thing like that yourself now ? "

" Don't speak of him—I don't want to blast my soul through him, don't, I ask."

" Ah well ! "

" I see they're taking some men on at the abattoir, why don't you try to get back there ? It'll be better than sitting in the house all day, you're only worrying yourself so."

Mick laughed. It was funny too—he hadn't laughed for such a long time.

" They don't take old horses nowadays," he said—

" why, look at me, I'm getting a hump on my back, and my old bones are very much worn out—ah yes."

She gave him a squeeze. He looked strangely at her then.

" Why you're still a strong hearty man," she said laughing.

He wanted to get away, to go back into the kitchen and sit down and think.

She let him go. He used to sit there for hours and hours thinking of Martha and Joe, and tears used to come from his eyes that were red and bloodshot. The landlord wanted another three pounds next Monday. He had to think of that too. And Mary was looking after the child —he had to think of that. Sometimes his belly obliterated the more serious things of life and he had to think of that too. There were so many things to think about. There was not much time left as a matter of fact for anything else. To-morrow would be the feast-day of St. Gerard. He would have liked to go the early Mass, but he was ashamed to go, because all the parish would know him now. And besides, hadn't he fainted at the Mass yesterday? Everybody would stare at him as he went up the aisle. He could even hear them saying to each other— " That's poor Mick—you know, Martha's Mick, Lord have mercy on her—she reared a devil of a son—he's living with a prostitute at the other end of the town."

Of course he could hear them talking about him. But why didn't they talk about something else? About their husbands or their children—or their daughters, or Theresa Corby, who was suffering from womb trouble. No, he couldn't go to Mass to-morrow. That would be impossible. He might go to bed and tell the woman next door he was ill—and she would go and tell John Magee, and Magee would come down. And he'd ask Magee to tell the priest that he was ill in bed. He really did feel ill. The only fit place for him was his bed. And perhaps the priest would come and give him holy communion there. That would be better. He wanted to ask a special favour of St. Gerard. Then he decided that he would go to Mass and face all the shame which would descend upon him as soon as he walked up the aisle. St. Gerard would never grant a favour to a man who was too ashamed to go into the house of God. "Well, I might have known—I'm going barmy all right, I can see."

Mary's husband is tall and thin, and his eyes nearly black, and his hair is curly. He limps because he got a kick from a horse one day in the stables. He drives a lorry and each night he comes home full of horse muck and smells so bad that Mary has to put out his clothes into the air for about two hours, to let the smell go away. On Saturdays you can always tell who is coming down the street in the forenoon, when you hear the jingle of harness, for he brings all the horses' trappings home, and he cleans them in the back yard, and sometimes children from the house opposite sit on the wall and watch him. He stops polishing, looks up at them, winks and says—

"What the name of hell are you doing up there? Get down out of it, you shower of bastards! Get home to your beautiful mothers—that's the style."

They all drop off the wall and run home. They rub their little faces against the coarse aprons of their mothers and shed crocodile tears.

Mary's husband had no children. He once said he would never bring children into the world, because he was only the fool for doing it—he was going to copy the big nobs, they never had any children, and they always looked well and fresh. But Mary fought like a tiger, and he told her if she was not satisfied to get away out of his sight. Mary's husband always liked Mick. She liked the look in his eye. Like that of a bull when it follows a cow. Magee had his eye on her too. But he was a lot older than Mick and herself. Her husband used to call Mick and Magee—"Fresh stuff. Irish closets." Mary said that wasn't nice. He said mind your own business. Then adding—

"Give us the stuff."

That was when he was hungry. He used to like steak raw, used to have it between bread. One day she

called him "·A bucketful of slops." He said—
   " A bucketful of slops is better than a bucketful of
——"
He often used to say that Irishmen were born in ——.
But he was a queer chap. Queer chaps said queer things.
Fresh people said fresh things. Nice people nice things,
and so on and so on. That was it. Shakespeare was a
man who wrote a lot of lines one under the other,
arranged in squares and oblongs.   That was queer too.
The only things he ever read were the words on the
newspaper that used to be wrapped round the meat. He
used to sleep all day on Sunday, and in the evening he
used to sit at the door, and watch all the Pope's good men
on their way to church. He used to grimace at them
when they went past. He was very proud of himself. He
prayed a big drum for the Billies. They always gave the
man who beat the drum plenty of ale. Liverpool found
its soul in ale. It was a queer place. Full of smells, and
beer. The women had eyes as dull as fishes' brains, and
the men had hard faces. They used to stare at anybody
with a pleasant, gentle face. It was funny. They waddled
along because nobody in Liverpool could walk right.
Perhaps it was the wind always blowing in over the river.
It was a very fine river, and sometimes the people would
go for trips down this river which was called the Mersey.
They used to bring bottles of ale with them, and the
children's faces were always full of sand and mud, and
they never blew their noses properly.   All the people
worked hard, like the devil himself ; that was because
money was a fine thing, and only respectable people had
money. Lime Street was a fine street too. The Big Belly
and the street Christs used to gather there.
   There was a concert hall too in Liverpool. People used
to go, wearing furs and fine coats. Then there were a
few papers run by bigwigs—these used to send men to
listen with their ears—they had to have long ears—to the
music. It was very hard for anybody to get a job like
that. First the editor asked you—" Did you know your
E.G.B.D.F. ? " If you didn't know that you couldn't get

a job. They used to work hard : the people with the long ears. Although they didn't know the difference between a voice and a hooter, they did very well, and all the people read industriously, and said, as they slapped their last slice of bacon into their bellies—" That's damn good —he knows his business." You see they had to know their business. There were some theatres also. The men running these were always full of genius, because they were able to make " Hedda Gabbla " look like a performance of " The Silver King." That was necessary, because the public had no belly for high stuff. You have to use the word belly in these cases, because it's known as a " fine word " in Liverpool, and the people are always thinking and talking about their bellies. There was a University as well. You could take a degree in football, tennis, racquets, boxing, and many other popular arts. They worked with monkish skill to make these things popular. Because they had to earn their bread. Now and again a rich man gave a lot of money to the University, and sometimes other merchants sent their sons to learn these things, as well as a little bit about science. When you mentioned science to a Liverpudlian it would make him flap his ears.

There were numerous monuments as well. The City of Monuments. They were very nice indeed. More people said this about them than they did about the Art Gallery, which was filled with rubbish and always empty. No, not of the rubbish, but of the people. The Museum was also agreeable. Lots of people went in to see a little seal swim about in a tank. All were great animal lovers. They used to have horses dressed up like peacocks, and lots of people tried hard to be funny. That was May-day. They had always held May-day in May, although in a little suburb of Liverpool it was held in June ; they were always a month behind Liverpool, which was a smart city. The men wore hats which made them look hard to deal with, and the women walked about as if they were carrying a load on their backs. They nearly all spoke nicely. The abattoir was in the south end of the city. All

the cattle off the Irish boats used to come to the landing-
stage. The men chased the animals up narrow dirty
streets, and wide filthy streets. There was always a smell.
Sometimes on a Sunday lots of young boys and girls used to
walk behind the bushes on the outskirts of the city. And
they said the same things as their grandfathers and grand-
mothers. Mick and Martha had come over once on a
cattle boat. They weren't blessed with too many of this
world's goods and they had to get among the bulls and
cows. They were pretty clever too—because they were
able to make themselves look like bulls. Joe was born
two years after they reached this wonderful city. Graft
was a fine art. All business men to be successful become
devoted to the patron saint of liars, St. Martin. They
used to rush about the place as if they were hunted beasts.

Magee had been in the city for twenty-nine years. He
had come over when young ; he went to help gather in
the harvest, and pick potatoes. That was a good living
for Irishmen. The English were too lazy to do the dirty
work, but the Micks were great boys. They wallowed in
dung. It was on their boots. They belonged to the bogs.
Magee used to work at a theatre, standing outside dressed
like Napoleon Bonaparte. The theatres had " leg shows "
each week. They were very stimulating. The news-
papers kept the theatres going. The theatres were afraid
to displease the papers. The critics were afraid to criticise.
That was the way of things. Mick had never been in a
theatre. Magee used to tell him great yarns about the
theatre. Mick's hair would stand on end then.

Most of the men went to sea. Some had white pasty
faces, and eyes full of a mysterious blackness—others had
very red faces, surmounting red necks, and blue eyes.
They used to swear by Liverpool as the greatest city in
the world. The next city did the same kind of thing. All
were the same. A white-livered humanitarianism domi-
nated everything. People from Liverpool were called
Bucks. Feminine, Buckos.

Mick twice made up his mind to go back to Ireland,
and then forgot all about it. He had been wishing and

making up his mind for years to have another look at the
grand old place. But he had never got there. It was now
dear to get across to Ireland, and then he hadn't enough
money. Last year Joe had gone and stayed there for
three weeks. That was before he lost his job in the leather
warehouse. Martha, too, often had a wish to go back to
Ireland. She never wanted to die in the land of the
infidels. But she could never go because you needed a
pile of money, and money was difficult to get over. But
she had some compensation, in knowing that she was in
England and that the people were slowly but surely
being converted to the only true religion. And now Mick
had an earnest desire to sell up the few pieces of furniture
and return to the old place. He would dodge the landlord. People often said that he wasn't clever, in fact that
he was a very dull chap, but let him dodge the landlord
—why, he'd show them ! It was proof of cleverness to
dodge payments of your debts. Debts were like bugs,
you couldn't keep them off you. Magee said he would
drop in about nine, so Mick poked the fire, and sat there
tapping his toe on the fender. He had grown thin with
all the trouble. And he had always been a man to enjoy
the best of health. But it was a sure sign when you
couldn't bend your back. The old-clothes man generally
called for people like that. The works run down. Finished.
Well, no one would call for him, because he wouldn't
be there long.

Mary brought back the dolly-pegs, and she was just
going to sit down by Mick when there came a knock at
the door. She jumped up in a fright and thought it was
her husband, but it was only John Magee who had
promised a chat to Mick. He smiled nicely when he saw
her. That's right. Keep smiling all the time. It didn't
matter what kind of an ache or pain you had. Keep
smiling.

" That owld Smiles feller, I think he was a bit barmy
meself—he couldn't have ever written so many clever
lines, for certainly they weren't witty—shades of Samuel
Smiles—no, he couldn't have done that if he had lived in

this confounded place, believe me," Mick had said to Magee one day.

Magee missed Martha too. He knew the good old times when he was able to baste his face with a fine slice of bacon and cabbage. They were times that would never come again. Ah no. They couldn't come any more.

"Sit down, John, don't be standing there as if you were a perfect stranger."

"Of course I will—of course I will," and he sat down with a thump.

"Well?"

"The same," said Mick—then he added suddenly, "I'm thinking of selling these few sticks and trotting off back to Ireland."

"Shame on ye, man—shame on ye, man—and your wife hardly cold in her grave."

"Well, it can't be helped, and it must be done some time; over there I'll have friends, but the devil of a lot I have here, and you would never like to see Martha's Mick walking bold like into the workhouse? Of course I know you wouldn't."

"Have you had a word from Joe yet?"

"No."

"I say, let's have a little walk—we might go as far as the jetty wall—much better than sitting here worrying all day—sure God Almighty would be vexed to see a fine man like you sitting here snuffing over other people's sins—away now."

"All right," said Mick. "Just sit yourself there until I go and have a wash."

Magee could hear him swilling the water over himself. He kept on spluttering and spluttering. John walked into the back kitchen to see what all the spluttering was about. Mick was wiping himself down with the towel.

"I hear that the abattoir is taking on fresh men," said Magee.

"I know—I heard yesterday—but even if they offered

me my job again I would never take it—my heart's set on going back to Leitrim, and that's an end of it. What is left for me, may I ask you ? Nothing. I've lived to see my home broken up by an infernal devil of a son—do you think I could stand it, living on here all by myself? Never, John—never."

" Shall we take the car as far as the stage? There's a fine new boat come alongside at tea-time ; I'd like to see her, she was built by the people over in Belfast, you know."

" Right you are," said Mick ; " by the way, do you know I'm as dry as a fish out of water ? "

" Damn it, man, why didn't you speak before ? Ah, well, we'll have a little drop on the way down. Georgie sent me an allowance this morning. He's having a great time is George, he always said he'd like to go with the army to India. It's queer the things that people like. Now there's that Theresa Corby—she likes nothing better than a slab of toffee—she's like a big kid, she is indeed."

Mick locked the front door, and together they walked to the bottom of the street to catch a car. Then they dropped in for a drink.

When they came out to catch the car Magee suddenly said to Mick—" Look." Mick looked like any man would but said he saw nothing. Nothing at all. " But it's your own son, I tell you, who has just walked past ye, and never set eyes on to notice you he didn't."

" God blast him," said Mick gruffly.

CHAPTER XIV

Joe had not seen his father. He did not know that Magee had seen him, and that his father had walked within a yard of him. They had been to the theatre together. It was not often that Jane took it in her head to go to any place like that, but Joe had insisted—it was such a long time, he said, since he had been inside a theatre. They had come out at nine o'clock, and each was cursing the show. It had been disappointing.

"Never mind," said Jane.

"Oh, there's better places than that," said Joe; "wait till we move out of this place."

They laughed and walked on. Joe wanted badly to have a walk down near the docks, but Jane would not do that because, as she told him—"You might be seen by someone who knows you, and you say you don't want to have anything more to do with your people." Joe had said that with the feeling of braggadocio, but there was a feeling in his heart that he ought to go and see his parents for the last time. Anyway, wasn't he a man? They could not prevent him doing what he wanted. And he confided to Jane as they went homewards that if they were moving out on the Thursday he would like to see his mother and father on the Monday or Tuesday. He knew they would be worrying about him. And then he had to consider the state in which he had left them. He visualised in a moment all the trials and troubles attendant upon his mother and father. It was indeed a hard, cruel world. But then every man for himself. That was the only thing. Follow your instincts, for to-morrow you die. Yes, that was the great thing—to follow your instincts. People were following their instincts and getting medals for it. Why shouldn't he? If only he had money. If only he was able to send his mother home something every week. He would be happy, because he knew then that they would not be worrying about him. Yes, it was fine to have money. When they turned into their street they both stopped. Jane asked—

"What would you like for your supper, dear?"

He said he would like a little cooked fish. So she went into a shop there and then and brought out two small fish. She looked at Joe. "Why, have you been crying? Oh, dear, Joe, you are getting as bad as poor old grandfather," she said.

"I couldn't help it," said Joe, and they walked on to the house. Larson was busy washing his little son and did not notice that Jane called softly to him as she passed the kitchen door. But when she had gone past, he suddenly got up, ran to the door, for he heard someone ascending the stairs, and knew it could not be anyone else but Jane. He was not aware that Joe accompanied her. He returned to the kitchen, for he heard Joe speaking to her as they closed the door of their room. The landlord had gone to the pictures with his wife. Fresh Redmond was out hunting scalps. Everybody had found something to do on this night of nights. Up in the room Joe asked Jane would she like to come with him to see his mother and father before they went away. She said she would, only there must be no row over the affair. She wouldn't stand for Catholics talking down to her. Not a bit. She was independent, and wanted to remain so. "You know, Joe," she said, "although I love you, I would never marry you."

He understood. He replied—

"I quite understand—marriage is not necessary to happiness. It is more of a bar if the everyday world speaks the truth."

They both enjoyed the supper which Jane had laid out on the table. She had bought a new white cloth, and there was a little jug containing flowers. Joe asked her where she had managed to get flowers at that season of the year. She said that someone she knew grew them in a hothouse. After a while Joe said—

"I think I had better go to-morrow and see my father."

"Why?" asked Jane. "Aren't you wishing to see your mother as well?"

"That's impossible now," he said miserably.

"Why?" she asked again.

"She's dead," he said.

A silence then, strange and profound. They looked at each other, and though her lips moved they spoke no word. She saw something in his eyes. She wanted to go and kiss him, as she watched his absolute misery.

"There's no going back on one's word of course," she said.

" She died of heart failure, so they say," he went on ; " but of course it was all through my wickedness. I have only you now in my misery of soul."

She went and put her arms round his neck. He seemed to feel in them a source of strength. He would have liked to remain like that for ever. If only he could blot out the sin on his soul. For now that he had heard the worst from Raynor, he knew that he must continue to suffer all his life.

" I'm sorry, Joe," she said, " but try and cheer up. You know that you too have to live—if I were you I would go and see your father, and try and make it up with him. He will forgive you. Perhaps even now he is weeping for you."

" That can never be," said Joe. " Never—never—I am finished now with him, I know. He will never forgive me—never," he concluded.

" Well then, try and cheer up—forget about all this trouble—after all it is not all your fault, you couldn't help being what you were, and if your father got the sack from the abattoir, whose fault was that ? Not yours, anyway."

" Well a man feels these things," he said.

They finished the supper, and both started to undress. Below Larson was busy packing his clothes in a box. The landlord asked him was he leaving altogether. " Yes," he said, " I am leaving altogether," and winked up at the big man.

A calm had descended upon the soul of Joe. He knew that here was one who would stand by him to the bitter end. There was feeling even in her. And she had never been credited with any. But he knew now more than ever. They talked of many things. But Jane was persistent in her attitude.

" You must really go home to-morrow and see your father—you must—you must."

Joe thought for a long time, then said—" Very well, I will go to-morrow.

"Has Larson given up the chimney sweeping?" he asked her.

"Well, he hasn't done anything much lately—he is thinking of going away to sea if he can get a boat," she replied, covering herself more securely with the blanket.

"But what about his child?" he went on. "Surely he won't go and leave him."

"That's all right, the landlord told him he would look after the boy for him. Don't forget, Joe, you must go home to-morrow—your poor father must be suffering terribly —you know I look upon myself as being partly the cause of all the trouble at home—I might as well say that I helped to kill your mother."

Joe frowned. When he spoke, he spoke savagely, and the words seemed to drop from his lips like a cascade of polluted waters.

"Whose fault? Not yours, nor mine—but their own. H'm—to think that they own their children. I tell you that it all started because I would not go to my Easter Duty this year, and would not attend the mission. And the books. What harm can books do a man? Why the worst books can help a man, the worst of them. They are as much man's food as the Holy Eucharist, believe me. My mother! And father! They bring the devil's wrath upon their own heads, not mine. I would have been quite normal if they had left me alone—but did they? No—no, they ranted all the livelong day, acted like dirty low-down, filthy spies—watched my every move— smelt my breath—thought I was taking to drink—followed me everywhere because they thought I was going about with a bad woman—that was you, and prying into my room, turning over the bed, picking up every scrap of paper, every book, scrutinising it, examining all these things with the skill of a monk—and what for? Because they thought they were trying to do me a good turn, save my soul—and then they didn't want to be disgraced. Fools. As if a little matter like disgrace counts in life. They were jealous for their own smug respectability. Respectability. I tell you it's the rope that hangs them, for they would suffer untold agonies for the sake of their pride. Pride. Ah yes, that is one of the seven deadly sins. Ha, ha! I'm sure they were often proud of their son. Oh yes, he was steeped enough in the mysteries of heaven and hell before he left the school-room behind him. I have nothing to thank them for, Jane, nothing whatever—I owe more to you, to Raynor, to Hugh, to those who are my friends. A good friend is worth all the parents in Christendom. Yes, do you realise that, Jane, you are more to me than my father and mother? What sympathy can you expect me to have for them? Well, there is only my father left. And I suppose he has been deserted by his cronies because of his rascally son. His rascally son is not responsible for what he does —he is not respectable, because he would sooner embrace the Beast than rest secure in the bosom of Christ. They are mistaken, because I will never look upon Christ again, without seeing the Beast too. Because you see in the abyss they mix up Christ with the Beast. See?"

"Well, don't talk any more," said Jane, "go to sleep —we'll have to be up early in the morning—don't forget to see your father, if only on humane grounds."

"If I go to see my father," said Joe, "it will be merely a young man visiting an old one—youth commiserating with age. It is a tragedy to be old in the abyss. The old wait so long."

"For what?"

"For death—at the least it is balm to them—but how slow even is death.

"I am sorry for my father as a man, not as a father— but a man grown old and with the weight of years bend-ing him to a stoop as any swine loaded with meal. I wish I could help him in some way. I really do. But there's nothing."

"Well, go to sleep. Good-night—sweet dreams."

The night wore on. They breathed heavily. Their breathing seemed to echo in the room. All was still. The window was half open, and the curtains had been drawn back. From his side of the bed Joe could look out on to the sea of roofs which looked like a great flat cake of slate. He could not see the moon, for the roof prevented him. The fresh air was good for him. He had been so ill during the last few days. He lay back. He could hear Jane breathing. He put his arm round her neck. She had fallen asleep. He could not sleep. The death of his mother haunted him. Sometimes he imagined he could see her and he tried to beat off the vision. She came and stood before him, holding out her hands, appealingly. Her hand seemed to descend and close, so gently, his eyes. He, too, fell asleep.

Down below, Larson was still busy packing his clothes. He looked at his watch, smiled, and went and lay down on the old hair-filled couch. It wanted only three hours. He would not have to wait long now.

He stopped and listened. Someone was moving up above. He wondered. He heard someone descending the stairs. The person had no boots on, but the stairs creaked just the same. He knew who it was then. He went out and stood at the bottom of the flight. He saw the form descending towards him. He said—

" You are sure that he is asleep ? "

" Yes," said Jane, " he is sound asleep. I will leave a note for him before I go."

They both went into the kitchen. She looked at the old band box which Larson had filled with all manner and style of clothing. She looked round her.

" Where is the boy ? "

" He too is asleep. But it will be all right. He will sleep all the way. He will not make a fuss, be sure of that."

" It is the best for us anyway—I feel as if I had killed that young man's mother—Joe's mother is dead, you know."

" Dead," said Larson.

" Dead and buried," said Jane. " I couldn't think of taking him away from his father. It would be cruel. But we have each other. Joe was a foolish boy."

" You had better go back and sleep—I'll come up and

tap at your door when the time comes. Good-night."

He watched her ascend the long flight of old wooden stairs, stairs without carpet or covering. When she got into bed she found that Joe was still sleeping. She was glad of that. He must not wake up. How could she do the best thing if he woke? If he found out. It was sacrifice on her part.

Larson had promised to take her away to his people; they lived in the South of Scotland. Yes, that would be for the best. She was tired. Very, very tired. She wanted to be quiet for ever. She did not wish to see another human face. She was tired of people. How fine it would be to go to the country. She knew Larson had people who owned a little farm. Why should she not go there? And as for Joe, that was impossible. She saw now the vivid truth of the old man's sayings before he died. The world was full of evil. Well, she was determined that she would add no more to the sum total.

She imagined she could see the surprise on Joe's face when he woke up and found her gone. He would burst into tears at first. But he would go back to his father. She was sure of that. His father would forgive him. It might be possible that he would become reconciled to him, and that he would lead a better life than he had done. He might even become a good Catholic once more. She hoped in her heart that he would, because she knew that he was young, and that time would bridge all the hard paths for him. She lay there thinking of these things. And then she asked herself—

"Do I do right by going away—what clearly is my duty—must I stand by him, or must I allow his father to look after him? His is the duty—mine is the option. Why should he waste the best years of his life with her? Of what use was she? She had been deluding herself—building castles in the air. Castles which fell down as fast as she built them. What right had she to expect him to love her? She thought of the many men who had loved her after their fashion. Then she shuddered. All those things were impossible. In fact she would lose

more than Joe. The reality of it would strike her more
forcibly than him. He would forget and live again. She
would never forget. She could only cherish the memories,
memories far distant and sometimes very indistinct of
the few happy years of her childhood. She saw before
her in a great line, the men who had loved her, with the
love of a moment. They passed before her in sad procession. Some were wealthy, some poor, some famous,
some unknown. She would add no more to the list of her
victims. Was she right in trying to persuade herself that
Joe loved her? Was she trying to persuade herself that
they would be happy together, for the remainder of their
lives? Fool, she thought, I have done the best thing—
the only thing. There is nothing else to think of. Only of
to-morrow, perhaps, and of Joe's discovery and his sad
earnest face as he realises that he has been tricked. But
it is for the best. He would know that. He would forget
about her in a short time. Jane would go down into his
memory like a blur, like a breath of wind. That was all.
She hoped he would return home. The sin was upon her
soul, for she had led him on. Still he was a man and had
control of his soul, and a little reason to boot. But he
must not blame her for doing what she thought was
right. He knew that all the trouble in the world was
caused by people who did not want to be told this and
that—they knew everything. He had often said that
everybody was right once in a while. Well, perhaps for
this time she was right. She would endeavour to forget
him. As even he in the fullness of time would forget her.
Everything was for the best. How soon had she made
up her mind? She marvelled at the quickness of her
decision. If he had not mentioned his mother's death
—everything would have been the same. They would
have gone away. Have been forgotten. They would
have grasped at the little happiness which was waiting
for them. Fate was master of them all. He knew what
was the best. He knew.

She lay waiting—waiting to hear the gentle knock at
her door. She was afraid that he would wake up at the

critical moment. God forbid that. It would be terrible. She must not be discovered. How terrible it would be to look upon his face when he had found out she had gone. Gone. For ever. She did not want to experience these things. She wanted to go quietly. He would forget. She would try. It was the way of life. A family is born, grows up, and is scattered to the four corners of the earth by the winds of Fate. There is no hope, no finding one another, all are lost. Never to return. The soul is dragged slowly through the furnace of sorrow. There is no escape. Do we throw off the body, we are tortured by the soul—do we throw off the soul, then we are tortured by the body. That is life. The agony of being is something profound, terrible, but what lies at the bottom of the wall? Forsooth, you look. Nothingness. From nothingness to nothingness. John Smith is John Smith all through thirty-five years, then he ceases to be John Smith. From one nothingness to another . . .

The dawn creeps in and Jane is out of bed and dressing hurriedly. She takes a last look at Joe and is gone. Silently she leaves the house with Larson and the child. They are going away. They will never return. They have passed out of his life. He will remember, then forget. He will live again.

The biting north wind catches them as they hurry on to the station. A train leaves at five-forty. They will catch that one. They will be in Scotland by mid-day. When they got into the train they all sat on the one seat. It was very cold, the carriage draughty. They huddled close to one another. The strain started off. The two looked at each other for a moment. Then the train entered the pitch blackness of a tunnel. All was dark and still save for the merry sound of the wheels clattering over the rails, the tattoo that beat upon the air as the train flashed over the sleepers.

They dozed off. The train whirled on through the morning. The windows were covered with frost. The telegraph posts whirled past. They stood out against the sky like so many hundred sentinels of heaven. The sky

was leaden coloured. The clouds low-lying and threat-
ening thunder. Bobby put his hand in that of his father.
Jane tried to speak to him, but the roar of the train
prevented her small voice being heard. Larson too tried
to say something but it was swallowed up in the vast
concourse of sound. Jane trembled. At last she was able
to ask him how far from Glasgow his old home was.

"About two hours' journey by train," he said, and
lapsed into silence again.

"Will your people be vexed with you for bringing
me?" she asked him.

The train had slowed down. It was better now to talk
to each other. Soon it would stop altogether for water.
He saw Jane's lips trembling. He wondered if she were
afraid—he wondered if she was regretting going away.
But it was done now—there could be no going back. All
was beginning over again, for her, and for him, and for
his child.

"There is only my old mother there," he told her;
"my father is dead; there is an odd man at the place
too, he helps to look after the bit of farm we have. I
used to send money home to her every week. That was
when I had it to spare of course."

She seemed more reassured now. She was glad that
she was going far away. She would be able to blot out
the memories of the past. They would soon be as dry
dust, to be dispersed by the first wind that came their
way. She took the child on her knee and hugged him to
her. Larson was watching her, and a smile flickered over
his face, which before had seemed to hold an expression
of doubt, an uncertainty lingering there. It was gone now.
He thought that Jane might have been imagining things.
He wanted to dispel that suspicion if it existed. It had
gone now, and he felt happier than ever in his life. He
had known her for the two years in which he had lived
in the house. He had come from the Midlands, and at
that time he had little money, but by dint of hard work
he had been able to earn enough to keep himself and the
child. Only last week he had written to his mother saying

that he was returning home after an absence of twelve years, and that he had decided to help on the farm. His mother had written him saying how happy she was in knowing that he was still alive and well, and that with the grace of God he would be home in a week. She was eighty-two years of age. She had worked on the farm on and off for years now that her husband was dead, and she had to have a man to help her. It just kept them both comfortably. When her son returned he would make things hum, she knew, and she had told the helper that her son was coming home to help make the farm pay. He had listened to this in stony silence. He had never known that she had a son. He had always lived in hope that when she died she would leave him the little farm. And now this man was returning to dash away his hopes.

The train took in water and roared on. Bobby sat on Jane's knee, ofttimes looking into her face and wondering no doubt what was the cause of all the excitement. For they were excited. They felt their hearts beating rapidly. They experienced a kind of mystic joy, in being hurled forward to something new, something that held for them a treasure house of hopes and desires.

CHAPTER XV

WHEN Joe woke up, the daylight was streaming into his room. He thought that Jane had gone down to make breakfast for them both. He did not suspect anything. Once, however, he had debated with himself as to why Jane had been so anxious for him to return home. But he was not suspicious. He got up and dressed, and stood gazing out of the window. He looked at his watch. It was nine o'clock. He waited until half-past nine. He wondered. He ran downstairs to look for her. No one had seen her. The landlord had gone into town on business. Fresh Redmond was still sleeping in her room. The house seemed terribly empty and deserted. He returned to the room and cut some bread. Then he went down and made tea. As he sat eating his breakfast, his eyes began to wander round the room, and, for the first time, he noticed that all her clothes had gone. Then he dismissed the idea from his mind, and thought " She has gone out to buy stuff for the dinner, of course she has ; why do I make myself ill thinking these things ? "

After breakfast he lay back on the bed and, taking up a novel that Jane had been been reading, he was soon engrossed in the story. All the stories he had ever read dealt with the same things. All the authors had the same convictions. All had the same style of treating their subject, which was about a man and two women or two women and a man. Nevertheless he liked the story. Then suddenly he threw down the book and looked again at his watch. It was nearly eleven o'clock.

" She'll be back any minute now," he said to himself and rose and began to pace the room. He was thinking now of what he should do. Should he take her advice and go and see his father before he went away ? It would be quite the best thing to do—his father would know then what he really was—would take him at his face value. He hated the thought of meeting his father. It would be terrible for instance to hear him saying—

" It's you that's the cause of your mother's death, you know—but I forgive you and hope you will be a good son and a good Catholic once again."

Yes, he could actually see his father standing before him, his figure slightly bent with age, and his trembling hand holding itself in the air with a forefinger pointed at him as if to say—

" Remember now, no more nonsense, you have to answer to Almighty God for your mother's death."

Perhaps he had better not go then. He would decide before Jane came back. He would ask her again. She would advise him for the best. He would do anything she suggested. He loved her and was completely in her power. Yes, he would wait. He sat down and began to twirl the pages of the book. At every sound he started. The footstep on the stairs was Jane's. The knock at the

door—that was Jane—the noise in the street—that was
Jane returning with the things for dinner. His mind was
uneasy. He did not know what to do with himself.
Perhaps he would go out for a walk. He might even
meet her coming home.

As if in response to this thought he went below and
washed, came upstairs again and began to dress in the suit
that Jane had bought him. He put on a clean scarf and
carefully brushed his hair. He wanted to look as smart
as possible when he met her in the street. But he would
have to be careful. Only the day before he had neatly
bumped into Father Dunny. He had been forced to cross
the road and look into a shop window to avoid him. He
hated to be seen raising his cap to a priest. Everybody
stared at people who did these things. Catholics were
such queer people. Often he used to watch the Sisters of
the Poor walking along the streets with their large white
bonnets, and he would feel suddenly ashamed to be
associated with them. Their dress and manner of going
about always seemed to him so ridiculous. He remembered how when one of them used to call on his mother,
he would clear off into the back-yard. She always asked
him a lot of questions, and she gave him a medal each
time she came, and each medal possessed greater powers
of healing than the preceding one. And she would open
her large basket which used to contain bread, eggs,
jelly, scapulars, medals, needles, all little things to take
to sick and poor Catholics, and she would pull from the
bottom of the basket a book and say to him in a sweet
musical voice—

" There is a nice book—tell me when I come again
how you liked it."

He would thank her in a gruff way, because he hated
these things to be done in sight of his mother. When he
looked at the book it was the life of some Saint or Angel.
He looked at himself in the mirror, put on his cap, and
he waited. Perhaps she had already come in. She might
be talking to Larson or the landlord, or Fresh Redmond,
although the last didn't like Jane very much. Then he

Q

heard a key being turned in the lock. Perhaps this was she. He waited expectantly. But it was only the big figure of the landlord. When he saw Joe he smiled, and laughed at the same time, then walked past him into the little office which he had in the kitchen. Joe had never seen him laugh like that before. He wondered if something had happened. A suspicion dawned on him, but he could not bring himself to believe it and he swept it from his mind. The landlord came out again and watched him standing there. He went up to him and asked—
" Did you see Jane this morning ? She's never this late. She only takes a half-hour to shop, for we don't live like nobles."

The landlord let out a roar. He had never met such a simpleton in his life.

" Jane ! Humph ! Why, she went away first thing this morning with Larson."

His head swam. He left the house. He wandered up and down the streets, wondering, hoping. His brain reeled. If only, if only . . . but blessed oblivion was not for him. So she had gone. He was left alone. Abandoned. Lost.

He wandered for hours, and he felt no physical hunger. At last he stumbled blindly into a man. And when he looked up into the man's face he saw that he wore his collar back to front.

" Are you a priest ? " he asked.

The priest stared at him. He thought he was drunk, or raving mad.

" I am, my child," said the priest.

" Then, hear my confession, father. Now."

The priest was silent for a moment—then he said suddenly—

" Come to the Church of St. Sebastian in half-an-hour and ask for Father Morran—I am the parish priest from Laytown, I am only on a visit here."

He left Joe staring after him. In half-an-hour. That was a long time to have such a load on one's soul. He must cast it off. But there was the river. What then. Its cool waters would bathe the bloody welts on his body. He felt like a man who has suffered ten thousand lashes. They would cool the white heat of his heart. " Oh give me oblivion," he muttered to himself.

For an hour he wandered. Then he sat down on a wooden bench near the park. Should he go ? He did not answer the question, but rose and hurried away in the direction of the church. When he got there he found that he had been in that church before. It was not so big as the other. It had two little altars, one to St. Joseph and one to the Sacred Heart. He stole up the aisle like a thief and knelt down near the altar of the Sacred Heart. He could not pray. He must confess—he must confess—he must rid his soul of every running sore—of every rotten seed. What a fool he had been. A fool. Did he not know—could he not have seen that he was only being led away by a woman who had treated love commercially, to be bought and sold like cattle in the market ? He cursed her in the depths of his heart.

After a time the priest came into the church. He saw the young man kneeling there and approached him. He looked at him and asked—

" Are you the young man who met me in the street this morning ? "

" Yes, father."

" Then go into that box there, see, with the name Morran over the door."

Then he went away to put on his surplice. Joe went into the box. He knew then that he was on the threshold —he was in the presence of Almighty God. It seemed an eternity before the little grille was drawn back so very silently.

He tried hard to speak but could not and burst into tears. The priest waited patiently until he had got over his fit of weeping. Then Joe spoke very slowly—

" In the name of the Father and of the Son and of the Holy Ghost, Amen.

" It is a few months since my last confession, father."

" Yes, my child."

"I have missed Mass a hundred times, father.

"I have told lies ten thousand times, father.

"I have missed my morning and night prayers for two years."

"Yes, my child."

"I have disobeyed my parents, my priests, and my superiors.

"I have stolen hundreds of things from my home and burnt them, father."

"Yes, my child."

"I have committed adultery, father.

"I have committed sins of impurity also, father."

"How many times, my child?"

"Hundreds of times, father."

"I have spat in the face of Our Blessed Lord.

"I have smashed the statues in my home and torn up the pictures of the Holy family, and the Saints Gerard and Joseph.

"I have committed murder, father."

The priest was calm. In the face of this catalogue which would ensure any Catholic eternal damnation, he was quite cool.

"Whom did you murder, my child?"

"My mother, father."

He burst into tears again, and the priest tried to console him.

"I have been a devil, father. I deserted a good home and went to live with a prostitute, father—I have wrecked my father's life and killed my mother by my action."

"That is not murder, my son," said the priest.

"In my eyes I saw it as murder, father," said Joe.

"I am sorry for all my sins—I only hope that God will forgive me, and that my father will take me back again—I wish to amend my ways—I have suffered, but never as they have suffered—I have known hunger, but never as they have known hunger—I have had temptations and given way to them, father. I did not believe that God was. I am sorry, father. I ask God humbly to forgive me. My soul is in torment. My body gives me no peace. For

I am damned in the eyes of Almighty God."

"Try, my dear child, to lead a better life—know that God in His goodness will forgive you if only you are sorry for your sins—try, my dear child, to look upon sin as something to be avoided, for there is only one end for those who indulge in sins of that kind. Pray also to our Blessed Lady to help and guide you. You have been led away by bad companions and by a woman. Try then and think of the enormous good you can do by keeping clean in the sight of God. God Almighty is merciful at all times, and try to keep worthy of that mercy. Now make a good act of contrition."

Joe said very slowly the Act of Contrition. He heaved a sigh of relief when he heard the priest say—"For your penance say a decade of the Rosary in honour of the Sacred Heart. God bless you, my child."

Joe waited to hear the slide shut back. But the priest was speaking again.

"How old are you, my son?"

"Very young, father."

"You are too young to commit such sins, my child.

"Where do you work?"

"I do not work anywhere, father; it is so hard to get work these days."

"Would you like work, work which will help you to lead a good life—work which will keep you in touch with good Catholic young men and women?"

"Yes, father."

"Then come to me to-morrow at ten o'clock. Would you like to work in Ireland, I have a brother there who has a fine farm? Have you ever worked on a farm, my son?"

"No, father."

"Where does your father work, my child?"

"He used to work at the abattoir, father—he worked there for fourteen years, but he got the sack because he was getting too old for the work."

The priest sighed and went on in the same monotonous tone as before—

"Well, I would like to help your father also, but however, don't forget to come and see me to-morrow morning—I will do my best for you. God bless you."

The slide shut back. Joy filled Joe's soul. For he knew now that his soul was clean and beautiful in God's sight. Ah!—if only he had taken notice of his mother. If only he had obeyed her counsel in all things. What a different person he would have been. Well, he would try to live better. He hoped that his father would forgive him. He hoped that they would be able to live in peace. But he would always be ashamed to look him full in the eyes. Anyway it would be all right if the priest got him over to Ireland. He had never been in Ireland. It would be a new experience for him. It would help him to forget the dark chapters of his life. It would open up new avenues for him—it might be the making of him. The world of to-morrow would be a new world. It was full of beautiful women. What reason had he to regret the loss of Jane? He left the confessional box and walked right up to the communion rails and knelt down. His eye fell on the golden tabernacle on the altar. God was inside that golden house—and His blessed Son was there also in Him. He could see Him now kneeling there, and He was saying to His divine son, "Pour forth Thy grace into his heart that he may live anew in the world of Thy Father." Yes, that was what He was saying. They were going to help him lead a better life. Oh, if only his mother could see him now. If only his father were to step into the church and see him kneeling there, his soul pure once more, the prayers of his childhood falling from his festered lips. Would he not forgive his son? Would he not try to help him over the rough ways of life? The priest had said that he had not murdered his mother. He gave more thought than ever to the question and found that there were the other things besides him which helped on his mother's tragic death. There was the worry of keeping the house—the worry of the debts hanging always over their heads—there was the fear of Mick or Joe dying and not being able to bury them decently. Then the landlord was brow-beating them. His mother could not stand all those things. He knew that it was these as well as his affair that had turned his mother into a frail old woman in a day.

Well, he would do his best. There was nothing else. Had Jane remained with him he would never have taken such a step. He was certain of that. In his heart and soul he was certain. He kept on praying and when he had finished his penance he went out into the street, but stood for a moment looking up and down the road. He did not know which way to go. What should he do with himself? He could not go home now, his father might be down at the docks. In his heart he was frightened of the consequences of meeting his father. He had a violent temper. He might kill him on sight. How near he had come to being strangled, he well remembered. He wished he could meet his father in the street. It would not be so bad, or if he went home now and John Magee were there, it would help to lighten the load. He returned to his seat near the park. He wanted to think it out. He could not decide in five minutes what to do with his life. He was not Jane, who could make a decision in a single moment. He watched the many people passing. He looked into all their faces and kept saying to himself— " Are they happy? I wonder ; they look well, though." Two or three times he recognised people whom he knew —they were fellow congregationalists at the church. He turned his head round whenever he thought they knew him. He sat there for a long time. One moment he was moved by the desire to return home at once—the next moment he had swept it from his mind and was contemplating suicide. But that was very difficult. Only brave men did things like that—he was a coward. He had no courage. He wished ofttimes that he could die suddenly—that death would overtake him when he least expected it. Even though he had cleansed his soul before the throne of God, even though he had done this, he was not satisfied—he was not happy. He had been fooled so many times, he did not know what to think. People used to say to his mother—"It's just laziness, that's all : he doesn't want to work." But they never offered him any just the same. If he had had something to do these things might never have happened.

In despair he got up and walked in the direction of Hugh's house. When he got there he found that he was alone. They were pleased to see each other. They shook hands warmly, and Hugh could see that Joe was bearing a burden of some kind. He looked ill and worried. He poured out a glass of ale and Joe drank it greedily. Hugh went and brought him something to eat. He ate ravenously.

"What have you been doing with yourself lately ? " asked Hugh.

"Nothing," replied Joe. "I am fed up with everything."

He told Hugh all that had happened. When he had finished, Hugh said—

"Well, now, you should go home to your father, he will be pleased to see you—don't you see, my dear man, that the spirit of sacrifice is not yet dead in this old world of ours ? Don't you understand that Jane has left you because she knows it is for the best ? It must have been a sacrifice for her—why then——"

"Don't mention her name to me," said Joe angrily.

"Well then," went on Hugh, he was laughing now, "go back home and settle down once more with your father, and everything will come right. I might be able to get you something to do down at our place. Would you like that ? "

Joe remembered that this was the second person who had offered him work. If only these offers had come before. He was thinking at that moment of his mother, of the sacrifices she had often made for him.

"It is you now who must make the sacrifice. Don't you see that because you loved each other the sacrifice was necessary. Don't you know in your heart that love demands a sacrifice ? Can't you even see yet how great and nobly she has acted, for you—for you? Try and realise these things for your own sake."

" I will try," said Joe, looking up into the eyes of his friend. He pondered over all what Hugh had said to him. Should he then turn his back to the darkness and face the light once more? He would be happy then like Hugh, like Raynor, like everybody in the world who made sacrifices every day of their lives. Now that he had listened to his friend, he saw in a different light the woman whom he had loved. And she had made a sacrifice for him. If he had known. If he had been able to read into her innermost soul. He knew he would have tried to prevent her making it—he would have urged her to go away with him. He would have tried his very best, in order that they could have each other through life. He knew he would never love any other woman. His friends could say what they liked, but he knew best, better than any of them, the dictates of his heart. " My heart loves where it loves." That is enough. Am I going to deny my heart life? No. Not while it beats.

Hugh, who was watching him closely, seemed to be able to read his very thought.

" My dear friend, you must cheer up and get all those silly ideas out of your head—no one wants to deny you life, but remember you must be at all times worthy of it. Do you understand? Now supposing I go with you to your father, it won't be so bad for you—I'll talk him over —tell him you intend to go the right path in future. All this trouble has arisen because you have certain ideas of your own, which you jealously guard, and I don't blame you in the least——"

" I have sold some of my ideas, I am afraid," said Joe.

" You what? " asked Hugh, who could not catch his words—he spoke so low.

" I mean I went to the priest this morning—went to confession, you know."

" I thought you believed only in yourself, Joe," said Hugh.

" I am afraid I am getting that way : that I will end

up in believing in nothing. You remember the old Italian philosopher ? "

" But of course that rests with yourself—if you decide one thing, I will not try to get you to decide something else. Every man for himself, Joe."

" Don't you understand how I've suffered ? " said Joe, in a broken, shaking voice.

" Of course I do, but here you are treading on all the old corns again, just after you telling me you had cleared yourself of them for ever."

" That's not my fault, Hugh," replied Joe.

" One has to suffer in life," said Hugh—" all life is suffering. We have to help one another—take one another's woes upon our shoulders and carry them down through the night."

" I carry mine alone," said Joe, and there was a gleam in his eye. Hugh wondered what had prompted him to say a thing like that.

Joe went down to the house with the queer smell. He noticed that the curtains on the window hadn't been washed for weeks and the glass panes were covered with dirt. It was just growing dusk. He stood shivering by the door. What was he to do ? If he told his father he had been to confession he might not treat him so badly —but when he thought of his mother, a mist descended over his soul. But he must do either one thing or the other. He had lost Jane to fall back upon God, the Catholic God whom he had always despised. He knocked loudly on the door. There must be nobody in, he thought. He knocked at the house next door. The woman got a fright when she saw who it was. " Good Lord, son, where have you been ? Your father's just gone in the back way."

Again he knocked at the door. He felt in his fob pocket. Of course he had a key. Why had he not thought of it before ? He turned the lock and entered. His father was sitting by the fire with his back to him. He saw in a moment that half the furniture had gone. It looked like an empty stable.

" I have come back," he said.

The figure by the fire did not move. He had a sudden desire to flee again. Anywhere—oh, God, anywhere, rather than see that face turned towards him. But it was too late. His father had turned round. He was looking at him.

" I have come back, father," said Joe again. But his father merely kept on looking at him, never saying a word—his small ferrety eyes were boring a way sure and clean right down into Joe's innermost soul. His stare frightened Joe. He thought he was going to spring at him—choke him—cut his throat. What then?

" You have come back?" said his father.

" Yes, father, I have come back."

" Why?"

God. God. He was caught there. Why had he come back? Jesus, why had he not thought of that before? His father had him now. He could never escape.

" Why did you come back to me?" repeated his father.

" I am sorry," said Joe.

His father rose and stretched himself. He seemed to Joe to have grown longer and thinner. His face was like a mask. He saw the thin hands stretched towards him, as if in mute appeal, but though the lips framed themselves to speak never a word was uttered. Joe backed up against the wall. He was afraid. He had once seen a man like that, and he had done the same thing. He strangled a child, and the police said he was mad. Perhaps his father was mad.

" Why are you waiting?" asked his father.

Jesus, oh, Jesus, he had him again. Why was he waiting? Could he not remember why he had come? His soul passed through an inferno and returned to him, white, pure and clean, but it had lost its strength. Words came not. " What must I say?" he muttered to himself again and again.

" Well?"

There he was again. He must be mad. He had never

known him to speak like that before. His eyes were strange too. Joe was really afraid. He wished he could say something, but no word would come.

" Are you still waiting ? " said his father.

" Good Lord," said Joe, " he is mad. Stark, raving mad." He looked at the thin face lined by suffering and grief. And yet had he not suffered also ? Whose the fault that the home had been smashed up ? It was every-body's. It was not the fault of a single man, it was the fault of everyone, everyone on the earth. Ah ! At last the words were coming. Soon he would be able to answer his father. He would not have long to wait now. No, not long.

His father coughed, and he looked comical as he shook all over. Joe tried not to laugh, but couldn't help it. The humour of the thing struck him.

" I am waiting," said his father.

His father was waiting. Of course he was. Why couldn't he speak. " Open your mouth, you bloody coward," he said to his soul within him. " Open, quick."

His father was waiting for him. Good Christ. He couldn't keep him waiting like that.

" Why are you waiting ? " he asked his father.

Ah, the words were coming better now. He had asked his father something.

" I am waiting for death," he said and buried his face in his hands.

Joe saw everything in a flash. He knew now that all was finished.

His father was waiting for death. Sitting by the fire that had no coals, and waiting for death. It was strange. If he had said that a month ago he would have laughed at him. And all the furniture in the house was covered with dust, everything was rotting away. No one came to see his father. It was just like a dead-house. He could do nothing now. His father was waiting for death. He laughed, for it was funny at first and then tragic. " The tragic sense of life in men," he thought.

His father turned round and looked at him again.

He shielded his eyes with his hand, to protect them from the gas-light.

"Go away—go away," he said.

And Joe went away that very night.

"The river of life is broad and swift-running. It sweeps on its way through the abyss. Let it take me too. I will go wheresoever it shall go. I will be with it always. I will rise no more. The Catholic God has done me. He has lied to me. The priest was only joking. Jane was a liar. The world was a funny place. There's a fine woman. Well, I'm after her.

"Hey you, how much do you want? Can't you hear? Can't you hear?

"Come on, you know what I want. Course you do. Christ, she's deaf and dumb. Ha, ha, ha! Which way must I go then? This way. I will walk for ever. I will never tire. I will walk unto the end of the world. What is it that I wrote on the fly leaf of ' Richter '? Oh yes, I remember it. It was this :

' The Light of Lights looks always on the motive,
    The shadow of Shadows on the deed alone.'
He could write those lines on his heart. Jane was a good woman, by God ! "

"Move along there."

"All right, I'm going now."

As he went, he communed with himself : " Yes, I'll walk on for ever. No one shall speak and ask me questions. I will not look upon the face of any man. I want to walk to the end of the world. My soul is the devil's soul. At last I am free. The world is a funny place. Ha, ha, ha ! How I diddled them about the holy Mass. They didn't think I'd spit out the Holy Eucharist. Not they. They have minds like camels. God have mercy on them anyway. The Eucharist tastes nice after you have had it in your mouth for two minutes. But you must not let your teeth touch it. Hell is for all those with black souls. Heaven is for saints and people with lots of money. It must be a fine place. Little John was in Limbo, that was a fine place too. He wished he was in Limbo. There

were lots of little children in Limbo. They stayed there
for ever, they never saw God's face, because their parents
have bad memories. Now that was very strange. Not
everybody could have a good memory. His father once
had a fine memory. But it was lost now. His mother
had no memory at all. The landlord had the best memory
of all. But a bug has a great memory for all that. It
remembers where it left off last. Oh yes, bugs were clever,
very clever things indeed. Well, I'll go down this road.
One gets into the country that way. To walk on and on
without ceasing : that helps a man to forget. To speak
with no man : that helps to keep a man's soul clear. To
wish for nothing is good too. From heaven my mother
can see me. She is smiling. She is three leagues away
from God. God has a little smile on His face too. But He
is stern as well. Father Dunny will be nearer God than
my mother. One of God's servants. What am I ? Rather
like a flea. Very small. God can't see me. People can't
see me. They only see big things. They wear spectacles
to see little things. The little things are near and seem
great—the big ones are far off and look small. But up
in heaven all is different. One is so deliriously happy
that one does not eat or drink—pray or do any mortal
thing except sing. The choirs in heaven are the finest
choirs of all. The people sing from pure joy. They are
never hungry. Hell is right underneath heaven. All the
people in hell could see into heaven, but they never saw
God's face. Only the people in hell could see heaven.
Those on earth couldn't see anything like that. The
people in hell had red eyes and red bellies. All as thin as
rakes. The devil they are ! St. Anthony and all the other
saints were a lot of liars. They couldn't help a crow.
Why didn't they help his father ? But perhaps they knew
he was waiting for death. He hadn't thought of that.
He used to hear his father say, 'Christ, save me.' He
couldn't save even himself. No one could. All were lost.
All were troubled with souls. Souls were a nuisance.
They made men act queerly. Kiss things and kneel down
like the black pagans in Africa. Christians were nearer

heaven than any other race. All priests were clever people. They had cleaner souls than ordinary people, that was why they wore a different kind of dress."

He walked on muttering to himself. He came to the edge of a wood. He lay down on the grass and looked up at the great rolling clouds. The rain fell. He lay on his back with the rain pouring on his face. His clothes were wet through. The water trickled down his neck. It was in his boots. His feet were sore with the long walk. All was still in the woods. Not even an insect outraged nature in her silent mood. The great trees stood over him. They were protecting him from the onslaughts of the storm. The world is a large place but one cannot escape a storm. It is the wrath of God. God was looking down at him there, lying drenched to the skin. God was so far away that even if He spoke to you you couldn't hear Him. Millions of miles away. The geography book was right, but the Catechism was a lie. A dirty, low-down lie. He sat up suddenly as a flash of lightning shot against the sky. And he hammered with his bare fists against the hard dry earth.

" Hey, God, hey you, God. Hey there, God!" he said again and again.

THE END